MW00438566

# THE THIRD FORCE

Brock Dahl

Copyright © 2017 Brock Dahl

All rights reserved.

ISBN: 978-1539109969

For Jessica, your patience and love overwhelm.

# CHAPTER ONE

Cordell Whitaker sat in the chapel at the American University of Beirut as he had every Sunday for many months. The Mass was one of the few in English in the city. Gaspar Vartabed, its regular officiant, spoke with a heavy Armenian accent that sometimes left the supplicant to fill in the liturgical spaces by memory. It was Easter of 1973, and Whit was nearly alone in the pews. Christ's passion according to John floated like incense across the silent chapel:

Pilate said to him, "So you are a king?" Jesus answered, "You say that I am a king. For this I was born, and for this I have come into the world, to bear witness to the truth. Every one who is of the truth hears my voice."

Pilate said to him, "What is truth?"

Whit's thoughts followed the question outside the open church doors and into the streets of Beirut. It was a city on the verge of collapse. Amidst the descent, he found himself searching for answers.

After the service, Whit drifted with those thoughts into the crisp morning air. It was the type of day that provides a window into the sublime. As he moved, a hand firmly grasped his shoulder. He turned to see Gaspar Vartabed directing a welcoming smile. "It's good to see you here, Cordell."

Palm trees swayed gently in the breeze behind the priest, who stood firmly in contrast to his surroundings. Tall, though slightly stooped by his age, the priest's thin figure retained a disciplined bearing. Several strands of his blackish grey hair floated gently, resting occasionally across his forehead. The same breeze that swayed the trees left in Whit's nose a hint of fish and salt. The smell still struck him as foreign, and part of Whit wondered if anything but the plains' winds - with their rhythmic aura of harvest, fire, and freeze - would ever feel familiar.

"Thank you, Father. I was supposed to meet someone for a date, but she stood me up."

Gaspar Vartabed, shook his head while smiling, "Ah, Lady Wisdom, she always seems to evade you." Whit laughed quietly to himself, but the priest's face grew stern just before he spoke, "You should come to confession soon in Bourj Hammoud."

"Lent just ended, Father; how bad would I be if I already had something to confess?"

The priest's smile was obligatory, but Whit felt the man's aging hand clench a little more firmly as his eyes turned sober, "We all have something to say." Silence passed between them before drifting away.

"You'll be at your church?" Whit hadn't been to the Armenian district, Bourj Hammoud, in months. There just wasn't much of interest to report on, and it was a city with no shortage of interests. Nonetheless, he sensed the gravity in the cleric's invitation.

"Yes."

Whit nodded, "Happy Easter, Gaspar Vartabed."

Gaspar turned his gaze towards the Mediterranean, over which American University was gracefully perched. The cedar-strewn hill beneath the spacious campus plunged precipitously towards the rocky coast. The priest spoke, whether to Whit or the sea, Whit couldn't tell, "I am not so sure happy days are ahead for this place."

Whit peered momentarily across the waters hoping to glimpse whatever oracle the priest gleaned from the distance. Seeing nothing, he patted the priest's hand amicably and departed. It was unlike the man to harbor such angst, and Whit wondered at its source as he strolled toward the gates of the university.

Minutes later, Whit took a slow walk around his star-crossed MG. He noticed the neighborhood children, kicking a soccer ball in an alley, stop and stare. He focused again on his car. What little dignity it possessed had long since been erased by the last eighteen months of fender benders on the streets of Beirut.

As Whit watched the children, he put on his sunglasses and retrained his eyes on several young men engaged in a fervent discussion in an alleyway three blocks away. One wore brown trousers with a yellowish floral print shirt. Another had a sweater, hanging shabbily over his shoulders, and black slacks. A third wore a green military fatigue jacket over a pair of khaki pants and boots. They pointed at one another, and Whit sensed that their conversation, as it picked up steam, was related to him.

Whit leaned back against the car and checked over his shoulder through the campus. He could see her from a distance moving gracefully across the square. She wore a flowing maroon dress, flecked with green, that hugged her figure as it bobbed like waves brushed against the shore. Her black hair wrapped around her neck and lifted intermittently in the same direction as her dress. Observing her, Whit almost forgot entirely where he was. He was awakened by loud shouts behind him.

Glancing back, Whit spied the men in the alley taking notice and exchanging some words. They slowly began moving towards her, which brought them incrementally closer to Whit, and his neck tightened as he felt the rush of cortisol through his system. They emerged from the alley into the street just as the woman, now just a few feet away from Whit, closed the distance with an illuminating smile.

"Whit, habibi," she shrieked as she lunged forward, hugging him and kissing his cheek. She held him a bit longer than she should have, as was her custom when she found him. The embrace, every time she shared it, sent a flood of relief through him, as though proximity to innocence was a salve for the weariness of life. As he opened the passenger door for her, she giggled and brushed the bangs away from her face, but he focused his attention over her shoulder. He could see them approaching, now about a block away, and shut the door after she sat. He moved quickly over to the driver's side and got in as she, oblivious to her surroundings, rummaged through her bag to find her sunglasses, looked up at him and blew a kiss. He ran his hand under the steering column and driver's side dash so swiftly that she failed to notice.

"How are you, Najwa?"

Whit started the car and saw the men in his rear view mirror start to slow down. He pressed the clutch and shifted into first, easing into the empty street and leaving the men behind, their nameless frustration unquenched, but noted. The group faded into the background and he trained his mind on the road, scanning constantly for Lebanese drivers who threatened at every turn to finish the job on his bumper that their brethren had prosecuted with merciless panache. The laughter of children merged into honking as Najwa fiddled with the radio, settling at last on a pop station that mimicked the nightly rhythms of Beirut's wild club scene.

Laughing and moving her arms, she said, "C'mon, Whit, let's go dancing this week!" They did not have far to go, but they would cover much ground before they arrived at their destination.

"Dancing in the midst of all this? Your father would shoot me."

"All this?! Nonsense. This is Beirut, habibi, there is always all this." She said playfully. "Besides, he always insists he'll shoot you, so you might as well have fun before he does it!"

"An excellent point. But seriously, the country is on the verge of civil war and you want to go to the clubs?"

"Well they're going to fight no matter what we do. I can't do anything about it, so at least I should have some fun?"

"Do you really want to be dancing when you die?"

"I can't think of any better way to go," she said, turning up the music and throwing her arms straight up, looking over her shoulder at him as she moved her entire body to the beat.

As Whit drove south through West Beirut, Najwa turned down the music and pulled a shawl over her otherwise bare shoulders. The streets, crawling with people, stood like dry ravines between the monochrome cement canyons walls of various apartment and commercial buildings. Women were clad with headscarves and men milled about fingering prayer beads. Somewhere in the distance a muezzin chanted an Islamic prayer. Some people hurried indoors while others seemed indifferent to the call to prayer.

"I don't like it here," she said.

"Why?"

"I, I don't know. I just can't understand. They look and all they see is a naked Christian prostitute."

"C'mon Na-"

"No, it's true. Look at their eyes. Months ago . . . no problem. Now, it's getting scary." Najwa peered with trepidation out the window as they lurched forward through the throng of moving people and cars.

"I don't get it – how it can change like that?"

"Everyone blames religion, but we've lived with them for years. A professor at school says its class . . . what does he call it . . . subju . . . I can't remember the word."

"Subjugation?"

"Yeah, habibi, you're so smart."

"You're not if you're hanging around with communists."

"I don't have a choice - they're half the school. I wouldn't have any friends otherwise."

Najwa looked at Whit silently and watched his eyes fixated in the rear view mirror. In it, Whit caught a glimpse of two men on a motorcycle four or five car lengths behind. Scarves shielded the mens' faces from the dirt swirling up from the streets. The thin machine spun forward on what almost appeared to be bicycle wheels. A yellowish metal bulk was nestled behind a headlight and low-set handlebars, with a black rubber seat extending a few feet behind it. The driver leaned forward, clenching the bulk with his knees, as a passenger held his arms locked around the driver's torso.

Traffic loosened as the streets cleared of the prayerful. The cars, an array of light blue, white, black domed and curved contraptions, fought towards their destinations. Whit shifted lanes and noticed the yellow flash move into his lane several cars to his rear. He placed his hand on Najwa's leg and swerved violently in front of oncoming traffic.

"Whaaaat are you doing?!" she screamed.

Whit veered left down a side street. The motorcycle almost tipped to keep pace with them. "We nearly got hit! Where are you going?! This is the wrong way!"

"There's no wrong way, habibti, just be patient."

His eyes were still intent on the rear view mirror; glancing back and forth, in front and behind.

"What is wrong?" her faced cringed with confusion as she turned to look behind the car.

"Nothing, Najwa, just be patient for a minu-," and he swerved aggressively towards the sidewalk.

"Whhiiittt!" Several people scurried towards a building where they came to an abrupt stop. An older man slapped the hood of the car, cursing Whit in Arabic. About twenty yards back Whit could see the motorcycle pull over behind a truck. He reached his left hand under the seat.

"Stay calm, Najwa, I'll be right back." It was a soothing voice, as though he was completely in command. He swung open his door, and she yelled after him as he hopped out.

Several younger men loosened themselves from the side of the building and approached the car. Whit pointed towards them, "Stand back!" His tone had turned ominous, aggressive, but returned to a gentle calm as he looked at Najwa, "Stay here." He shut the door and walked briskly down the road in the direction of the motorcycle.

Approaching the truck from the driver's side, Whit saw no one in the cab. He removed a piece of chalk from his left pocket, and then shifted it into his right hand, sliding it into his palm, unnoticed. The muezzin's song reverberated off the buildings on either side of the street. It was a single, male voice intoning a prayer in Arabic.

As Whit moved cautiously past the cab of the truck, a smallish, bearded man peaked his head around the rear. Whit recognized the sweater and black pants. A blackened scarf hung awkwardly around the man's neck, as if it had just been pulled down from his face. The man crouched suddenly, looking shocked to see Whit, and then disappeared in an instant. Whit neared the end of the truck and slowed.

The motorcycle burst forth from behind the truck, almost hitting Whit as it threw dirt into his eyes and nostrils. He instinctively covered his mouth while his eyes pinched shut. Time seemed to slow as he responded without thinking. He extended his arm and let the chalk slide out of his palms in between his clenched fingers. The chalk grazed the tire. Then the instant spun away as the motorcycle ripped down the next turn.

Whit rubbed his eyes and walked around the end of the truck. There he saw two little boys sitting on the curb. In Arabic, he said, "I have a toy for you if you tell me something?" He showed them the piece of chalk and they reached out with interest, but he pulled it back and smiled as they giggled. "Please," the younger of the two said.

"Did they say anything to each other while they were here?"

"Who?"

"The two guys on the motorcycle."

"One said,"

"Which one?" Whit interrupted.

"The man driving told the other one to check."

"Check what?"

"I don't know."

"Did he say anything else?"

"No, the man just ran over and ran back."

"And when he ran back, did he say anything?"

"Just screaming."

"Screaming what?"

"Go, go!" The two boys began to laugh and scuffle, miming the motorcyclists haste as one slapped the others back.

"What about a name? Did he say a name when he yelled at the driver?"

The boys seemed to think, and the smaller of the two finally spoke up, "Ah, Sayyaf!"

"No, no it was Sayyid!" the other yelled. As they giggled again, Whit smiled slightly and broke the chalk in half, giving one piece to each boy. They grabbed the pieces, laughing, turned and ran. As they fled, they crossed the path of two police officers approaching on foot. The men, lumbering lazily down the sidewalk, wore thin khaki uniforms, shifts open halfway down their chests and soaked in sweat. Whit turned and walked away from them. "Mister," one officer yelled. Whit continued walking briskly.

When he returned to the car he found Najwa outside of it in a throng of onlookers hurling insults and pointing their fingers at her. "What are you doing?!" he yelled and the crowd, immediately shocked, began to step away from the car. He walked confidently over and pushed her back inside as the throng closed in. He then moved patiently to his door, got in, started the car, and pulled away just as the two police approached and raised their hands. They coughed as they shrunk in Whit's rear view mirror.

"What is wrong with you?!" she was screamed. "You nearly killed those people and left me! What the hell is wrong with you, Whit?!"

"I told you not to get out. . . ." he yelled back, "I though..."

"You thought what? Are you crazy?!" She was so frantic that she began crying and put her head in her hands. The sight of her crying stopped his anger and his heart slowed. He reached up and stroked her hair gently.

"Are you ok? I'm sorry, I didn't mean to scare you."

"Yeah, well I'm scared, ok! What is my mom going to think when she sees me crying?!"

"It's okay. We're okay," he spoke calmly, and her breathing slowed as she looked at him. But as she grew calm, Whit was quietly anxious. It was not okay at all.

# CHAPTER TWO

"I can get you all the guns you want, that's not the problem." The man spoke quietly through a full beard that laid across the top of his torso. As he squinted under the sun, wrinkles assembled around his eyes like dried clay, masking his youth.

A clean-shaven, slightly pudgy man sat next to him on the bench. "Then what's the problem, Jawad?" The question came uncomfortably, as to one more accustomed to speaking in commands than playing the supplicant.

"I don't know what you're going to do with them. They say you're never getting out of here, and I'm not working with any other of your stumbling mor-"

"The PFLP does not stumble. We strike fear into the Israeli occupier."

"They don't seem to be trembling down south, Sadiq."

Sadiq's face reddened as he pursed his lips. He paused for a moment, then spoke after his chest rose and fell more slowly again, "The occupier is the enemy. But we are focused on something else for now before we can take the snake head on."

Jawad turned to him, raising his eyebrows and waiting for a moment, "Are you?"

Roughly ten to twelve feet away, on either side of the two men, sat two groupings of five to six men. All of them wore baggy gray jumpsuits without pockets. Each grouping scanned the recreational yard where the rest of the block's prisoners milled about. The groupings also eyed one another.

"The enemies of the revolution have to be dealt with first."

"Be careful, Colonel. I am still Lebanese."

"Lebanese. Pha," Sadiq said, as he spat on the ground in disgust. "Egyptian, Syrian, Palestinian."

"Jordanian," Jawad interrupted, and Sadiq stared at him, his eyes widening and mouth pursing again.

"None of it matters," Sadiq raised his voice tersely between clenched lips, "There is us, Arabs, and there is them!" His voice roared, and he saw several of Jawad's men begin to approach, as his own turned towards them, moving forward slightly. Jawed Keswani held out his hand in disapproval; all stopped.

"Sadiq, please," Jawad pleaded quietly but sternly, lowering his hands as the men turned back to the yard. "You think I do not understand that. You may think they all mean nothing, but they do not. And you have to have them all," he paused, the last word sharpening his staccato cadence, "on your side if you want to do anything about the Jews."

"Your problem, Jawad, is you think your religion is going to carry you against the Jews."

"And your lack of faith is something stronger?"

There was a pause. "Well at least we both know who the enemy is. That is why I know I can rely on you."

Thunder clapped in the distance, and Sadiq's thoughts drifted over the walls of Roumieh prison. They moved south over the fields of Lebanon and the slopes of Mount Hermon, winding back and forth over lake Tabria near his ancestral home, which the Christians called Galilee, and crossed from there into Jordan, settling in a small bunker in the hills near a town called Jerash. By road, a four hour journey around Israeli controlled territory; by bird's flight, a little more than a hundred miles; by memory, seconds away.

The explosion, sounding like thunder, rumbled in the distance and shook sand from the bunker ceiling.

"We must push back here . . . and here," Sadiq yelled desperately to the men huddled around a map, punching two spots as most stood silent. Several flinched as another explosion sounded closer and clumps of sod fell from the ceiling onto the map. They all wore fatigues, though in varying shades of green. Two men wore black and white checkered scarves wrapped around their heads. Others wore military caps, AK-47s hanging over their shoulders.

A burly man in an unlabeled fatigue jacket started, "Colonel Sadiq," then a pause accentuated by gunfire sounding closer, "this is over – "

"For the traitors it is over!" Sadiq bellowed.

"What would you have us do?!" came the response, "The Jordanians have us surrounded and outnumbered from the south and the east!" The man pounded the map as he yelled. "If they close off the north, we have to flee to the hands of the Israelis or die fighting!"

"Then we shall die fighting, an-"

"And what of the resistance?!"

"It will die anyway unless we fight, you fool!"

"We won't force any more of our men into suicide. The real enemy is still the Jews. We will have nothing left to fight them with."

"The enemies are those who do not support the resistance."

"Enough," a man at the end of the table raised his hand, and all grew quiet.

"But, Abou Ammar," Sadiq plead, "we-"

"I've heard enough," Abou Ammar spoke plaintively. "Colonel Sadiq, you have fought valiantly," he raised his hand again as Sadiq opened his mouth to speak, "if you feel you must fight to the death, no man here will stand in your way." Abou Ammar shook his head slowly, as if disbelieving what he was saying, but finding it necessary to say, "But we cannot fight the Israelis from here, and we choose to fight another day." Explosions rang out directly over the bunker. "I hope you'll choose the same. We'll need you and your men in Lebanon. And that is the only place left for us."

Sadiq spoke more quietly, "And you think they'll let us fight from there?"

"I know we can't fight from here." With that, the man turned and was followed by four additional men. As the door opened, he turned back to look at Sadiq, and behind him the night sky flashed brightly, turning his form dark. As the sky darkened again, his figure blended into the darkness.

Sadiq turned to look at several of his men, crammed into a corner in the bunker, and slowly nodded. Immediately upon exiting the bunker, they received fire from the darkness. The Jordanians were upon them. Two of Sadiq's men fell immediately, and Sadiq turned in the opposite direction of the fire, running up and over a small berm, as several Palestinian fedayeen provided covering fire. The night flashed hot and angry, and Sadiq's veins ran with rage. He turned to take one last look at the mountainous region, alight with tracer bullets and explosions, and sprinted to a nearby jeep that was pulling away to the north.

"Sadiq . . . Sadiq." Jawad spoke calmly as Sadiq's memory faded. Jawed looked back out across the yard. "You get out of here, and I'll work with you. But I have plans, too. And when the time comes, I know you will remember." Sadiq stuck out his hand to shake Jawad's, and Jawad looked out into the crowd without extending his.

"Have your men contact this man. He will handle things form there." Jawed handed a small slip of paper to Sadiq. It read Farouk Abou-Hamza, Banque du Liban,

Sadiq tapped the card on his leg, "You've chosen the right partner," and looked out into the grouping of prisoners milling about.

One jittery man looked back at Sadiq several times. He had bushy, black hair and his grey jumpsuit hung open, soaked in sweat. His form loomed over the others around him, like a mountain peak against surrounding foothills. Finally, the man seemed to catch Sadiq's eye, and froze, as if awaiting a command. Sadiq sat, his forearms hanging over his knees where his elbows rested. A slight twitch in Sadiq's finger seemed to trigger some switch within the man.

As if a robot, the moving mountain turned around and began walking briskly towards the opposite end of the yard. As he did so, other prisoners began to speak loudly, and then shout at him. Sadiq rose to his feet, turning briefly to Jawad, "I'll see you soon."

Puzzled, Jawad said, "I'm getting out of here tomorrow. I don't know how I'll see you so-," but Jawad halted as the man plunged into the crowd in the distance, drawing a makeshift knife, and sinking it deeply into the throat of another inmate. Prisoners rushed from every direction into the melee, and Sadiq walked calmly towards the scruff. As he did so, he pulled a small white kerchief from his pocket, and tied it around his wrist. Sadiq then held his hand in the air as he walked slowly, but confidently, to the grouping.

Men screamed and swung their arms, blood spattering the middle of the yard to the chaotic cadence of their rage. Blare horns wailed around the walled echo chamber. Peering beyond Sadiq's raised kerchief, Jawad briefly perceived a guard in a far-away tower hunch over a long-barreled sniper rifle. At that instant, Jawad's men yanked on him to get him to the side of the yard. As they pulled him, he looked over his shoulder, saw a flash from the barrel, and saw Sadiq crumple to the ground. Sadiq clinched his right forearm, from which blood surged forth.

Sadiq's men surrounded him, wrapped his forearm and pulled him towards an open space on the other side of the yard. The side walls of the yard opened, and guards in riot gear surged into the crowd, beating men indiscriminately. As Jawad's men pushed him towards the open door and back into the safety of the cell block, the last thing he saw was Sadiq leaning calmly against the wall, flanked by four or five men, watching the chaos ensue.

# CHAPTER THREE

By the time they arrived at her parents' house, Najwa had calmed and the good humor that invigorated her soul had returned to her eyes. Nadia, Najwa's explosively vibrant eight-year-old sister, was peeking over the balcony of the Khoury's third floor apartment. It was a position she always occupied, waiting anxiously for her sister and Whit, the only person she knew who had a bigger English vocabulary than she did.

Nadia and Whit liked to use big words together so no one else could understand them. He got her a thesaurus for her seventh birthday. She was a little confused at first, because she didn't like dinosaurs. But when she opened it there were words and words! Whit whispered to her – nobody else knew – that it was their secret code book, and whenever she needed to say something in English without anyone else knowing except him, she would run to find her code book - already dog-eared and browning from use – and choose just the right secret word.

Nadia also used the thesaurus to write letters to Whit. Every Sunday she had a letter for him, sometimes two paragraphs, sometimes a full page. He always had extremely important questions that his newspaper needed answered, but because he was an American, he confided (she learned that word from the thesaurus), he just couldn't concentrate long enough to find an answer. So, he relied on her to do it, and even though it was difficult, she thought it was important enough to spend her time doing properly.

As Whit pulled to a stop, she waved anxiously and then disappeared from the balcony, only to reappear outside the front door within seconds.

"Najwa!" Nadia exclaimed, plunging towards Najwa's leg as if a moment's delay would be fatal. She then rounded the front of the car, and came to a stand-still as she saw Whit, poised with his knees bent and his arms outstretched, fingers wriggling back and forth in a tickling motion she joyfully feared. "Baaghhhhh" she screamed and turned to run as he grabbed her and tickled to her laughter and smiles. Najwa laughed and they all mounted the stairs together. On the first floor they met a familiar character.

"Hello ladies," a slightly pudgy man with thick-lensed glasses and a dark black mustache said. "And Mr. Whitaker, how are you today?" Whit nodded, placidly, lips pursed.

"Bye Marius," Nadia squeaked as she dropped out of Whit's arms and ran up the stairs. Marius looked to Najwa and Whit, a little awkwardly, and excused himself with family obligations.

"Have a good day, both of you."

Najwa looked curiously at Whit, and they continued up the stairs. Najwa and Whit approached the second floor door to her parents home, where Nadia leaned against the door jam.

"What am I thinking right now, Whit?"

He thought for a second, "Abandon all hope, ye who enter here."

"HA!" came an immediate, boisterous laugh from inside the room. Nadia, turned and standing in the middle of the open doorway, looked on quizzically. A large and tired-looking man appeared, his left hand on her head and his right hand extended to Whit.

"My good Whit, you must be remembering the sign at the airport."

They all laughed together as Whit grabbed Boutros Khoury's hand and they embraced each other's backs with their free left arms.

Whit, in a hushed tone that the girls could not here, asked, "Marius?"

"Later," Boutros responded. He wore a white shirt opened around the neck and brown corduroy slacks. Sweat lightly dotted his shirt. He was an inch or two taller than Whit, and his black hair hinting at grey, showed more signs of stress than of age.

Backing up, Boutros motioned dramatically into the room, "I introduce the third of my three angels for you today."

"Whit, get in here and sit down, haven't you eaten at all since last week? Look at you." Martha Khoury, Boutros' wife, was a paragon of Lebanese motherhood. She embraced Whit warmly and then disappeared into the kitchen, directly across a dining room table from the entryway to the apartment. Her slightly plumping figure embodied the dangers of dabbling in one's own hospitality.

The air was stuffy from the lack of ventilation in the apartment. Yet a dash of spiced aromas broke the thickness, and Whit's mouth began to water.

"Look, I have some hummos for you," she proudly exclaimed in a high-pitched voice.

"Martha, let the man sit down first," Boutros began as Whit interjected excitedly,

"How did you know I like hummos?!"

Nadia, "You ate almost the whole bowl by yourself last week."

"Indeed my little pretty! But only to save you from a stomachache!"

Martha nudged Whit's shoulder with her arm and moved across the table to embrace Najwa. Grabbing Najwa's cheeks she began talking to her, and Whit and Boutros stepped out onto the balcony as Boutros lit a cigarette. Nadia followed.

"Nadia, habibti, go inside and help your mother, the smoke is not good for you."

"Then why is it good for you?" she asked.

"It isn't."

"Then why do you do it?" He turned, eyebrows raised to look at her open, olive eyes. Lowering them, she turned and ran inside. Boutros closed the door and turned to look out over the city.

"She's right you know. It will kill you." Whit started.

Boutros issued a brief laugh, "In this city many things could kill me. This," he raised his intonation and his cigarette, holding them both suspended for a moment, "this is the least of my worries."

"Marius looked embarrassed in the hallway," Whit said.

"He should have been, the dirty weasel. They are going to take the whole damn country down with them."

Whit leaned against the balcony banister and turned his back to the city, crossing his arms over his chest as he looked inquisitively at Boutros.

Boutros, turning from the city to see Whit, said, "They are trying to expand the militia."

"Which one is Marius with again? I can't keep them straight."

"I think they call themselves the tigers or something."

"Ah, yes, ok."

"Khalil," Boutros continued, speaking about his 17 year-old son, "asked me, no told me, earlier this week that he was going to join."

"And what did you say?"

"What any father in this God-forsaken city would say," Boutros said, averting eye-contact with Whit as he took a drag on his cigarette. "I forbade it."

"His response?"

"Called me a coward. Said I'd never fought for anything in my life. Said he didn't want to be like me. Then he stormed out. That was last Tuesday. We haven't seen him since."

Whit tried to reassure him, "He'll be back soon. Didn't he do this same thing a couple of months ago?"

"Yeah, it's starting to get old."

"He hardly knows what he is saying. He is too young to know what courage is."

"Maybe he's right. This country is burning to death and I just want to get my family out."

"So what will you do?"

"The same thing I've been trying to do. Keep saving for visas and some way out. Get to Cyprus and then America."

"Lucky for you, you won't have to bribe the American guards."

"No, but the plane tickets, visas, and every thing else is pure extortion. Six years we've been saving and I'm beginning to worry we'll never get enough."

"I thought the Port job would have been paying enough to put more away."

"Not after the union takes their share."

"You must be the only man down there paying his due."

"That's how they get you, Whit. Set the traps along the way so if they ever need to trigger it they can. If you accept their 'gratuities,'" he made air quotes with his finger, "then that's the moment they own you."

"You're an honest man."

"It isn't helping my family any."

"It will."

"I can't be so sure."

"Don't change, Boutros, whatever you do, don't change that."

"Hard to survive these days if you don't."

Whit paused a moment, letting the thought float away with the smoke Boutros exhaled across the balcony rail. "Does Martha want to leave?"

"She's a woman, what do you mean?" Boutros laughed as his tone calmed and softened, "She wants everything at the same time. Wants to be near her family. Doesn't want to be in the midst of this," he said, sweeping his hand again across the city, "but mostly she doesn't want her babies to end up scraping like us. That, in the end, is why she'll go."

"Ah, the woman – how capable of creating a world of her own vision by sheer force of will."

"That's for damn sure," Boutros turned to Whit, "particularly when that will is brought to bear on one man alone." They laughed as the balcony door opened and Najwa leaned out. "What are you two laughing at?"

"Ourselves, baby, ourselves."

"Well quit being so selfish and come in, mama says food is ready."

Whit feigned shock, "Isn't that always the case?"

Najwa smirked and closed the door. Boutros noticed Whit looking after her.

"She loves you, you know." Boutros said, without agenda.

Whit was stunned, and stumbled a bit, "I - I would be a lucky man, Boutros."

"But?"

Whit smiled jovially, dodging Boutros' attempt at sobriety "I'm just afraid of that iron will, my friend."

Boutros laughed it off, "Well she comes by it honestly." They were quiet for a moment, watching the city breathe, "Why are you always lonely, Whit?"

Whit contemplated the question. "Did you go to Mass today?"

"She willed it."

"Haha. What is truth?"

"You think you can answer that?"

"I think I need some, I don't know, time, to figure out what it is I can do – what it is I'm supposed to be doing."

Boutros retorted, "That's your problem – you think too much. You won't think your way into the good life, Whit – you live your way into it." Boutros looked out again across the city, teeming with the same uncertainty that resonated within this young American friend who had blessed his family. Whit had come at a time when they were falling apart. The rage of teenage years, the financial difficulties, the feeling that he wasn't the role model he had hoped to be as a father. He tried so hard, but the world wouldn't let his kids recognize what his decisions meant. Maybe they would some day; maybe it would be too late.

Boutros' thoughts wondered back to when Whit first walked into his family's life. They were visiting AUB when Najwa was applying to colleges. She had applied in the United States, as well. Boutros had hoped to be able to save enough money by that time to get to the U.S. and an American college. But life moved on and the time for her to choose arrived, and Boutros could not pull together the cash to make it happen. Life had gotten more expensive since the unrest started, and every pound he earned had halved in value.

Boutros had been carrying these frustrations with him as the Khourys approached their car several blocks from AUB. Adding to his burdens, four young men got up from small tables at a café and crossed the street towards his family. A motley mix of green and khaki clothes, wild and slicked back hair, they had the the distorted countenances of those warped by habitual vice. Upon first seeing them, Boutros told Martha to go to the other side of the car and get the kids in quickly. He avoided eye contact for as long as possible.

Martha opened the door and shooed the kids in, closing it behind them.

"Well, well, well – you think you own this block my friend?" a wiry youth, wearing black pants and a fatigue jacket, asked in a menacing voice.

"I'm sorry," Boutros said calmly, "I don't understand what you m-"

"Yeah, yeah. You Christians are all the same. You think you own every inch of the country and can do whatever you want here."

Boutros responded, "I think you're mistaken young man, we j-"

The youth lunged forward and stuck his finger aggressively in Boutros' chest. "You don't talk to me in my country, you just listen."

Nadia began to cry inside the car and Khalil put his hand on the door handle. Najwa grabbed his arm and shook her head, but Khalil pushed her off and opened the door on the passenger side, getting out next to Boutros.

"Oh big man coming to help his coward dad. C'mon big man what are you going to do now?!" The vulgar youth nodded to one of his accomplices, a tall, thick-set man wearing khaki pants and a long-sleeved black shirt. The accomplice hit Khalil, knocking him to the ground. Boutros began to step forward and Martha screamed. The man standing over Khalil had pulled a handgun and pointed it at Boutros. Boutros scooped Martha behind him with his left arm and held his right hand out.

"There is no need for thi-" and the leader slapped Boutros across the face.

"Shut up, I told you," his voice rose in volume and tightened with anger, "You don't speak." Then he closed his fist and hit Boutros, who slumped a little and straightened back up, blood now trickling from his mouth. Najwa screamed inside the car.

"Sayyid," one said to the leader, who turned and stared at his accomplice. The man shirked back, but nodded with some trepidation to Najwa sitting in the car.

Sayyid turned and laughed the laugh of a man intent on evil, "Tell her to get out of the car or we'll shoot your son." The man standing over Khalil pressed his gun into the back of Khalil's head.

Boutros said, "Please, just take my money or whatever, but leave my family alone."

"Oh, we're not interested in your money. We just want to talk to her."

Martha blurted out, "You should be ashamed." Boutros moved slightly and a second youth pulled a gun, pointing it at him. He held his hands open before him. Sayyid moved to the car, opened the door and grabbed Najwa by the arm, pulling her out. Khalil tried to jerk up but a boot was now on his neck. Boutros moved slightly forward and Sayyid pulled a knife, pressing it against Najwa's throat as all froze again.

"Now habibti," he said in Najwa's ear, grinning knowingly at Boutros. "Why don't you come have some coffee with me."

As Sayyid began to pull Najwa, a voice came in broken Arabic, "Let go of her and leave the family alone."

All turned to see a foreigner standing in the street.

"Oh, an infidel yabanji coming to the rescue," Sayyid said, using the derogatory curse for a foreigner, "What the hell are you going to do all by yourself, yabanji?"

"You know," the man responded, taking slow steps towards one of the armed youths, "I was having coffee with Yasfir yesterday," they all exchanged nervous looks, Yasfir Hadi was the head of the military wing of their movement. Then Sayyid smirked and said,

"You don't know Yasf-"

"Don't interrupt me, Sayyid," the man said coldly. Sayyid swallowed deeply and stared at the foreigner. "Yasfir was lamenting the presence of so many fools in the PFLP ranks." The man paused, returning Sayyid's gaze, then continued, "He said that discipline had gotten so lax, that they've had to take everyone's ammunition away to keep these fools from starting a war." The three henchman nervously looked at one another again, but Sayyid's eyes remained on the challenger. "My guess, Sayyidi," he continued, adding a playful Arabic ending that meant "My Sayyid," "is that you are just the sort of fool that Yasfir hates."

Sayyid squinted with disgust and trepidation, "Yeah, you don't know Yasfir because these guns are loaded. So what are you going to do now?"

"I think I'll give you one more chance to put your empty guns away. If you don't, I'll start by breaking your friend's arm." The foreigner was now within arms length of the armed man pointing his gun at Boutros, and motioned his arm toward the man. "Then I'll wait a second and, if he," pointing towards the other armed youth, "doesn't drop his gun, I'll have to shoot him. So . . . you can go back to your coffee and leave this family alone. Or . . ."

The unspoken threat lingered in the air momentarily until Sayyid responded, "Or what?"

"Or we can do this right now," the foreigner said, his smile dropping.

Sayyid's smirk evaporated. He stared for a minute longer as his face grew ashen. The man holding the gun on Boutros was visibly shaking, and began to lower the gun to his side.

"You know these people?" Sayyid said, dropping the knife from Najwa and stepping away though still holding her arm.

"That's what I said, so take your hand off of her and walk away."

"Well tell them they don't park on my street anymore." Sayyid motioned for the others to back off and move away. The foreigner stepped in between Najwa and the men. Martha ran over to Khalil to help him up as Najwa gripped the stranger's arm tightly out of fear.

"I'll see you again, yabanji."

"I won't be so patient next time."

Sayyid swallowed deeply again and the men turned and briskly walked back towards the coffee house.

"Thank you," Martha began to say to the foreigner in English, but he interrupted.

"Sir," he said, looking at Boutros, "I am going to get in the front with you, ok?"

"Yes, yes, of course," Boutros responded.

"Ma'am, please get in with your kids, but you," Whit placed his hand on Khalil's shoulder, "you get in and sit on the outside, right behind me, and you and I will watch these men as we drive, off, ok?"

Khalil almost grinned, "Yes sir."

"Ok, everybody in."

Boutros hands shook as he started the car. As they pulled out the foreigner and Khalil stared straight towards the men. They eased off the block, and into the rush of traffic. Nadia began crying.

The foreigner turned to the back seat and looked at Nadia. "Are you ok sweetie?" She nodded as she cried. He pulled a piece of candy out of his pocket and handing it to her said, "I personally think you deserve a prize for being so brave."

Boutros questioned, "What is your name? Who are you, my friend?"

"I'm Cordell Whitaker. I work around the area – so I've seen those guys before."

"We can't thank you enough," Martha said. "You have a place in our home forever."

Whit responded, "I am grateful. But now, if you don't mind my friend," he looked at Boutros, "I should probably get out at this next corner."

"Yes," Boutros said, not sure what to do next. "Yes, of course."

Martha stepped in, "No, wait, can we have you to our home to thank you?"

He paused, as if considering something, and looking them over, said, "I would love to visit you on some other day." He took a piece of paper out of a small spiral notebook and wrote down a phone number and the name "Whit" below it. He handed it to Boutros. Whit got out of the car and nodded to Boutros. Leaning in the open window.

Najwa started speaking, "Are you ok here?"

"Of course." He tapped the hood, but Khalil rolled down the window and grabbed Whit's arm. "Wait, do, do you really know Yasfir?"

"Hm," Whit looked over Khalil's head for a minute and smiled while shaking his head from side to side, "Nah." Khalil laughed as Whit shook his shoulder and turned away, disappearing into the crowd. Khalil got in the front seat. As soon as he shut the door, he put his hand on Boutros' shoulder and shook it, laughing. Boutros looked curiously at Khalil, and then refocused on the road. He pulled out quickly into traffic and towards home.

Boutros's attention hurtled back to the present as Martha opened the sliding glass door to tell him that Khalil had returned to the apartment. Boutros stood quickly and nodded at Whit, who smiled and leaned against the banister, looking out across the city as Boutros walked inside.

# CHAPTER FOUR

A man with a soft, pock-marked face, hunched with his forearms on a set of cross bars. He had bushy hair and a black beard that wound out of his mange like an unkempt garden. It terminated in various shoots and tendrils upon his collar bone. He looked, with one blue eye and one brown, over his shoulder towards Jawad, who was perched on a long bench alone with his thoughts. The man gave a slight nod, and at the moment he turned back to the hallway, a prison guard came into view, leaned slightly towards the bars, and spoke briefly into the man's ear.

The guard had dressed sloppily in a sweat-stained khaki uniform with a khaki cap and an unpolished, black visor. Like the visor, the uniform had the appearance of having been intended for some more presentable purpose, now lost after years of inattention. Pressing himself up from his inclined position after hearing what the guard had to say, the mangey prisoner turned and walked slowly across the cell taking a seat next to Jawad, whose eyes never left the hallway or the prison guard.

In a hushed voice, the man began, "They say your release can be arranged, and no prosecution will be brought, on the condition that you grant free passage to the PFLP in the Arqoub." Jawad held his cold stare through the guard, which said as much as his words momentarily would.

"If there is anything to negotiate with the PFLP, they can do it with me directly. Those making this offer should understand several things. First, they have no basis for a prosecution. Second, I will soon be elected as minister for the Arqoub, and will occupy the Prime Minister's current seat in parliament. I will remember friends, and I will remember those who are not."

The man looked at Jawad, shocked, "Are you sure you want me to-"

"Tell him what I said, Marduk. We will not permit them to interfere with our plans."

"Yes, ok." Marduk began to walk away, and Jawad said,

"Oh, and Marduk,"

"Yes?"

"After you're done with him, get a pass to go call Kasim, and tell him to be here immediately. And not to come alone." A wry smile grew across Marduk's face.

Marduk returned to the bars, and quietly spoke to the guard. Jawad could see the guard's eyes grow in exasperation and then squint with rage. The guard stared at Jawad, and then turned and burst down the corridor without further word.

--

"The infirmary is there just behind and to the right of the arched gate." Sayyid held the binoculars to his face a moment longer then passed them to a man in the driver's seat. The man had a scar running from below his left eye to his ear. As he took them, Sayyid continued, "He'll only be there for another day or two, so we don't have much time."

"Tonight?" the man asked.

"No," Sayyid shook his head slowly, "they're going to have to double the guards for the next few evenings after the fight in the courtyard." A car zoomed past and the men jerked quickly to look. Satisfied there was no threat, Sayyid continued, "No, we have to do this in broad daylight." He received a perplexed stare in response.

"Everyone must know that no one can control the PFLP. They cannot imprison us, and they cannot defeat us. We can act as we please . . . even in broad daylight."

Momentary silence followed. "So how do we do it? It's going to be like trying to drive a truck bomb across the Israeli border."

"Precisely," Sayyid said, as he scribbled something in a notebook, "so we do what they'd never expect – we go right through the front door. We'll work it out tonight."

Sayyid looked through the back window and saw two tan Land Rovers approaching rapidly and kicking up dust. In an instant, they blew past Sayyid's car towards the gate to Roumieh, appearing to speed up rather than slowing down as they approached. Sayyid gripped the dash board as his driver began to speak:

"What the –"

Sayyid held up his hand abruptly, "Watch how they react." His mind was racing as he spoke. Who were these people and why were they driving expensive Land Rovers in the middle of Beirut? He was nervous for what would come next, but excited.

As the cars sped towards the gate, a small portal at the base of the massive steel frame opened and six guards sprinted out and pointed machine guns at the cars which, roughly ten yards from the gate, came to a screeching halt. The cars sat, revving their engines.

"So we need more guys?" Sayyid's driver asked.

"Or a better approach."

At the gates, a voice came over the loud speaker, "Turn off the engines and step out of the cars." For a moment nothing happened, and when the guards all cocked their machine guns and three of them lowered to one knee, the car engines went silent. The driver's side doors of both cars opened, and men stepped out of each, their hands half-way raised in non-committal submission.

Sayyid could see someone still stirring in the back seat of one of the trucks. He saw a guard gesticulating wildly, jerking his rifle as if to command an immediate exit. One heavy-set man stepped out, one arm up and the other inside the door. The guards clearly thought he had a weapon, and surged forward two to three steps as the man held his hand out for them to stop and yelled something. Sayyid still saw faint movement. He leaned forward with interest as a woman, with bowed head was yanked out of the car by the man.

"Let's get the hell out of here, this is going to turn ugly."

"No, wait." Sayyid replied, and his heart raced with hopeful anxiety. The front gate started opening more fully. While his companions focused on the man slowly emerging from the gate, Sayyid took in the structures behind it. His mind created a series of imaginary polaroids he could use later: long wall to the right, two doors, a window in between. Snap. Following the wall enters a courtyard. Snap. Snap. The left side beyond the gate was not visible, but there appeared to be cars parked on that side. Snap. Through the window on the right side wall he barely made out a nurse walking past. Snap. The doors closed.

Immediately, Sayyid's focus shifted to the man coming out of the gate, with full beard laying across his chest, who was now crossing between the guards. He turned and waved his hands sideways, and they all stood down. He entered the car first. The others began piling back in, as one man grabbed the woman forcefully, pushing her into the car. All the doors slammed shut.

"Who is this guy?" Sayyid asked.

"No idea, but everybody else seems to know," came the answer from the back seat.

As the Land Rovers roared past, Sayyid looked in the car, but saw only a furious look on the face of the newly freed man. It was a focused anger, with plans behind it.

"Alright, let's get back. We've got work to do."

# CHAPTER FIVE

"Kadir, before you go on, let me exp-"

"Explain? Explain? You nearly cost me my job. Hell, the way things are going these days, it could have cost me even more than that." Whit sat across from a man in a khaki suit. A white shirt with small black dots hid beneath his jacket. He had long hair, with grey streaks amidst dark black that contrasted with a youthful face. Dark circles absorbed the light beneath his eyes, as his forehead wrinkled with practiced anxiety.

"It will never happen again."

"You are damn right about that, because I'm never going to give anything to you again. I trusted you. Dammit, the U.S. Ambassador was in our office chewing out the Prime Minister. What the hell is wrong with you?"

"Kadir, I drafted the story and never mentioned you or any of Wael's plans."

"So how the hell did the Ambassador know?"

Whit was nodding, "After it ran that night, they cornered me. The Ambassador's deputy was in our offices in an hour demanding to know what we knew. My editor called me and I told them they knew I wouldn't divulge secrets, but they assumed I had a source inside. Someone else told them the Prime Minister's office was planning to agree to some concessions to give the fedayeen freer movement." Kadir gritted his teeth and shook his head. "Kadir, I have to tell my editors more details than goes in the story so they will let it get published. They're not supposed to say anything. It's the only way, and you guys wanted word leaked about how outrageous some of Abou Ammar's demands are so you could keep pressure on him, if you remember."

"I trusted you."

"And I trusted them."

"Now you owe me, Whit."

Whit stared back, hating the part of Kadir that he saw in himself. There was a ruthless streak that found leverage and exploited it to the fullest extent. Kadir's streak was born from a survival instinct; Whit always envisioned his own as serving some higher purpose. At this moment when he could see the table being turned on him, he wasn't quite sure which was more justifiable.

"What do you have in mind?" Whit asked, begrudgingly.

"There's a new movement down south." Kadir began.

Whit immediately recognized where this was headed. "You don't say?"

"C'mon. You know it."

"And it just so happens to be in Wael's district?"

"That is incidental." Whit was always impressed at how Kadir's English tightened when he was seeking the kill, so that his speech morphed into a pellucid arrangement of syllables that expressed his sentiment as clearly as a native speaker.

"Well I can't get down there to do a story, so . . ."

"We need to know where he's getting his money, and what he's doing with it." Kadir interjected, ignoring Whit's excuses.

Whit laughed and started a response, "You've got to be kid-"

"Penance is never going to be easy, Cordell." Kadir interrupted, again. The two stared at one another, Kadir in anticipation; Whit, in disdain.

"Penance is between me and God, Kadir. For you, it's just a favor."

"That's the least you can do."

"Just so we're clear, I don't owe you anything." Kadir laughed indignantly, as though in control, but Whit continued, "And your boss is losing votes with every Israeli bomb down south, so I'd exercise a bit more discretion."

"You let me worry about his prospects."

"It sounds like you are."

Kadir stared at Whit as Whit rose to leave.

"I'll see what I can find out."

"I'll walk out with you." They moved out into the halls of the parliament building, reaching the doors and stepping out into Nejmeh Square. The sand-colored buildings, each four or five stories tall, glowed soft orange in the early evening sun. Square was somewhat of a misnomer, as the area sat at the intersection of roughly eight streets which met in a circle around a large statue.

"How much time do you think you have, Kadir?"

"What do you mean?"

"Look around." Men in suits and women in elegant dresses walked back and forth across the square. Wild-print purple and orange ties, khaki suits, violet and red dresses scurried to and fro. The streets were lined with banks, cafes with outdoor seating, and conspicuous consumption. "You've got communists ready to tear this all apart and camps with no running water or electricity just a few miles away."

As Kadir contemplated the question, Whit watched the front door to the Banque du Liban open. A thin-built man with wire-framed glasses emerged and strolled into the street.

"Do you recognize him?"

Kadir looked over and shrugged his shoulders, shaking his head no. The two shook hands and Kadir got in a car near the Parliament and drove away. Whit followed the Banque du Liban employee for several blocks. The man eventually turned a corner, and when Whit reached it, he peered around. The door to a tan Land Rover was slamming shut, and the car lurched forward behind an identical SUV.

# CHAPTER SIX

"In the name of the Father, and of the Son, and of the Holy Spirit," Whit said, as he knelt in the confessional, beginning the rite.

"Amen," they said in unison.

"Forgive me Father, for I have sinned, it has been," Whit hesitated, then proceeded ambiguously, "quite some time since my last confession."

The confessional booth contained a small wooden kneeler with a rectangular purple cloth, tattered at the edges. It was embroidered with a yellow cross and hung from a rusting rail. The screen in between the confessor and the priest was wearing thin. It was pocked with the dirt of the streets that swept into the sanctuary with the increasingly infrequent opening and closing of the doors. Several candles were lit, throwing the lives of saints and sinners into relief on the walls around the chapel. In one frame, a man lifting his eyes to heaven in permanent contemplation, held a pen in his hand. A skull stared blankly at him from a crude desk. Nearby, a statue of the

Virgin Mary stood looking mercifully upon her children. Her hands were held open, welcoming the suffering with the frail beads of a rosary jingling loosely in the occasional breeze passing beneath her left hand.

An old lady or two knelt in contemplation. The darkness was punctuated by the flickering candlelight and the earthy pungency of incense. It was a distinct scent, like a resinous wood kindling slowly and mixing with a deep, thick spice that filled your lungs rather than simply scratching the nose.

That scent was the same Whit had smelled a thousand times before, and always it was associated with his first consciousness of regret and mercy – that inexplicable tension that wound about the ballast of reconciliation in every human's life. He was seven again, and preparing for his first confession. Each penitent prepared to meet the terror of self-revelation. The way each confessed presaged how their journey would play out. At eight, Rick Ebbers, who had four older brothers, thought the whole affair a riotous joy, and looked forward to confessing having sex before marriage. Whit wasn't sure what that meant, but it sounded bad. Others were completely oblivious to any wrongdoings. Some, like Whit, bore heavily the accumulated guilt a second grader carries, convinced of certain damnation for a lifetime of inequities. So nervous was he to confess that he became sick to his stomach when the time neared. He examined his conscience just like he had been taught.

The examination. Step one. Memorize the ten commandments. Step two. Ask yourself how you have broken each commandment and prepare to confess it. Step three. Be truly sorry for your sin and intend never to do it again. For a child of seven, this often led to a great deal of hard thought, particularly since Sister insisted that you have at least one thing to answer for with each commandment. She couldn't know what she was asking; how hard a thing she demanded. She probably sinned once, maybe twice in her whole life. Though Whit had seen her sneaking cookies once between classes.

Thou Shalt Have No Other gods Besides Me. That one was hard to think of anything to say. How could he worship any other god? Over time, though, this edict became shocking in ways. How direct was this demand; almost like a jealous lover fearing infidelity. He found it difficult to reconcile the Yahweh of the Old Testament with the image of the God he had come to know when older. He wondered what kind of God would lower himself to man's stature the same way he wondered why a man would let himself fall in love. Exposing oneself to the vicissitudes of disappointment and heartbreak.

The God of the Old Testament seemed so different. God saw what he made, and it was Good. Really? Would God have felt it was Good had he known that Eve would take the apple? Or did he know, and still think it was Good? If so, why was it so bad that she took it? If he didn't know, how is he really God? And what kind of God loses his temper with beings so infinitely inferior to him? How could he nearly erase creation, then regret it and promise, with a seemingly over-emotive kaleidoscope of colors, never to do it again? What kind of loving Father commands someone to kill his own son and then stops him in the middle of the act? What kind of all-powerful being grows jealous when people build a tower and curses them with linguistic chaos? Who tortures a man throughout his life because of a bet that the sufferer would keep his faith.

"How many?" the frail but friendly voice on the other side questioned.

"What?"

"How many years?"

"Oh, Gaspar Vartabed, you'd be disgusted."

"Nonsense."

"Too many."

The feeling of guilt rushed back like a returning tide and the rip curl submerged him in his childhood once more. Sister lifted her aging hand towards him. The moment had come. The index finger rolled inward in a motion of beckoning towards that terrifying mystery that lay beyond the wall. How could he avoid it? What could he do? As she raised her eyebrows and clamped the finger again tightly to her palm, he knew the time for thought was over. Timidly, he walked into the room. A priest in black vestments and a purple stole around his neck was facing the other direction quietly, awaiting the horrible truths he had to tell. But the man's voice was gentle and welcoming.

For what seemed like hours the seven-year-old Whit listed off every affliction he had chosen, and even some he had not. The guilt of years of silence flowed forth like a torrent, and then, just as abruptly, he could not think of anything further for which he was responsible. In the dramatic crescendo he had been taught – the graceful catch-all for those forgotten peccadilloes to which we've become so accustomed we do not even recognize them – he recited, "and I am very sorry for all my sins." Instantaneously, as though thrashed by an incredulous God, candles stacked on a wall came crashing down to the floor, scaring young Whit and rousing the aging priest from his somnolent watch over the gates of youthful indiscretion. Remembering the fall, he was awakened from his reverie.

"For tonight, I will agree with you, Cordell. But one day soon, I will not."

"Have the sisters and children been safe?" Whit was asking about the orphanage and school attached to Gaspar Vartabed's church.

"You know they don't cause problems in the Armenian areas."

"What can you tell me, Father?"

"The sisters did a tour of one of the refugee camps with medicine again yesterday."

"They need to be careful. The PFLP doesn't care what clothes they wear. Which camp?"

"It's their calling, Cordell. It was Tal Za'atar," the priest said, describing one of the larger Palestinian refugee camps.

"At any rate, they noticed a room with a lot of armed men coming and going. As one of the sisters was giving a shot to a child, the door stayed open for quite a while. Inside she said she could see men standing around a table and pointing at something on the table."

"Did she know who they were?"

"No."

"Could she describe them if I gave you pictures?"

"Perhaps you should speak with her."

"Probably better for me to communicate through you. They're probably following the sisters and watching what they do. If they ever stop them and ask them who they talk to, it'd be important for them truly to know nobody but you."

"Ok. And what if they want to talk to me?"

"You just tell them you have hundreds of parishioners all over the city. Did she say anything else?"

"She said three or four had thick beards and all of them were wearing soldiers' uniforms."

"Hmm," Whit could not expect much detail from the sisters, but at least they could alert him from time to time about what they saw.

"Could she hear anything they were saying?"

"Not really, but she thought they were standing around a map. And they were shouting and arguing about something. And that's really all she said."

"Ok, thank you, Father."

"Whit, now for your confession."

"Not tonight, Father. But thank you."

The old man sat with an almost bereaved, lonely look on his face. Whit rose and stepped outside of the confessional. He turned towards the altar, and his memory lifted like rising incense, wafting through years of examinations. There were other sins to consider. Though Shalt Keep Holy the Sabbath. Thou Shalt not take the Name of the Lord in Vain. Honor Thy Father and Mother. Thou Shalt Not Kill.

This fifth had been the most mysterious to him as a child. In his youth, it seemed laughable. He failed to understand how it could ever be relevant. It was not until he became a man that its full severity would be apparent. It was not until he came to Lebanon that he would confront the moral weight of the irrevocable.

# CHAPTER SEVEN

The young man looked towards the front of the line impatiently as the floodlights blinded those waiting to be checked. He was an aged looking youth with a goatee and long hair hanging down to the middle of his neck. The shadows from the floodlight blended with the dark circles under his eyes to create a hollow, exhausted appearance. His glasses betrayed an academic bent that forced others to take him less seriously in a world where a violent temperament was valued above all else. He was in line at a checkpoint entry to the Tel Za'atar camp, and could see the irritable Palestinian fedayeen guards picking their way through those waiting.

He noticed as he looked around that it was a mixed crew of people, with mostly men coming from a long day's work wherever they were in the city. These were the lucky ones who had the work permits required of Palestinian refugees by the Lebanese state.

The exhausted youth noticed a young, slight man in front of him also looking intently at the guards and down at his watch. The man had a brown suit and a light blue shirt. He checked his watch so frequently that he made his tired neighbor increasingly anxious.

"I don't think it will make this go more quickly," the tired man said to the slight man, who then turned and smiled.

"It doesn't even work," he said, laughing as he showed the watch to his new friend. "I just check it every time they look this way to keep from making eye contact." Then the smaller man extended his hand, "My name is Salman."

"Ahlan, Salman."

"Are you saving your words up? What is your name, my friend?"

"Michel," the tired man responded.

"Well, Michel, how long have you lived in the camps?"

"I am just visiting."

Salman started immediately at hearing just a few more words, "You speak with an accent – you didn't grow up in the camps?"

"No. My parents fled to Europe after the Nakhba and I was raised in France. I came back to go to the American University."

"What are you studying?"

"I'm writing my PhD on camp life. You were raised here?"

"All my life I have lived in this squalor. I don't know how much longer I can take it. Ah, my friend, I am tired tonight, but please come soon and we will walk around the camp together."

"That's very kind of you, Salman."

Michel and Salman stood together talking as a figure emerged from under the flood lights at the camp's entrance. Michel took notice over Salman's shoulder. At first, Michel could not make it out, but the form moved so aimlessly and slowly that he mistook it for a guard inspecting those waiting. As Salman talked and gesticulated, his voice faded from Michel's senses. Michel was focused on this figure moving slowly from the light. The fedayeen guards grew quiet as the figure drew alongside them.

The guards were an edgy group of mixed deportment. Two wore full army fatigues that would have been better suited to hiding them in a Cambodian jungle than urban Beirut; though their signature black and white checked headscarves placed them appropriately enough. Another wore brown pants with a fading greenish jacket and a khaki hat. They stood somewhat lazily, one with an AK-47 slung upwards over his shoulder, one with a holster on a belt, and a third, seemingly unarmed, with the khaki pants and a thick black mustache that fell over the front and sides of his mouth. Michel watched as the two armed fedayeen spoke to each person and the third stood a few feet away, his attention wandering. They motioned, and the elderly man nearest in line produced a grouping of papers that they shuffled through nominally before waiving him onward.

Then, a shadow, extending fifteen feet across the ground passed across his feet, and Michel's attention was again drawn to the floating figure pitched in relief against the low-set floodlights. As the figure moved closer, Michel could make out the build of a man, turning his head to the line while continuing to move slowly beside it.

The shadowed man, whose face was still shrouded in darkness, moved closer to Michel. The powerful floodlights captured every particle of the chalky air, but through it Michel finally made out a middle-aged man, hard-worn by the sun but with a chilling vacancy in his eyes. The man did not stop walking, moving slowly beside the line. He was wearing tattered jeans and a white linen shirt. The shirt was threadbare and had not been washed in months. Grains of dirt had accumulated in the cuffs and waste line, dirtying the edges of the cloth. Across the shirt, from the upper left shoulder through the middle of the top of the stomach was a deep maroon streak that was fading to black. His forearms were scarred.

As the man neared Michel, a chill ran through the latter in visceral recognition of something horrifying. He couldn't quite identify it, but felt he had sensed it somewhere before. The man's face was receding perpetually. But it wasn't just vacancy; it was a look of indifference to life. He seemed to be looking not just at Michel, but into him, and even still while into him, also completely through him.

The man's unwavering stare settled on Michel's eyes. As Michel felt a sickness rise in response to this seemingly unearthly gaze, he said a prayer to himself. The shadowed man let out a long gasp, as though slightly in pain and laboring even to breathe. Then, in a monotone, drawn out wheeze, he whispered to Michel, "It will not help you."

"What?" Michel gasped quietly but almost involuntarily, stunned. Had he prayed out loud?

The figure cackled and then grew serious again. "Do not hope." Michel felt his heart plunge to his stomach. The man's eyes opened wide, still staring through Michel rather than seeming to really be attentive to him. He whispered again, "Do not hope."

Michel noticed that everyone in line had turned to watch, even the fedayeen. A drop of sweat rolled down his face, but he refused to look away. Michel silently began praying again. The man winced and for a moment seemed to focus on something over Michel's shoulder. The man let out another audible and shocked gasp as though he had suddenly become reacquainted with the world and made some authentic connection – whether wanted or not – that momentarily filled his vacancy.

The man turned away, almost as if to cry in pain, grimacing and squeezing his eyes shut. Then he slowly walked into the darkness beyond the reach of the floodlights.

Whether out of pure exhaustion or some other motive, Salman and others quietly shuffled forward in the line. Before they came to the guards, Salman turned to Michel and said, "I hope to see you soon. I live four streets in next to Fayed's bakery. Ask anyone around there for me and they will show you the way."

After a few minutes, Salman passed the guards and paused to look back. He then turned away and walked into the camp.

----

It was close to midnight as Michel finally passed through the gate into the camp, but still there were a host of people, mostly men, smoking, sitting in the street, and chatting. Armed fedayeen, headscarves, jackets hanging open, and guns hanging lazily over their shoulders, walked back and forth like extras on a poorly-lit stage. Out of his pocket, Michel drew a metal flask and took two swigs. In the distance he could see a small hut with a makeshift tin roof hanging low over several wooden poles. Inside there was a gathering of men in various camouflaged fatigues.

As Michel moved closer to the gathering, he tripped and stumbled several steps forward. He bumped into a fedayeen soldier who pushed him, "Watch where you're going, fool."

Michel then staggered into the doorway of the gathering. Men were shouting back and forth over a table and pointing at various portions of a map. No sooner had Michel woozily leaned into the door than a young fedayeen grabbed him by the armpits and pulled him up.

"I know you."

Michel stammered, "I – I don't, haven't remembered you."

"You sit and write in the coffee shop outside AUB all the time."

"I'm student . . . student . . ." Michel said, with a feigned inebriated smile.

"What are you doing here?"

"I s-stay here s-some nights, I'm writing my diss- my diss, my dissertation on the camps."

"Sayyid, get over here and look at this," someone yelled from near the table.

"I'm watching you," the young fedayeen said as he pushed Michel up against the wall, knocking the flask out of his hands and onto the ground just inside the door. The young man walked towards the table. Michel stumbled out of the doorway and towards the end of the building. As he rounded the corner, he miraculously regained his balance and dexterity. Immediately, he pulled what appeared to be a cassette player out of his pocket and once ensconced in the darkness of the alley, he leaned against the wall and slunk down, putting headphones on and pressing the play button on the cassette player. In his ears the sounds of the room crackled alive. A loud, percussive thud split his ears. Someone must have kicked the flask. Then voices slowly came into range.

". . . you do not know what you are doing. The first thing they'll do is attack the camps."

"They have been attacking us for years, it's time we showed them they don't control us."

"We're here," fuzz and crackling again interfered with his hearing, ". . . the enemy. But you want to use all," crackling, "the Lebanese Army."

"They're keeping us from fighting in the south, we have to carve out space for," crackling and fuzz. Michel winced as the loud noise ripped through his ears. He pulled the earphones away momentarily, putting them back he heard, "weak – now is the time."

"What are you talking about? They have tanks and mount-," crackling, "we have a bunch of spent skeletons just off several years in Jordan. It will be the same thing all over-" Michel could tell that the voice arguing to fight was definitely Sayyid's, but did not recognize the other voice.

"Abou Ammar does not condone your strategy . . ."

"Abou Ammar?! We're fighting a world revolution and he loses everywhere. He just lost us Jordan, but we won't let him lose Lebanon. The time is now."

Then a muffled word was spoken, perhaps a name, "You cannot fight a war with everything that moves. Remember we are trying to regain our homeland."

"If it moves and it is not Palestinian, then it is the enemy."

Silence again. "You dig your own grave, but we will not let you bury us, too."

"What the," fuzz again, "mean?"

"Think about what you are doing. We have to fight the enemy, and we cannot beat them if we're fighting everyone else."

"The people refuse to be subjugated to Zionism and economic imperialism. They hold us in these camps and barely let us out to work. They are no better than the Jews. We will end them all."

"You," a loud clang interrupted, ". . . warned."

Michel then saw a group of men walking rapidly past the alley and getting in several trucks parked across the street.

"You don't warn me," Sayyid yelled from the doorway, "you are with them or with us."

A man in the lead truck got in the passenger side and stood for a minute on the rim, looking towards the building. Michel thought for a second that the man looked at him, and leaned over as if in pain in the alley. When Michel looked back up, the cars were pulling away rapidly.

Michel removed the earphones and put the cassette player back in his pocket. He waited for a few minutes and when he saw Sayyid walking away from the building, he stumbled out of the alley and back around the corner. He tripped his way into the door of the empty room, and leaned over to pick up his flask, but as he did, he stopped and stared at the map on the table. On it was a circle with three arrows. Michel turned to look and saw no one near the building. He quickly stepped towards the map, and taking a small rectangular box from his pocket, he pointed it at the circle and turned a tiny knob on its side. He leafed through some other documents, stopping to point and turn the knob.

When he heard footsteps outside, he rushed back to the door and bent over again and scooped his hands back and forth until they came to rest on the flask. At that instant, a boot came crushing down on his hand, the rough sole tearing his skin. He winced in pain, and looked up to see Sayyid.

"What are you doing, ass?"

"I dr, dr, dropped my f–f–f–flask."

"If I don't see you carrying a gun next week, I'm not going to let you in this camp anymore."

"I w–write, Sayyid, I just w–write. Not everyone shoots a gun."

"If you're not shooting than you're a Zionist donkey," Sayyid said, spitting on the ground.

Michel slowly unwrenched his hand from underneath Sayyid's boot.

"You c-can't k-keep me out," Michel stammered. Sayyid struck Michel across the face with the back of his hand. Michel wiped a drop of blood, "th- this is Abou Ammar's camp and I'm here with F- Fateh's permission."

"Fateh?" Sayyid said, disgusted. "Their days are numbered. A new world is coming and you'll see who the real revolutionaries are."

Sayyid looked on scornfully as Michel drug his bleeding hand across the floor, grabbed his flask, put it in his coat, and lurched towards the door.

"Find a gun, Michel. You join the revolution or deal with the consequences."

Michel and Sayyid stared at one another for a long moment. Then Michel turned his eyes to the floor, stepped outside and walked with some unease towards a dark street across from the low-set building. Sayyid turned to look in the room and noticed the map was still on the table. When he turned back, Michel was gone.

----

Minutes later, a man sat in a hotel room overlooking the main gate of Tal Za'atar. He watched as Michel exited the gate and stood next to a phone booth, lighting a cigarette. Michel quickly threw it down and stepped once with each foot on it. The man picked up a phone and dialed a number.

"It's him – we have something." The man grabbed a jacket and hurried towards the room door.

In the street, Michel stepped once more on the cigarette and started walking down a long alley. He crossed three more streets, rushing through traffic and drawing the ire of the cab drivers moving slowly through the dense Beirut night, then entered a lively café. Music was playing as men sat watching soccer on tv and talking. Women sat intermittently amidst the crowd caressing some of the men. Waitresses moved through the room serving tea. Cigarette smoke wafted through the air, and the patrons' attention was focused on so many distractions that Michel slipped through virtually unnoticed.

Michel walked straight to the back and entered the restroom. He looked around, walked to the third stall, stepped inside, removed a small block from the heel of his shoe, and placed it behind the toilet. Walking out of the bathroom and seeing a man in a blue jacket in the entryway to the cafe, he turned and exited out the back.

Small with slicked black hair and tortoise-shelled glasses, the man with the blue jacket went into the restroom, walked to the third stall and shut the door. He reached back, feeling for something. Then stopping, he pulled hard and looked at the block in his hand. He put it in an envelope, which he placed inside his jacket pocket, and then returned to the open café, leaving out the front door.

A taxi cab was sitting out front. A young couple started opening the door and the driver told them he was off duty. When they stepped back angrily, the man in the blue jacket slid into the cab through the open door. The young man stepped towards him in disbelief, but backed down as the cab sped off. The couple looked at each other in surprise, laughed and clumsily ambled down the street towards an unknown destination.

In the cab, the driver turned to the man in the jacket, "What is it?"

"I don't know yet."

Through a lens the man looked at a thin ribbon of film that he had pulled out of the little box.

"Drive faster, drive faster!"

# CHAPTER EIGHT

"Trust me, if we knew what it was we would have already tried to stop it. It's a phantom the people make up. A bed time tale they tell their children. The third force will get you, eat your hummus. The third force will get you, don't talk back to your grandma. The third force . . ."

". . . will get you when it blows a hole through the wall and kills your parents."

The man sat smoking across from Whit, unimpressed with his grim humor. Tufts of black chest hair rolled out of the man's orange shirt, which contrasted even more strongly with his khaki suit. The blackness of his hair gave way to a saltier thinning of his mustache and head. Bags hung under his eyes; the deposit of years of accumulated exhaustion.

"Look, the truth is we don't have enough men any more to fully understand what's going on. This is off the record, right?"

"Of course, Camille."

Smoke poured out of Camille, hovering around him as though he was forced to speak secrets through a dense fog. Camille offered a cigarette to Whit, who declined. He offered one to the American sitting next to Whit and furled his brow, as though in pain, as the American took the cigarette, "What did you say your name was?"

"Royce." The man was a smaller figure than Whit and Camille, with brown hair and a square-set jaw. His jaw sat atop a mantle of muscle passing as a neck and shoulders.

"Why does it take two journalists to interview one guy?"

"I'm actually not a journalist. I'm an archeologist."

"Whatever you are, none of this is getting quoted or it's the last time I see you guy . . . wait, an archeologist? Why on earth are you with him?"

"Camille," Whit said, "we've been over this before, I never quote you. We wanted to catch up, but we also wanted to get your signature on some permits to go down south."

"Why do you need to go south?"

"He," Whit motioned to Royce, "wants to look at some ruins and I want to interview villagers down there to get a sense for the climate. And neither of us want to go alone."

"Neither of you should go at all. It's getting out of control down there."

"How do you mean?"

"The fact is they've won."

"They?" Whit and Royce shifted. Whit was wearing a light khaki jacket and jeans. He had on a collared polo underneath the jacket.

"The PLO. Ever since the Cairo Accord. Once President Chehab left office, the Deuxieme Bureau started to lose our budget and our manpower. We used to have eyes and ears in all the camps throughout the city, and all over the country. But in just two years we've lost probably two thirds of our resources. Now it's all we can do to find out what's going on at the same time you guys do – and you probably have a better idea of who's responsible." Camille spoke impeccable English which he learned in Maronite schools and polished off at the American University of Beirut.

Whit noted off hand, "Well if that were true, my editors wouldn't be asking me to do this story. So how can it remain such a mystery how the violence always flares? I just don't get it, Camille. For what, three, four years, random outbreaks of violence and no one can trace the source?"

"Your guess is as good as mine," Camille paused for dramatic effect as his sense of humor returned, "maybe it's the devil."

The three laughed and Whit grew animated. "Now I think you've got it. I'm done here, Royce," Whit held his hands up, and he looked majestically towards the horizon through the imaginary headline his fingers framed, "American journalist wins Pulitzer for uncovering the source of Lebanon's violence: Satan."

Camille and Royce laughed, "C'mon, you two, as weak as we've gotten it might as well be the devil out there. We'll never know the difference."

"In any case, Camille, we want to go south."

"Even if I gave you permission, only God knows if the PLO will let you through."

"We're going to the Arqoub," Whit said, speaking of the mountainous region in the southeast part of the country that stretched away from Mount Hermon and was bordered by Syria on the east and Israel on the south.

"The Arqoub?!" Camille blurted in shock. "Why not go straight to hell? It would probably be just as safe."

"I thought you guys had control down there?"

"In hell?! No, we're just the gatekeepers." They laughed again as Camille continued, "Look, according to the official line we do." Camille dusted his cigarette in an ash tray, thought for a moment, then leaned forward, prompting the Americans to do the same. Lowering his voice, Camille said, "It's no secret that we're losing control down there just as much as we are here. The truth is we're not strong enough to stop anything they do down there, and their numbers are increasing. Our military is under-resourced and divided along sectarian lines, and our hands are tied by bickering parliamentarians."

"So let me go down there and write about it – expose the problems."

"We've got even more serious issues than that, Whit. I'll give you the permit, but you're on your own for getting around, and given everything else that's going on, I would officially caution you not to visit the region."

"Everything else?" Whit said as his eyebrows' raised and he exchanged glances with Royce. Camille grimaced and simply shook his head no.

"C'mon, Camille," Whit said, "you can't drop that and then leave me hanging."

Camille again sat pensively. He looked at Royce and then back at Whit. "There's a renegade strongman down there, not fedayeen, he's Lebanese. Supposedly building a near cult-like power base, mixing religion and militancy in a way no one has done before."

"I thought it was just Shi'a and Druze who are angry about the constant fighting?"

"He took his own people away from another militant group, and he's supposed to be real sick. He's recruiting the youths in the name of fundamentalist ideologies. Not really representative of the religion if you know what I mean. Hell, he's even running for parliament. You know what else," the two Americans leaned further towards Camille, "he was in jail up here in Beirut, but was just released. The prosecutor says they don't have enough on him, and the prime minister's office is livid." Whit stared motionless as a light clicked.

"You don't say?"

"Yeah. But of course, none of his constituents know about what goes on behind the curtain. He's just out spreading money all around, and no one can figure out where he gets it."

"What is his name?"

"Keswani. Jawad Keswani."

Camille lit another cigarette while he watched the name sink in. "What are you guys doing here, anyway? If I was born in America, I'd be sitting on the beach drinking a beer."

"But you wouldn't be surrounded by Lebanese women."

Whit and Royce laughed as Camille shook his head, embracing the humor with a certain irony. "Get 'em while they're young," Camille shouted, "before they look like that!" he pointed at a picture of a heavy-set woman roughly his age.

"I don't know what you're talking about, she's an image of beauty."

Camille extinguished the cigarette, "She's the third force, I'll tell you that much." And the three laughed again.

"So you see, Whit," Camille continued, "even if we get the resources, the political climate has turned against us. It's gotten so bad that if we found out that Sa'iqa was going to gun down the President, the President's office would be too afraid of Parliament to let us do anything. Any move I make against the fedayeen, I have to answer up and down the chain."

"So what do you do?" Whit asked.

"I move against them every time I get a tip." They all laughed.

"Where's that gonna lead?"

"Either I'll get fired or someone will blow me up in my car."

"So the same outcome either way." Royce said dryly.

They laughed again and Camille interjected, "Now I know why you brought him, he has a Lebanese sense of humor. Anyway, I've got work to do. You come back tomorrow and get your permits. May God have mercy on your souls."

# CHAPTER NINE

The next morning Michel woke early. He poured water from a tub on the floor of his nearly barren apartment, and removed a straight edge razor from his bag. Rubbing a small amount of shaving cream onto his face, he scratched the stubble that had begun to grow after a long night.

He finished shaving, splashed cold water on his face, and threw on a dark brown, cotton shirt as he grabbed his bag. He turned to take one glance for anything forgotten in the apartment. The only visible items were a mattress on the ground and a chair and a desk that stood empty against the wall. As the sun broke across the horizon, he walked with a purpose out the door.

A few minutes later, Michel made out a fading sign with Fayed's name on it. As he slowly approached, he heard an enthusiastic voice, "Michel, my friend, good morning!"

Brock Dahl

Michel turned to see Salman. "Wow, habibi, did you sleep in the streets last night? Next time we have a couch you can use."

The dust, only loosely resting atop the parched streets, swirled and rose. It brushed across the cement block buildings, leaving a residue of rootlessness through its unceasing abrasion. The streets bustled with people moving back and forth while shielding their eyes from the abusive air.

"No water again last night," Salman said, "if they think they can kick us out by cutting that off, they don't know what we can endure!"

"How many days have you been without water?"

"I lose track, this time maybe eight. We had it for just a few days. I'm not sure if it's more difficult to go without that or electricity."

Michel looked around to see a series of low-slung wires crisscrossing the air between the cement buildings. On some, various flags or banners hung, turning a makeshift effort to electrify the camp into kitsch revolutionary art. The banners heralded the fighter-leaders, ironically displayed on empty wires.

"Can we build our own generators?"

"Phah," Salman said, "Where have you been living? The fedayeen use the few we have for their munitions factories. If someone wants to bake bread, let him wait his turn. But if it's a bullet you need, well my friend, have a light!"

"Why aren't you carrying a gun, Salman?"

"Like I said last night. I've got plans. I'm gonna get out of here. There's a girl, my friend."

"Isn't there always?" They both smiled.

"Not like her. Fatin is the one."

"So what's holding you back?"

64

"You really are a foreigner. Look around. I go to work and make barely enough to eat. Her father is a proud man. He won't even consider talking to me until he knows I have enough to pay a decent dowry and get an apartment on my own. And . . ." But Salman hesitated, as though he didn't want to contemplate something further.

"Yes?"

"He's a local Fateh commander named Musa Rasoul. I think, maybe, he expects me to join the movement and become a soldier."

"Well it seems like there are plenty of those walking around. Steal her away and get out of here!"

"I wish, but we couldn't hide. Musa Rasoul is my uncle!"

Busily walking to and fro, women wore small headscarves around their heads. They were not fully covered, but tied around their necks and chins. Many wore all black with white head coverings. The men wore a range of jeans and pants, as though ready for a days work. Instead, most stood in the streets talking without opportunity. The women seemingly constructed the daily basics for their family out of the dirt on the ground.

Fedayeen guards stood around wearing a kaleidoscope of uniforms and AK-47's slug around their shoulders. All seemed to be waiting, waiting, waiting.

As Salman and Michel walked, several people passing by greeted Salman. A young man and woman, probably in their early twenties, stopped. The man was the physical opposite of Salman, muscular with hair combed back across his head. The woman, modestly covered, possessed a striking beauty and the type of eyes that seemed to have seen too much of life, despite their youthful energy.

"Michel, these are my cousins, Adib and Fatin."
Michel was startled for a second, but as they spoke, he
watched a car full of fedayeen several blocks away race
up to a building. Four men jumped out and began
unloading several crates. He could not tell their contents
from so far off, but they were so long and skinny he
thought they must be rocket launchers of some make,
probably Russian.

Michel knew from his research that by this point
Lebanon had became an armaments bizarre. Guns were
flowing in from every patron in the region and beyond.
Syria armed it's own militia, Sa'iqa, as well as others.
The Russians helped the fedayeen and Lebanese
communists; the Egyptians stayed close to Fateh. The
Americans and the Israelis aided some of the Christian
militias.

"Michel, Adib and Fatin want to know if we can join
them for dinner."

"Ah yes," Michel his attention reverting, "I could
come for a bit this evening but have to be back on
campus late tonight."

"Oh, you work too hard!" Adib jested, "Come when
you can, though. You are always welcome." As the
group shook hands and Adib and Fatin departed, Michel
saw Sayyid walk outside the buildings in the distance.
Salman noticed.

"Do you know this man?"

"Only from seeing him around AUB."

"I suppose he spends a lot of time there. He's a local
PFLP henchman. His commander is currently in jail and
he's just been harassing everyone in sight. But forgive me
for speaking out of turn."

"No, it's quite alright. I've heard this. What do you
know about him?"

"We had been friends when we were children. There was only one school in the camp, and we're roughly the same age. We studied and played together. At some point Sayyid's family moved south, and when he returned to Beirut in his teens, he was different. I remembered him being so happy before, but after coming back he was just full of hate. I heard his father was killed in fighting in the South. He told me once he joined the PFLP because it was the only group that really stood up for our people. But, that was really the last I ever talked much with him. He's become increasingly impossible since he joined."

They spoke as Salman showed the camp to Michel. It was a self-contained community, with substantial production capacity for such a rudimentary place. Michel also noticed the unique layout of several nicer homes in the camp. They consisted of a doorway passing through to a courtyard, with the home aligned around the courtyard on three or four sides.

"I grew up in France. I don't understand the courtyards."

"It is a private space. The family's refuge from the world."

It was into just such a courtyard that Michel and Salman were ushered after they showed up at Fatin's home that evening. Adib was the first to welcome them. In the courtyard there was an array of plastic chairs around a low table. There were a number of middle-aged men sitting in a few of the chairs. All wore various iterations of suits and dress shirts without ties. Adib patiently introduced them one by one as they gave the faintest acknowledgement of Salman and Michel, one or two tossing their prayer beads up in minute recognition.

While the group waited, Adib, Michel and Salman sat in one corner. The sun streamed low through the latticed portico between the courtyard and the street. It was the time of day when shadows cast long across the ground. The sun had started to burn a phosphorescent orange that bathed the land in a sideways light. A soft glow filled every open space with a dream-like sheen, conjuring wistful memories of one's past, plated gold in the declining light which, like memory, brought forth new shapes and images from an otherwise familiar landscape. In the courtyard, it had the disorienting effect of casting the entire area in shadows while a burst of rays streamed through the doorway and the tiled glasswork. The middle-aged men continued swinging their prayer beads, quietly sitting at the other end of the courtyard from where Salman, Adib, and Michel sat.

Adib carried on, "So, Michel, how long have you been here in Beirut?"

"Only a year. I am here doing research."

"Ah, and what do you think of our fine city?"

"It is charming."

"Liar!" Adib roared with a smile. "It is a furnace, and we are at its center."

"Nonsense, it is the anteroom to paradise!" A loud voice boomed as a man, standing roughly six feet four inches tall, ducked through a doorway and strode proudly into the courtyard. His torso spread wider towards his hips, but his suit jacket hid the bulky frame. He carried his hands around the room like factory gloves, outsized and awkward, as he embraced and clasped the seemingly miniature paws each risen guest had offered him. He was clean shaven with deep set eyes, and his thinning, slate colored hair, was combed back in wisps across his head. Musa Rasoul worked his way around the gathering until he arrived to Salman.

"Salman, welcome to my home again. We haven't seen you for some time."

"Yes, uncle, I have been out working much these days."

"Still working outside the walls?! We need all our men in here. Why would you work for them?" Musa intoned, as Salman stared blankly.

Musa Rasoul excused him his perplexity without pressing, turning to Michel, "And who is this long-haired journeyman?!" the uncle said again with a comic bellow.

Adib answered, "Father this is Salman's friend from the University. His name is Michel."

"Welcome to my home, Michel. What brings you to Tel Za'atar?"

Salman regained his confidence, and spoke before Michel was able, "He is writing a dissertation on camp life."

"Aha – then you have come to the right place. We can discuss it all you like. These men," Musa Rasoul swept his hand towards the four men seated in the opposite corner, "have lived here since soon after al-Nakhba, when we were kicked," his volume and intonation rising, "out of our homes by the Jews."

"I am grateful for your hospitality, Musa Rasoul."

Musa turned back to the elders, and took a seat in their midst. Michel waited for them to start speaking so he could return to a conversation with Adib and Salman, but they all just sat quietly. Musa Rasoul broke the uncomfortable silence, but not in the way Michel had hoped.

"So what exactly are you writing, Michel?"

After a pause, Michel proceeded, "I'm trying to understand the situation in the camps now. To understand how it has come to be this way."

"How it has come to be? This is a story we all know, Michel."

"Respectfully, Musa, it is different every time I hear it."

Musa Rasoul detected the tone of mild antagonism in Michel's voice. "Well then," Musa said, lowering his voice as Salman shifted nervously, "here you can hear the truth." Musa paused for dramatic effect, clearly posturing before his audience.

"It started, Michel, when I was a little boy. My parents had a home and a small olive garden west of Jerusalem. They would take what they grew and sell it to the merchants in the city. My father also worked as a cobbler. Between the wars, the Jews had been coming to Palestine in increasing numbers. They had already been working to push us out of the country. Sometimes they bought our land, sometimes they simply occupied it. We were disorganized and not prepared for how efficient and determined they were to push us out for good in 1947. But we began to fight back."

As he spoke, the elder men nodded their heads and listened, one leaning on a cane and shaking his head from time to time in disgust. Musa's words, hanging like a thick fog with the pain they contained, floated slowly across the evening breeze and stoked embers within Adib and Salman. As the words brushed against the embers, Michel could sense an incandescent glow. In the brush of one conversation, he saw how they waited here with smoldering, unquenched expectations.

"When the fighting reached its height, and they overpowered us, some fled north into Lebanon and set up temporary camps. Many others went to Jordan. There were thousands of us at the time in Lebanon, maybe a hundred thousand, and I think it must have scared the Lebanese."

"How long did you think you'd be here?"

"We refused to believe we would stay here. I remember, at first, there were all kinds of rules. The entire camp had to be constructed of temporary buildings, because we knew we would return home. Our elders even forbade us to plant trees – as a symbol of the fact that we were uprooted and would not lay down root here."

"So I understand you are the Tal Za'atar commander of Fateh, sir. If I may ask, why did you join Fateh?"

"Fateh was committed to act. They didn't talk politics, but just pure revolution against the occupier and getting us home. I joined the local militia, then still very secret, here in Tal Za'atar. The years passed. We fought with the Israelis and angered the Lebanese. The Deuxieme Bureau, that's the military's intelligence department, started putting more spies in the camps and the Lebanese restricted us more and more. It all came to a head in 1969, when the Lebanese tried to silence us."

Michel knew that, as with any story, this one had many versions. From others he had heard the Lebanese Christian version: that the Palestinians had pushed the state to the brink of collapse by inviting Israeli reprisals and intolerable turmoil. At some point, the state had to act to constrain the Palestinians; and the battles in 1969 was the result. But the other Arab states, Egypt foremost amongst them, forced the sides into a truce.

"So we signed the Cairo Accord," Musa Rasoul continued, "which provided us with new authorities and constrained our actions in certain regions in the South."

"Well," Michel responded, "it seems as though much is changing now, though. The civil war in Jordan . . ."

"A tragedy!" one of the old men suddenly got excited. "The Arabs – our own blood, deny us safety and hunt us like dogs!"

"So if I understand," Michel continued, "the Jordanians fought your various militias and kicked you out of the country . . ." the men nodded in assent, "and they came here to Lebanon . . . and there has been an influx of fedayeen fighters over the past few years," the men were still nodding, and though one lifted his hand to speak, Michel continued briefly, "but there are also the communities that have been here for two decades and –"

"We have bled here! We fought the Lebanese and the Israelis. We have built homes and our own army. In the last few years, thousands of hot-heads have streamed into our . . ."

"Haj Muhamat," Musa Rasoul interrupted, "please, he is a guest."

"What is that to me? I am old and do not care anymore. If he is going to write, he needs to know the truth." Muhamat turned back to Michel, "Young man, in the last few years thousands of fedayeen have flooded our alleys and streets. They bring disorder. They disgrace our leaders, like Musa Rasoul."

Musa started, "That is not . . ."

"They rob banks. They rob shops. They rape women and nothing happens. It is a disgrace – and there is no law. No order from the Lebanese or from Fateh."

Another man started pleading with Muhamat, "The Lebanese agreed to let us run our camps, and Fateh risks civil war if they fight them too aggressively."

"Then let there be war," the old man said, "all we have done all our lives is fight."

Musa Rasoul began again, "Haj Muhamat is expressing a frustration felt by some who have been here a long time, Michel. You are right that things have changed in the camps since the Jordan tragedy. But we are working out these differences. We are all a people displaced and we cannot simply reject our brothers in arms."

Michel watched as the women came and took their seats. Fatin sat next to her father. The old men got up to leave, and Michel rose, as well. Adib rose – "No, please, stay a little longer to speak with just the family."

Michel shook the elders hands as they left, and returned to his seat. Fatin loosened her headscarf, revealing dark, flowing hair. Michel could not help but stare for a moment, then turned intentionally to Salman, who was caught in rapture. When Michel turned to look at Adib, the young man smiled and nodded his head knowingly, winking at Michel. Michel laughed a little and reached into a bread basket.

"Michel, my friend, what do you really want to know? Why would you come here from France?" Musa Rasoul's tone was cold, but curious. In it, Michel sensed a forlorn longing of one who had caught a glimpse of a dream in his youth and spent the remainder of his life chasing after it.

And then, Fatin spoke. "There is not one of us in this camp who wouldn't gladly trade places with you. If we could, we would run away from here so qui…"

"Fatin!" her mother exclaimed, "This is your home. How can you say such a thing?!"

It was Salman's turn to step into the fray, "But aunt, what if we want something more for our own families?"

"Something more?" Musa took offense. "You have family. Is this not enough? The only thing more," he said with emphasis, "would be finally returning home. That is what I have committed my life too, Salman."

"But uncle, we have never even seen this home. We were born in these camps and in these camps we will die."

"You lack faith!" Musa Rasoul boomed.

"No father," Fatin said gently, "Salman is realistic. How many years have you fought? If I have a child some day, do you want it to be raised like we were?"

"I think we did just fine for you, Fatin," her mother said, looking with embarrassment at Michel as though she had to apologize.

Adib lit up, "You did mother. And I for one don't know any home but here. And so that is why I fight with father. But – I cannot blame Salman and Fatin for wanting something different. How can you ask them to give their blood and their lives for a dream they have never tasted?"

"Because that is what a dream is, my son. I am sorry, of all the things we could never give you, that we could not give you a home."

"But we have Musa, this is our home," his wife pleaded.

Now Fatin stepped back in, "And what a home it is, with our women bleeding to death in child birth because we don't even have water or electricity. Is it so wrong for me to want something better?" Her mother grimaced.

Salman stood up and Adib grabbed Michel's forearm, shaking it rapidly in anticipation.

"Sayyid Musa Rasoul, I am a simple man and the son of your brother, for whom I know you have no love left."

"Save yourself," Musa Rasoul said as he looked down at the fire and waved with the back of his hand, "not again, Salman."

"Please let me speak, uncle. I may be of little consequence and will probably never lead a group of men across the border-"

"That is certain my son, please sit and don't embarrass yourself further with thi . . ."

"Let him speak, father," Fatin said eagerly. Michel looked at Adib, who smiled with entertainment and nodded his head eagerly. Michel realized this scene had played out before.

"But I love your daughter, uncle, and I will take her away from here and make her hap-"

"Take her away?!" Musa boomed as he rose to his full height. "Make her happy?! You think she would be happy without her family?! And how do you plan on getting out?" He took a step towards Salman, towering over him. Fatin stood up and put her hands on her father's shoulder. Adib stood and stepped closer to Salman, who was now looking almost straight up at his uncle.

"Now father, Salman only-"

"Silence, Adib. This is between me and little Salman! Do you think you are better than the rest of us?"

"No uncle."

"That you can just disappear with my daughter and never return again?"

"No uncle that is not what I meant, but it . . ."

"I won't let you take her away – you have to prove to me that you deserve her!"

"I will prove it to you! Tell me what to do!"

"Pick up a gun dammit and act like a man! Our enemies are everywhere, Salman, and we need all the help we can get. Look around these streets – the Israelis are the least of our worries now!"

"That is why I refuse to pick up a gun, uncle, because they are the least of our worries. But if that is what you want – if that is how I can be with Fatin, then I will do it right now. Tell me what to do."

"Tomorrow morning, then, you will meet Adib and come to the headquarters."

Salman trembled as he spoke, "So be it." And he turned towards the door in such a ferocious fit of emotion that he completely forgot that he had come with Michel. He flung the door open and disappeared into the darkness.

"Well, Michel" Adib shouted, unable to contain his delight, "welcome to another family dinner!"

Musa Rasoul turned his wrath on Michel, "And you, Doctor Michel, when will you join us?"

Michel was silent for a moment, and as Musa visibly calmed, sensed his opportunity, "It appears, Sayyidi Musa, that you have no other daughters to inspire me."

As the men laughed, Fatin left through the side door, her mother chasing after her.

For a few minutes the men revisited the baba ghanoush instead of speaking. Adib finally broke the quiet, "Do you think he will come father?"

"I don't know, Adib, but I love that little man." They laughed again. Michel rose, and the two men rose with him.

"Please don't go, Michel," Musa Rasoul implored, "forgive my anger I have much to consider these days. My family is my only comfort."

"It is not because of you I leave, Musa Rasoul, but I must return to the campus before it gets late. Adib, I will see you soon."

"I look forward to it, Michel."

Musa Rasoul walked with Michel outside of the courtyard and into the street, waiving off the armed guard who stood outside the door.

"What you witnessed there, Michel, it was about much more than just my daughter. Salman's father and I, there is . . ." but Musa paused, seemingly unable to finish the sentence.

"Much history," Michel finished it for him.

"Yes."

"This whole place is filled with history, Musa. And history is taking some strange turns."

"I'm afraid it is."

Michel waited, and locked eyes with Musa Rasoul. His tone turning serious, chilling Musa's spine as he sensed a young man before him who spoke with uncharacteristic gravity, "The days are turning dark, Sayyid Must. You don't have to be without friends."

They shook hands and Michel disappeared into the darkness.

# CHAPTER TEN

A group of men huddled over a table and disagreed about what they were viewing. The first picture simply had a map of Beirut with various dots around it. They could make nothing of it. The second film provided by their informant was still being developed.

"There is nothing on the map?" A skinny man said from a desk near the wall. He was reading a paper and appeared to ask out of occasional obligation than any real interest.

"No, Karim." a young man said to the questioner, "Just a bunch of dots. Maybe there will be something in the other images."

"How long is it going to take?" Karim asked.

"Another thirty minutes or so."

"Ok, I'm going out. I'll be back."

They all stood, blinking in wonderment. "Going out? We have to figure out what's going on here."

"And there's enough empty heads around that table to do it – you don't need me."

"Tamam, Karim, but if we find something we will have to go to Camille without you."

"Yeah, yeah." The man walked to the door and exited.

"The biggest payload we get in weeks and he goes out?" one of the other men said. "Some great manager."

"She must be really worth it."

"Karim couldn't get a hooker if he paid double." They all laughed as the next image fell from the machine. One of the men in a brown shirt, marked with sweat on his back in the heat of the room, picked it up off the ground and looked at it.

"Seriously, what does he do? It seems like every time we're onto something he disappears."

"Yeah, because we've had so many hot leads lately," a younger, bespectacled man said, but looked a little nervously towards the door.

"C'mon Sherif," another participant said, "What has he done since they made him manager?"

"We're not going to discuss –"

"They should have left him out in the camps where he belongs and given you the position."

"That's enough. You know Camille had no choice, it was Parliament."

The men hunched closer to the table, "Sherif, take a look at this. It's the same map, but a few of the dots are connected."

"What is this?" Sherif said in a hushed tone to himself, moving the paper back and forth in his fingers.

A smallish man leaned over the documents with a cigarette in his mouth; ashes hanging precariously over the print.

"Idiot," Sherif slapped him back, "you're gonna catch the thing on fire." The smoker looked indignantly at him, then threw the cigarette in an empty ash tray on the next desk, returning to the maps.

———

In an upstairs room, Camille sat. "I got these permits for you, but I can't be responsible for what happens down there."

Whit, who had arrived moments before, responded. "I understand. We'll be extra ca-"

Someone knocked on the door.

"Yallah."

The door opened and the small smoker entered. "Sir, we got a shi-" the man stopped upon seeing Whit, "I'm sorry, I can wait outside."

Whit said, "No, I'll step outside."

"No, no," Camille said, "what does it matter anymore?" he asked, rhetorically. "What is it?"

"We got some...." he thought pensively, "some items downstairs Sherif wants you to see."

"Where is Karim?" The man shrugged his shoulders and Camille leaned back against his chair in frustration. "What is so special about these items that I need to come down there?"

"We don't know."

"You don't know what is special about these items. Karim has not looked at them, and you are coming up here because – why exactly?"

"Well, because," the man looked hesitantly at Whit, "because of the source."

Camille sat silently staring. "Whit," Camille rose out of his chair and pushing it aside, said, "You might as well join me to take a look at this."

Whit rose without speaking, reverencing the sudden show of confidence.

Camille grunted and turned to the youth, "Let's head down."

There were no lights in the hallway and a window at its end permitted a dank, brownish aura through its opaque panes. The acrid scent of human sweat and stress accumulated and hung like an unwelcome phantom in the stuffy hallway air. Without the cool fans of Camille's office, Whit began to perspire almost immediately.

As they walked between the hushed whispers and odors that clouded the dimness, Whit could make out the vague profiles of people waiting in chairs, and a soldier or two leaning against the walls. The soldiers snapped to attention as Camille passed. Their escort pressed the elevator button, and Camille pushed him onward, "Let's take the stairs, the elevators around here make me nervous."

They descended several flights of stairs to the basement, where Camille took out a key and unlocked a door at the bottom. He motioned for Whit to pass through.

———

Karim walked nervously outside the building and smoked rapidly. He looked over his shoulder several times, and finally rounded a corner where he stopped at a pay phone and unwrapped a piece of paper. He glanced around again and, seeing no one that captured his attention, dialed the number on the paper.

"What?" came the voice on the other line.

"It's me."

"I know. What is it?"

Karim nervously considered what he was about to say, and said, "Can we meet? I need-"

"Shut up and just tell me what you have to say."

"Over the ph..."

"Goodbye.."

"No, wait. Ok, Ok."

"Ok, what? Speak."

"We got something here last night."

"What is it?"

"I don't know. It looks like a map with markings on it."

On the other end, Karim could hear a commotion and some hushed but fervid and angry discussions taking place.

"Do they know what it is?"

Karim realized the question was addressed to him, "Not yet, but they are working on it."

"Call me back if they figure it out." The line went dead.

On the other end of the line, with his hand on the receiver, Sayyid stared at a man sitting at the next table.

"How did they get the maps?"

"I don't know, Sayyid."

"We'll deal with that later. They haven't figured it out yet. We're going to go now."

"But, Sayyid, if we rush it we may have to-"

"I know you fool," Sayyid stopped him from speaking further, "but if we don't do this now it may not happen at all."

Sayyid and the man went outside where a group of armed men hovered. They all spoke together, then piled into three Land Rovers and sped off towards the camp exit.

---

"You better have the missing gospel or I'm going back to my office." Camille yelled as he entered the room.

Sherif was sweating. "We don't know what it is but . . ."

"Give me the documents."

Sherif interjected, "Mr. Camille, perhaps this man shouldn't be—"

"It's time we started showing the world we're not impotent. After the Israeli raid they've been saying we just sit here and do nothing." He was speaking about a raid the previous month where Israeli commandoes had snuck under cover of night into downtown Beirut and killed several fedayeen leaders. "Not next time, not if I can help it." Camille looked, and said, "This is just some lines on a map."

The group sat dumbfounded, and Nouri Shehadi huddled scribbling over a piece of paper. Shehadi, with the look of a mad scientist, black curly hair exploding from his crown, continued crossing and circling. He dropped his pencil and looked closely at the printed image of a map on the desk in front of him. As they were speaking, an additional image emerged from a nearby printer and Nouri ran to grab it.

He looked at Sherif and Camille, "It's a map with arrows . . ." He walked to the other map and laid them side by side.

"What on earth is it?"

Shehadi looked more closely. "Both are of the same area . . . dots on one and arrows on the other."

"What are the arrows showing?" Camille asked.

"Just streets."

"Where did we get these from?"

"A source took these images from documents in Tal Za'atar." Sherif said.

"When?"

"Last few days."

"Ok – who's in Tal Za'atar these days?"

"Well, Fateh,"

"Thanks genius. They're everywhere. Who else?"

"PFLP." Whit saw a grimace pass over Camille's face.

"What of them?" Whit asked.

"You've been here long enough, Whit. They're the most unpredictable and violent group. But we nabbed their Tal Za'atar commander, a guy named Sadiq, a few weeks back and they've been eerily quiet since then."

"Wait . . ." Shehadi interjected.

"What?"

"If you trace them back far enough, all of them head out like spokes from one central area."

"What is it . . ."

Shehadi looked up blankly at Camille, "Roumieh."

There was a momentary pause, then Camille's eyes widened, "Sadiq's in Roumieh."

"Yeah, and they just moved him to the infirmary after the recent riot."

"The infirmary is right by the front gate?!"

They all shot a look at Camille as a realization simultaneously lit each face in the room. "Let's go!" Camille screamed. "Whit you're with me!" The men all started grabbing guns and running for the door.

As they ran towards the door, Camille turned to the youngest, "Omar stay here and call Colonel Chartouni. Tell him we think the PFLP is going to hit Roumieh prison to get Sadiq."

The group ran up the stairs and outside to two parked cars. Sherif hopped in one with three men. Camille and Whit hopped in the next and Nouri and another man got in the back seat. As they sped off, the men started loading weapons. Shehadi passed a hand gun up the front seat to Camille, who took it and put it in a holster under his jacket. The other man, with a bushy moustache and a gold chain, offered a gun to Whit. Whit looked at Camille, "Just to protect yourself, in case." Camille said.

Whit grabbed it and checked the chamber and the cartridge. The man then handed an M16 and two magazines to Whit. Whit took tape from the man and arranged the magazines so they were facing opposite directions, taping them together. Camille looked curiously at Whit through his peripheral vision. Then Camille refocused on the road and honked as he sped through the streets.

# CHAPTER ELEVEN

The prison gates were slowly closing. Sayyid grabbed a walkie-talkie and said, "When they start opening next, I go. Take positions and be ready once the shooting starts." He checked a cartridge and then reinserted it into his AK-47. Roumieh's huge grey walls loomed over its surroundings. The entrance faced a heavily treed forest that sat strangely untouched amidst the buildings of Beirut, which crowded up against the giant edifice on its other sides.

After a few more moments, Sayyid opened the car door and stood cautiously, sliding the AK-47, with sawed off stock, under the jacket which looked strangely out of place in the warm morning air. He slowly walked down the road that abutted Roumieh, neither walking straight towards the entrance, nor away. A small, blue prison van approached and the front gate started to open. Two guards stepped into the road.

As Sayyid approached the gates, one of the two guards motioned for him to stop and let the van through.

The man held a small automatic weapon by a strap over his shoulder and was dressed in military fatigues. The van pulled up between the two gate doors and stopped, and an inner-gate slowly started to open. Sayyid did not stop walking and, as the guard held up his hand higher for Sayyid to stop, Sayyid pulled the rifle from under his jacket and shot the man in the forehead. The second guard, stunned for a moment too long, stared at his dead comrade, and Sayyid shot him twice in the chest. Several guards from inside began firing wildly out the front gates. Gunfire exploded on both sides of the van, and men screamed as glass shattered in all directions and the sound of bullets hitting metal and concrete ricocheted off the prison walls. The prisoners inside, awakened to the maelstrom, began beating wildly on their bars and screaming.

Running and sliding over the front hood of the van into the gateway, Sayyid began firing through the second gate towards a group of guards running through the courtyard. Two fell; the others scattered behind walls and a crossfire ensued.

Sayyid turned to a guard just inside who was cowering, frozen in fear, and yelled for him to continue opening the inner gate. The man reached up and pulled a lever and, as the opening widened, Sayyid shot the guard and sprinted inside to the first door. As he plunged into the infirmary, more guards emerged into the courtyard, but Sayyid's men had run inside behind him and opened their weapons. They created a defensive perimeter between the courtyard and the infirmary door.

Inside, Sayyid ran to a nurse who was ducking behind a desk, "Which room is Sadi-"

"C'mon you idiot," Sadiq yelled as he stumbled into the hallway, pulling a needle and tube from his arm. He ran towards Sayyid, who smiled briefly before shooting at a guard over Sadiq's shoulder who had emerged into the hallway. Sadiq plunged to the ground, and Sayyid ran forward, lifting him. Sadiq limped with one arm over Sayyid's shoulders.

———

"They're already inside," Shehadi yelled as the cars screeched to a halt about fifty yards from the gates. The men opened the doors and sprinted towards the prison. They fell to the ground when firing emerged from the tree line across from the exit. Whit honed in on the source almost immediately, and unleashed a volley with his machine gun on the clump of bushes, which turned silent.

As he looked up again, Camille was running towards the gates, and then stopped and fired at six men emerging with guns ablaze. Camille ducked behind a car in the middle of the street that was burning, and watched in horror and then awe as he saw Whit running and firing about ten yards away.

Two heavily armored Land Rover jeeps swung around the corner and fired mounted machine guns towards Camille and his men. Camille returned the onslaught and Whit put his M-16 carefully on the hood of the car he had been using as a shield. He fired one shot. One of the fedayeen's heavy machine guns stopped.

Camille jumped up and sprinted towards the car where Whit was firing.

"Where the hell did you learn to fight like this?" Camille yelled over the cacophony.

"Playground!"

"Bullshit!"

A frenzy of fire burst forth from further down the road as two more jeeps of fedayeen sped towards the gate. Whit and Camille, distracted by the firing, did not notice Sayyid, with Sadiq limping alongside him, hobble out the front gate into the first Land Rover.

Turning to his left, Whit saw the man with the bushy mustache run out into the open as he attempted to advance towards the other Land Rovers and, though Whit didn't know it, stop it from escaping. He fell almost immediately.

"Nasir!" Camille yelled, and got up to go after him. As he did, Whit pulled him back down.

"Too much open ground, Camille," he yelled above the cacophony as Camille looked back, he saw Nasir leaning on his side and reaching for his gun. The gunfire had become so heavy from near the gate that Whit and Camille stayed pinned to the side of the car.

"Do we have anything besides the guns?!"

Camille yelled back, "Like what?!"

"Grenades, an RPG?!"

"No, but we got a message out to the army. They will hopefully get here any minute," he screamed back over the fire.

Whit leaned over in the other direction and as Sayyid's jeep sped off, he took careful aim and shot the front left tire. It screeched to a halt as a second jeep, with gunners hanging out the windows, sped up, firing wildly.

Whit could see two men jump out the side door and start running to the rear jeep. He quickly fired at the latter, who fell to the ground. As he took careful aim again, gunfire raked the hood and he ducked behind it, bumping into Camille.

"I hope they get here soon," Whit screamed. As he looked back, he saw the second jeep racing away and turned and fired.

Camille did the same, fedayeen began firing from another car. Suddenly, a barrage of fire tore down from the sky, and Whit could see a helicopter speeding over the scene and then away.

"Cavalry's here!" Camille yelled. The rest of the fedayeen loaded into the remaining jeep. Whit and Camille fired, and as a rocket whizzed over their car, blowing up the one behind them, they were both knocked over. When they looked back up, the remaining jeep was fleeing. Both men stood and immediately began running towards the fedayeen on the ground, hoping they could find one alive.

After they checked those they could find, all dead, Camille said to Whit, "You have to get out of here. I shouldn't have brought you."

Whit started to turn, but as he began to say something, another voice interrupted.

"Who's this, Camille?"

Both men turned to see a tall man in full battle gear walking towards them from the direction of the fighting. "Colonel Chartouni," Camille said with a surprised voice. "This . . . this is an American reporter, Cordell Whitaker. Mr. Whitaker, this is Col. Emile Chartouni, the most reliable man in the Lebanese Army."

"Mr. Whitaker, you'll need to leave, please. No reporting allowed." The man had the classic soldier's build. Square-jawed with broad shoulders and a narrow waist. He had the burnt look of having spent years standing watch in the heat of the sun.

"Indeed." Whit turned to go, but hovered slowly to listen.

"Camille, we have the area secured. My men are in a firefight near here with a truck full of fedayeen. Any idea about the target?"

"Sadiq. They had him out already by the time we were getting here."

As the two men continued talking, Whit nodded to Camille, who blinked knowingly and returned his attention to the Colonel. Whit turned and walked away from the prison as more soldiers ran past him.

The Colonel turned back to the two fedayeen lying on the ground, and noticed their weapons disassembled at their feet with the ammunition set aside. He also noticed the jackets lay slightly open, as though they had been searched.

"Did you search them?" the Colonel asked, nodding in the direction of the deceased.

Camille looked at the bodies, not having noticed them situated so previously. For a second he said nothing, then spread out his hands, "Had to take care of it myself – you guys were late."

"Did you find anything in their jackets?"

Camille paused momentarily, "No, no I didn't." He then walked away and made a mental note to find Whit as soon as he could.

# CHAPTER TWELVE

"Ali Ishaq, at your service. Where to, sir?"

Whit wasn't even sure, and listened without hearing.

"Sir, where are you going?"

"Oh, sorry, Ali, was it?" He thought again for a moment. Where did he need to go right now? Where did he have to go? "Sourp Pergitch."

The cab driver paused for a moment, perplexed. "Where?"

Whit said, "Bourj Hammoud." The man looked again as if thinking.

"The church," Whit said, "the Armenian Catholic church in Bourj Hammoud."

"Ah, ah, ok, I thought you were drunk at first. Are you ok?"

"Yes, I just . . ."

"Did you hear about the fighting at the prison?"

Whit paused for a moment, "No . . . what happened?" But as the man spoke, Whit's mind drifted to the past. People moved back and forth through Grand

Central Station. Whit checked a map and looked at the board for the Hudson line.

"Are ya lost?" A middle-aged man with tortoise shelled, circular-framed glasses looked at Whit as he spoke. The glasses were the first thing Whit noticed. The man had grey streaks through light brown hair. Whit had been on the east coast long enough to spot an Ivy-Leaguer on sight. Yale or Princeton, he thought. Certainly not a Harvard man; he had initiated the conversation.

"Where are you headed?"

"West Point."

"You don't say," the man jumped immediately, "I'm headed there as well."

"For the conference?"

"Yes – are you a student?"

"I'm a grad student at George Washington."

"Ah, well you should come to my panel. I'll be speaking on the Middle East."

"So will I. It sounds like we're on the same panel."

"Oh I doubt that very much, this panel was only for people with experience in the region."

"Indeed – I just got back from several months of field work." The man was silent, and gave an awkward smile.

"Well then, we'll have much to discuss, mister, well I don't believe I got your name?" said the man extending his hand.

"Cordell Whitaker, but my friends call me Whit."

"Thurlow Grinaker, Whit, but my friends call me Grins." The two laughed as the public announcement for the Hudson line rang through the cavernous hall.

"Sir," the driver said, pulling over slowly and parking the cab, "sir, we are here." The man extended a card to Whit.

"Of course," Whit said, reaching into his wallet and handing the man twice the desired amount, which was a measly sum in US dollars. The driver said, "Wait, this is too m…"

"I have your card, Ali, that's a down payment on the next time I call for a ride." Whit smiled. Ali began to respond, but Whit had already shut the door and was walking slowly to the church.

Whit felt a queasiness arise as he approached the door, but a strange breeze blew through the square adjacent to the church, and his resurgent unease broke against an icy alertness to something amiss. He turned slowly to survey the surrounding area.

A cigarette vendor across the street sat staring at him, calling out with a pack in hand. Diners sipped coffee at a disheveled cafe, boys kicked a soccer ball, and several dogs sprinted down a side street.

"Aaggghhh" Whit heard a man screaming, but saw no one. He turned quickly in the direction from which he thought it came. A voice, distinct from the scream and sounding familiar also emerged.

Suddenly, the church door moved slightly, simultaneous to another scream and a thud. He knew the voice – it was Gaspar Vartabed. Whit ran towards the church doors as the vendor watched without caring.

Whit ripped open the doors and beheld a man pinning another to the ground. He could only see black clad legs and immediately realized it was Gaspar. The scream came again momentarily before the aggressor choked it off. Whit sprinted two to three steps and hurled himself forward. The next moment of horror seemed to happen in slow motion.

In the brief second before he hit him, Whit saw a seemingly animalistic face turn towards him. The eyes were simultaneously bloodshot and jaundiced, bulging in inhuman fashion from the face, profuse with sweat. The teeth flashed in the light of the windows like a wolf snarling as it sinks into its prey. Then time seemed to speed back up and Whit's contact with the man was more like hitting a wall than a human.

The man didn't budge, but turned and with both arms grabbed Whit and hurled him three feet away. Whit tumbled into a wooden pew and noticed three other men pulling themselves off the ground and surging towards the assailant. They pushed him off Gaspar Vartabed like a rugby scrum crushing the opposing force. As the man pushed back, maniacally intent on attacking the priest, Whit joined the fray and helped pin him to the ground.

Strangely, as they held him to the ground, Whit noticed the man's shirt, though white, had a fresh, red, blood stain streaking across it. Then, it slowly dawned on Whit what was happening. It was something he had always heard of growing up but never known to be real; this was an exorcism.

"In the name of Jesus Christ," Gaspar Vartabed was now on his feet and standing over the group, holding a vile of holy water above his head in a suspended staging before the sanctified attack. Abruptly, he ripped his arm forward vertically and horizontally in two quick swipes that emblazoned the sign of the cross upon the pinned demoniac. The man screamed in agony, as though the water were fire searing his flesh and burning through to the marrow of his bones. "In the name of Jesus Christ, you are commanded to be still."

Suddenly the fighting and trembling stopped.

"Don't let him go," one of the men said in Armenian. The four men stayed holding the man down, who now seemed to breathe deeply, wheezing heavily.

"The power of Christ compels you," Gaspar Vartabed said in a subdued tone in Latin, "to leave this man at peace."

All was quiet. The labored wheeze sounded like a wounded reptile gasping for air, yet paralyzed. Then the man turned his head slowly, one by one, waiting to peer into the eyes of those holding him, none of whom made eye contact. Whit, however, somewhat in shock, stared straight into the inhuman eyes. He could not remove his gaze. It was then that the man locked eyes with his and laughed, whispering slowly, "Lie. Lie. Liiieeee!" But the last lie erupted loudly as the demoniac hurled the four men forward. Gaspar Vartabed flung holy water and in the moment it contacted the man, he screamed in pain and ran past the priest straight towards the wall.

Screaming, "All sinnnerrrrssss!" the man leapt sideways, ran six to seven steps along the wall, appearing to defy gravity. He continued this acrobatic exchange between the floor and the wall for another four to five seconds, arriving at last in the front of the church.

He suddenly lowered his head to the ground and shuffled forward, mumbling to himself. He dropped out of sight in front of the first pew. All the men looked to Gaspar Vartabed who peered with a seeming comfort and knowledge that perplexed Whit.

"We are almost done for today," the priest said in Armenian. The troop walked ahead of Whit, who saw them all freeze as they rounded the corner.

Whit walked forward to the front of the church and rounding the corner himself, saw the man's shirt lying next to him and his chest drenched in blood. He was leaning back with his shoulders against the church pew, his head bobbing up and down slowly. His chin occasionally touched the space between his collarbones. Whit could not tell what had caused the injury. The man's hands lay at his side without any blood on them.

The group moved closer behind Gaspar Vartabed, who walked swiftly to the man and knelt beside him. The man looked up into Gaspar Vartabed's eyes; the countenance of a human being had returned to his face. Tears streamed down his cheeks, and his formerly jaundiced scleras were wet and reddened. Profound pain haunted this man's face as much as any diabolical force.

Then, Whit saw it, as one of the men in the group whispered in a hushed and awful tone, "Father – my God." Blood was issuing forth from a small line on the man's chest, but as Whit looked closer it was clear that the line was slowly moving. It was as if an invisible hand was drawing a nail across the man's chest, cutting him as it moved.

The priest reached into a bag he was holding and set out the holy water and a book. He opened to a page sliding his hand to a certain spot, and then, finding it, began again in Latin, "Go back, Satan!" He emphasized the command in his voice and crossed the man with holy water. The growing line stopped for a moment.

The man began to rouse and become more alert, and as he did the four men assisting Gaspar Vartabed moved forward, but the priest held out his hand to signal them to stop. Whit could see the line on the man's chest start to move again, but it made a slow and deliberate turn.

"Go back, Satan!" the priest intoned. The line stopped moving again. For an entire minute, the group stood fixated, staring at the man and the bleeding cut on his chest. For a minute they sat exasperated and exhausted, waiting and unsure of what to do; unsure, that is, except for Gaspar Vartabed. The priest moved to the man and, placing his palm on his forehead, spoke a low prayer that the others could not hear.

The man went catatonic. A chilling breeze rushed through the church and the lights momentarily flickered, casting a darkness broken only by a strange glow that seemed to emerge from the placement of Gaspar Vartabed's hand on the man's forehead. The lights returned, and the man's eyes rolled upward. He grew so still that Whit thought he might have passed away.

For a minute more they waited; for a minute the priest prayed. For that entire minute Whit forgot where he was. He forgot that he had just killed men; forgot that he was thousands of miles from home, in a city he barely understood, surrounded by people whose lives were so different from his own; yet so similar.

"Go back, Satan." Whit heard Gaspar Vartabed issue the command in a confident but quite voice, "Go back, Satan." As the minute came to an end the man's eyes relaxed. Rolling forward, as if released, they set on Gaspar Vartabed. The demoniac seemed to recognize Gaspar. His chest continued to bleed, but the line had ceased moving.

A low, tortured sob issued forth from the man that appeared to be his own. As the tears dripped from his cheeks, they mixed with the blood on his chest and flowed down his body, eventually falling onto the church floor, soaking it in a pinkish water that one of the attendants moved forward to wipe up with his own sleeve.

"It hurts," he mumbled.

"We are here. We will fight it together," Gaspar Vartabed said.

Crying still, the man stared at the priest. He started to look around at the others. Realizing he was shirtless, he swept his arms slowly around and Gaspar Vartabed moved the ragged shirt within reach. When the man pulled his shirt on, soaked by the fresh blood, Whit beheld a streak in the linen from old, dried wounds. The new blood set with the old.

Without a word, the man rose and stumbled down the aisle to the door, opening it into the flooding light of the Beirut afternoon. Etched in black profile against the blinding white sunlight, the man blurred from vision and faded into the day.

The group spoke quietly with the priest and then exited.

Whit hardly knew where to start. "Are you ok, Father?"

"Are you?"

"Yes, just . . . shocked." The two were silent, contemplating the cross that hung from the front wall of the church.

"Why did you come today, Whit?"

"Just . . . I don't know . . . trying to get my bearings after a rough . . . day."

"Well, I'm sorry; this could not have helped."

Whit laughed briefly, "No, Vartabed, to the contrary. I think I'm confused."

"Well there's nothing to be confused about. Shocked; absolutely."

"Why that man?"

"I don't know."

The priest waited. Whit watched the altar in contemplation, as if an answer would emerge from the flickering candlelight.

"Do there have to be men like you and men like me in the world, Father?"

The priest turned to look at Whit, his eyes closing slightly. "What kind of man are you, Whit?" Whit was silent, raising his eyes to the cross over the altar.

"When I was a kid, my grandfather used to take me out shooting." The priest clasped his hands across his knee as Whit paused. Shaking his head, Whit continued, "Every time he put the rifle in my hands, he used to say, 'This is a powerful tool, Cordell, you only use it when you must.' I didn't pay much attention then . . ."

The priest waited again, then asked quietly, "But now?"

It was Whit's turn to wait for a few moments, after which, he inquired, "Did that man choose the evil?"

"Hard to say, Whit. Maybe it chose him."

"Is there a difference?"

"Significant."

Whit, almost whispering, asked, "What?"

The priest unclasped his hands and held them open, towards the altar, "Whether redemption is still possible."

Whit looked intently at the priest for a few moments more and then placed his hand on the man's shoulder, squeezing it tightly. Without another word, he rose, turned and walked towards the door. The priest knelt, leaned his forehead against his hands and closed his eyes.

Across the city of Beirut people sat together speaking, laughing, eating, loving, hating, forgetting and remembering. All of them were separate, yet together. In the camp Musa Rasoul dipped bread into a dish of baba ghanoush as his family laughed and traded jabs. Twenty feet away Salman stood guard outside the door. Twenty yards away men were frantically rushing in and out of a building, and trucks feverishly pulled up and waited as their hauls were unloaded. Twenty blocks away Boutros sat with his family and handed a dish of chicken across the table to Martha. Twenty minutes from there Camille sat with a group of men, speaking and listing various items on a chalk board.

Families and friends, vast and unnamed, exchanged food and words and laughter. Across the city embers burned with the warmth of a people alight. Across the city the embers turned to flames and lit the darkness on the kindling of anger and frustration.

Whit walked through the streets of Beirut, finally getting into a cab. The driver pulled into the hectic night traffic. Whit looked out the cab window and thought about the events of the day. He didn't notice that he had said nothing to the driver about his destination, but the man drove silently and with a purpose.

# CHAPTER THIRTEEN

After checking there were not threats in the street, Salman entered the small building where Musa Rasoul and Adib were meeting with Sadiq, Sayyid, and several other PFLP members.

"You throw gasoline on the fire today and now you want to toss in a hand grenade? No – a nuclear bomb?!" Musa boomed in anger as the men stood across a table with multiple maps.

"The imperialist pig spies are going to be coming for us all."

"Because you will have brought them here!"

Sadiq looked on scornfully. "I presume you'd prefer me here to Roumieh."

Musa paused momentarily, "I don't want any of our revolutionaries imprisoned. But we're not ready for all out war with the Lebanese."

"The Lebanese are weak," Sadiq continued hatefully, "if we don't act now, we'll miss our chance to take control of the revolution."

Men were running back and forth in the adjacent rooms, loading weapons and bringing boxes inside. The lights flickered overhead.

"Our enemies are the occupiers, Sadiq! You keep fighting every ghost that passes by your door and we'll be dead before we're even at the border."

"Colonel Sadiq has ordered our men into action," Sayyid slithered to Musa Rasoul with a smug look on his face, "the time for total revolution is upon us. We missed our chance in Jordan. We won't make that mistake again, Musa."

"Colonel Musa Rasoul to you," Adib said to Sayyid, as the two glared at one another.

Musa Rasoul interjected, "If you make war on the Lebanese state, these people will turn against you. We will have no place left to fight."

Sadiq responded, "They have always been against us. At least now everyone who is a man will have to pick up a gun and use it. Not like your pathetic excuses for soldiers who don't even come armed." Sadiq threw his hand in the air towards Salman, who had since stepped inside and was carrying a wooden stick hanging from a belt. As an initiate, he had not yet been given a gun. Sayyid shook his head in disgust. He walked over and attempted to thrust a gun into Salman's hands, but Salman placed his stick on it and pushed it away.

"Abou Ammar," Musa Rasoul started, using the nickname for the PLO leader, "won't permit your thugs and criminals here any more. You can't use our homes to do this."

"Some good it's done you all this time, Musa. What do you have to show for your revolution against the Israelis? A bunch of pathetic little shanties and subjugation to the imperialist, Western powers." He waited, but after no response continued, "You don't have to like it, but you are too weak to do anything about it."

A look of cold hatred passed between the men. Musa Rasoul turned this threat over in his mind. Sadiq had been a rash and offensive man all his life; and in chaos rash men could make good on their decrepit imagination. Musa, having lived through the chaos too many times, knew this. Men like Sadiq come and go. They are born and die in blazes of self-immolating bluster, but they do much damage on their way.

"You've been warned for the last time. You do this alone." Musa turned and stormed out. The few young men with him followed, and Adib backed out slowly, never turning until he was outside the door.

Sayyid turned to Sadiq. "Do you want me to kill him?"

"No," Sadiq responded. "Before he dies, we are going to make him feel pain for his treachery." Sayyid's face took on the guise of a twisted satisfaction. "Hurt him in the worst way, then bring him in, but wait until we've done what we have to do tomorrow."

"Wait? Until what is done?"

"Do you not pay attention to anything, Sayyid?!" Sadiq yelled, "It's time to implement our plan. Musa may be weak, but he'll get assistance from Abou Ammar unless the whole city is in chaos. It will be once we make our move."

"And what about our friend in the south?"

"We still have to satisfy him. It's your job to find the presents. Have you?"

"Yes."

"Good. Contact him and make sure he'll have the rest of the weapons ready for us. Then find a way to make it happen."

---

"We need to act quickly. They are going to bring a curse upon us all." Adib was vehement, controlled yet angry at the offense they had caused to his father.

"Patience, son. The time will come when we must act."

"Maybe we should talk to Abou Ammar?" Salman said sedately, half asking, half suggesting.

"Why?" one of the older men asked. "He doesn't care about those of us who have always been here."

Musa Rasoul rose to his feet, "Salman may have the right idea my friends." There was grumbling and restlessness, which Musa Rasoul sensed. "No, listen. Salman, why do you suggest this?"

"Sirs," Salman started, looking around pensively, "there is no turning back now. How can we ever win back our land if we cannot win our own people's hearts? Sadiq's men – they give the fedayeen the name of bandits – or worse. Look at how the shopkeepers shut their doors, the children run inside, and the women flee from the streets when they come. No, there is no turning back from them, and if we ever want to get back to our home, we will have to destroy them. But to do what we need to do, we have to have Abou Ammar's blessing."

Musa Rasoul looked around at the group, rapt in attention. They began nodding, and several looked to Musa Rasoul, showing their assent.

Musa Rasoul began, "He has spoken wisely, my friends. If any man amongst you disagrees, let him speak now. If not, I will go to Abou Ammar." The group rose, and exited one by one, patting Salman as they left. Some of the younger men nodded in acceptance, and stood aside waiting.

Adib walked to him and embraced him, "Welcome, brother."

Musa Rasoul had disappeared, and Salman looked around at the other young men standing around the courtyard. All held weapons except him. Finally, Musa Rasoul emerged holding something in his hand, but Salman could not tell what it was. As Musa Rasoul neared, the light from rooms outside the courtyard revealed a kalashnikov in his hands. The butt of the gun was of a beautifully carved wood with inlaid golden etching. Musa stopped before Salman, and said, "You are one of us now, my son."

The blood rushed through Salman's system in his excitement. As Musa Rasoul lifted the weapon straight out, Salman beheld the hand carving in the wooden stock. It was of a landscape. Salman did not recognize the landscape.

"It is the fields around our home. Carry this with you as a reminder of the only reason you carry it at all."

Salman reached out to accept the gun. After he had grabbed it, Musa Rasoul clasped his hands around the youth's neck and embraced him. Stepping back, the other men did the same. Over Musa Rasoul's shoulder, Salman could see Fatin in the doorway to the courtyard. She turned and ran inside.

"Now my friends, leave my family and go home tonight. We will have much preparations to make." The remainder of the men departed, as Adib and Salman took seats near Musa Rasoul.

"What do we do now, father? Even if we get Abou Ammar's permission, he will not publicly provide any support to us."

"I know. We have to think very carefully."

"I've been watching them, sir." Salman confessed in a hushed tone, "The truth is they have had weapons coming in for three weeks."

"What kind?"

"Rifles and rocket launchers, mostly. I can't tell with certainty, but most of them look Russian."

Adib joined in, "The question is when will it happen. If they make their move before us, it could be too late."

Musa Rasoul nodded. "I have feared it for a long time. They want to provoke the government. Once the government is attacking our camps, what can we do? We can hardly fight against Sadiq and his men with the government."

"Are you saying we have to join them?"

"No."

Salman grew nervous as a heretical thought welled up in him, but he interjected, anyway, "Why don't we let the Israelis kill them?"

"What are you saying?!" Adib shouted and started to rise, but Musa Rasoul looked on quietly and placed his hand on Adib's shoulder. Adib, in shock, sat back down and waited.

A moment of silence passed between them, and Salman's heart beat rapidly with the fear that he had been too bold. "Salman," Musa Rasoul finally broke the silence gravely, "I want you to be honest with me."

This could be it, the final rift where his uncle sent him away, bereft of any hope from now onward, but he was tired of shirking this fear, and would face it like a man. He sat more upright in his seat, "Anything, uncle." Silence again, for a moment.

"Your friend, Michel, do you really think he is a student?" Adib and Salman's faces distorted with confusion. "I . . . I don't know, uncle. He's certainly not, uh, not going to join us if that's what you mean. He only asks me about the cam—"

"Precisely. Asks you questions."

Salman waited, confused.

"Tell him I would like to speak with him. Don't make a big deal of it."

"But why is he important?" Adib, dumbfounded, questioned.

"I suspect he knows many people – even outside the camps. Find him. Bring him by. We're running out of time."

The cousins exchanged glances, and Salman rose, "Yes, uncle."

# CHAPTER FOURTEEN

The driver continued down the main artery. Headlights intermittently illuminated the inside of the car as Whit's mind floated aimlessly away from the road and over the day, the month, and the years.

"Tough day?" the driver asked, only momentarily shaking Whit out of his thoughts.

Whit finally responded, "Just ready for some sleep."

"I bet." The driver took a turn down a quiet residential street and the lights dimmed gradually, barely shining through the rear window. As the darkness enveloped them, Whit finally grew more aware of his surroundings and recalled that they had not discussed his destination.

"Where are you going?" he said sharply. There was no answer. Whit's pulse quickened. "Hey, I asked you what you are doing? This isn't where I'm going."

"We're taking a different route tonight." Whit looked around. There were one or two old men walking the street and aside from the soft light still glowing, reflected on the closed gates and darkened windows of the buildings they now passed more quickly, nothing more.

"Like hell, turn around." The driver accelerated and Whit pulled a gun from his pocket and put it to the man's neck. "Pull the car over or the last thing you see is going to be your blood on the windshield."

"Hold it, hold it!" The man shouted and quickly pulled to the side.

Whit moved to open the door, but finding it locked, cocked his gun and stuck it in the back of the man's head.

"Ow," he exclaimed. "Calm down, dammit, we're on the same side. They just wanted to talk with you!" The man exclaimed, holding his hands up.

"They? What are you talking about?" Whit, his eyes finally adjusting to the darkness, felt a sense of something familiar as he looked in the rear view mirror at the top half of the man's face. The nose and eyes were non-descript. Without the rest of the face he could not distinguish this man from any other. Then he noticed the glasses. They were a unique rectangular shape that he had seen earlier in the day at the Deuxieme Bureau offices – it was the analyst Nouri Shehadi.

"Ah – you're with Camille?"

"Yes." He said, wincing. "Can you take the gun off my head?"

"I'll take it off once we're back on the right street and you're driving in the direction I tell you."

"No, they want to see you tonight. I can't let you go."

"You tell them I was going to kill you. And I said if we're really working together, there's no need to kidnap me."

"Kidnap?!" The man said, exasperated, almost yelling more out of fear than argument, "I was just giving you a r–" Whit thrust the barrel into his neck. The man lifted his hands off the steering wheel, trembling.

"Drive me back to the road and then turn right."

"Ok, there's no need. Why don't I just take you all the way home. It's not like we don't know where you live."

The man turned the car around and headed back several blocks turning out again into the lights. As the brightness filled the car and Whit felt it becoming visible to outsiders, he removed the gun and placed it back in his pocket.

"That's enough, right here."

"C'mon, I'm just–" Whit pushed hard against the back of the seat, and the man immediately pulled over once more.

"I'm not supposed to be doing this crap." The man was speaking quickly. "I got hired to be an analyst, not get killed out in the streets."

"Alright, I'm not going to kill you – but tell Camille he knows how to contact me. We can set up a meeting like anyone else." Then, about to get out, Whit thought better of it and pushed his hand against the back of the seat again. "Why would he need to bring me out like this, anyway?"

"I don't know, just leave me b–" pressing again. "Ok, ok. He wanted to introduce you to some other guys."

"Who?"

"No! I can't say more and you know it." Whit pressed again and Shehadi responded angrily and scared, "C'mon stop, I know you're not going to kill me.

Why can't you just . . . " But before he finished Whit got out of the car. He walked a half block away and leaned against a pay phone. As he dialed the number, he held the receiver to his ear and watched Shehadi.

"Alo?" a voice on the other end of the line said.

"When I want to meet with a friend, I don't send someone after him like he's being arrested."

"Oh, sh–, wait, Wh–, wait."

"One more time like this and I won't be hel–"

"Wait, please. We just need to talk very soon and I was rushed. Did you hurt him?"

"No." Whit looked back at the car and could see Shehadi moving slowly through the sclerotic, lava flow of traffic.

"We need to talk, immediately."

"Not like this we don't. I'll be in touch."

"No w—"

Whit hung up the phone as Shehadi hastily passed him on the street without seeing anything but the road directly in front of him.

Whit dialed another number and waited as it rang several times. "What?" Royce's voice, sounding exhausted and angry, came scratched over the line.

"Thirty minutes." Whit checked his watch – it was 7:15p.m.

There was silence on the other end of the line followed by, "Do you prefer water or coffee?"

"I'm a little dehydrated."

"Shut up."

Whit got in a cab and directed the driver to Ayn al-Roummaneh. He rushed up to his apartment. The lock was not broken and it didn't appear anything had been tampered with on the inside. He grabbed a duffel bag and threw a change of clothes and a few additional items into it. He checked his gun and grabbed several magazines. He went to the two windows and shook some foot powder around the base of each. He did the same near the front door, and then carefully and slowly closed it behind himself. He checked his watch – 7:45. Just enough time to make it.

# CHAPTER FIFTEEN

Sayyid pulled slowly into the lot and, stepping out of the car, was frisked by several armed men. The two men with him were also frisked. One of the guards motioned them towards a building, and the three walked together. A door opened as they approached, and inside a slightly built man with glasses motioned for them to sit down.

"My boss tells me we have some business to conduct."

"So does mine." The room was austere. Bright white lights reflected off clean white walls. The bespectacled man had black hair, slicked back across his head. There was nothing on the brown desk that he sat behind except a metal lamp. A set of file drawers sat awkwardly against the wall behind him.

"You know the price."

"We are ready to pay."

The man looked at Sayyid for a moment, then tilted his head in curiosity. "What would require this much firepower?"

"It doesn't matter to you."

"It might."

"We're paying you for the weapons, not for advice on how to use them."

"When . . . my boss . . . is elected, you have to agree to refrain from violence at his request."

"I cannot make that promise."

"Then we have nothing further to discuss. Ikhwan, show these men the way ou–"

"Wait. How can we trust you'll do what we need?"

"Mr. Sayyid, that is your name isn't it?"

Sayyid squirmed, "Yes, but I don't believe I know yours."

"That is not important. What is important is that to work with my boss, you have to commit to cooperating with him fully. He can get you all the guns and other tools you need. But he cannot permit you to use them indiscriminately if he is trying to orchestrate peace."

"Is it peace he wants, or just power?"

"They can co-exist."

"We won't be his puppets in the revolution."

"And we're not requesting that you be such . . . puppets. But if he is able to orient the government towards a greater level of . . . support for your cause, you will not have any need to fight it anymore."

"What does he get out of it?"

"He is interested in supporting the revolution."

"He is interested in supporting himself."

"Be careful, Mr. Sayyid. You need the help of his constituents in the south."

"I find it difficult to trust a man who is committed only to his own interests, and not the revolution."

"Fortunately, Colonel Sadiq has a better sense of the revolution's interests than you, and that is why he has sent you here."

Sayyid was silent, absorbing the man's cold stare.

"You will bring the . . . down payment to us the day after next. You will receive the next installment of your weapons at that time. Once we know you are . . . reliable . . . you will bring the next set of gifts to us and we will have the remainder of what you need."

Sayyid nodded and rose to leave.

"Oh, and Mr. Sayyid. Make sure you keep your word. My boss does not take kindly to broken promises. In fact, he punishes them quite severely."

Sayyid turned and left with his accomplices. As he walked through the hallway, his blood curdled at the sound of an almost inhuman screaming, muffled by walls and doors, but sounding as though it emerged from somewhere nearby.

Back in his office, the bespectacled man picked up the phone and dialed. "It's Farouk. Let me talk to him."

"Yes, sir. I have met with them. Are you sure you want to do this? They are Neanderthals." He sat and listened. "Yes, yes. I warned him. Oh, and sir, I spoke with our man on the inside. Our other plans are all still on track. I'll come down in the next few days to discuss."

Farouk hung up the phone, then rose to a file cabinet and extracted a folder. He opened the folder, noting some paper checks inside, and returned them. He then picked up his phone, whispering, "Ikhwan, back in here please."

As Ikhwan entered, Farouk held up the envelop. "This needs to go down to our friend at the Port tonight after it closes."

"Yes, sir."

# Chapter Sixteen

Royce looked out across the Mediterranean. He checked his watch and, deciding he could wait no longer, rose to leave.

A voice broke the silence, "Fancy a moonlight stroll?" Royce, annoyed, knew it was Whit.

"Why do you always do this? I've been waiting here . . . you're late."

"Right on time, in fact. But we don't have much time, so let's walk and talk." Royce's car was about two hundred yards in the distance. That should give them five to six minutes.

Royce started, "Please tell me you weren't involved with that today."

"Forget that. We've got bigger issues."

"You can't shrug this off. If you weren't getting such fantastic stuff they probably would have yanked you already. We just can't afford to let go of you at this point. You're one of the only lifelines we have left in this madness."

"About that, I got cornered—"

"Who?"

"It was bizarre. It was a few of our Deuxieme Bureau friends."

"Why? You can go into their offices any time."

"Precisely. They must have something else going on. There are others they claim they want me to know, but the way they approached it made me uneasy. It doesn't look like they got into my apartment, but I can't sleep there until we find out what is going on."

"Okay," Royce said, "you have somewhere to go tonight?"

"Yes."

"I knew it, you animal."

Whit stared, "I don't have time to talk to a girl let alone sleep with one the way you guys are running me."

"Good. It'll keep you focused."

"Can you arrange something with Camille?"

"Do you trust him?"

Whit nodded, "After what happened today, I'm pretty confident he's on the right side of this play."

"Ok. I'll tell him you want another interview to follow up on some things and we'll see how he takes it."

"Ok," Whit continued, "and we need to get down south immediately. We've got to find out what the story is."

"I still don't get why it's so urgent. Whatever happened today - don't you think these guys are going to lie low now?"

"If all they were going to do was lie low, they wouldn't have been so desperate as to walk right into a prison. We've got to see Shlomo."

"Ok. We've been getting a lot of info from him about this Keswani that Camille mentioned." Whit's interest was piqued.

"What kind of info?" Whit said.

"You know I can't tell you that."

"Dammit, Royce. I'm exposed. You guys left me hanging when the Embassy hit Wael Ghanem."

"What is that to you?"

"I've got to mend some fences or some of my magic you love so much is going to vanish."

Royce thought, but decided not to ask. "Trust me, you'll find out more if we go down and talk with Shlomo."

"Ok, set up the meeting with Camille for tomorrow afternoon and see if we can take a day trip to see Shlomo after that."

"Are you giving me orders now? I thought I was your boss?"

"Hey, you insisted on being the archeologist. You're just along for the ride the paper is funding."

Royce laughed and shook his head. The men were now about half way to Royce's car. Across the street several youths milled about in a coffee shop. Down towards Royce's car two lovers sat on a bench under the moonlight. The sounds of the waves crashed from the right, reverberating off of the buildings to their left and sending sound waves back across Whit and Royce, who walked slowly and deliberately, scanning their surroundings. The surf echoed in a consistent refrain, coming indefatigably out of the darkness.

Whit looked at Royce. Graying hair fell lightly over a tan, thick-set face. Wrinkles had started to accumulate around his eyes. He had the look of a man who knew, and whose knowledge burdened and aged him.

"Final thing," Whit, with uncharacteristic nervousness, continued, "I need to get a few visas to the U.S."

"How many?"

"Five. Three adults, two minors."

"What?!"

"Don't ask, please just get them for me."

"I hope you're getting something good. These things aren't candy. It's getting harder to get ahold of them here. How badly do you need them?"

"I'm close to getting some critical stuff, but it's going to cost us."

"If we get these, you're probably not going to get any more for a long time – so it better be worth it."

"You handle your side of things. I've been handling mine just fine."

"Don't get pissed. I'm just telling you they're getting tight."

"Loud and clear."

The surf filled a few moments of silence until Royce spoke again. "Any idea who it was today?"

"PFLP."

"How the f–"Whit glared at Royce. "Sorry," Royce stopped himself. "Just, how confident are you?"

"Why?"

"So I can tell the bosses. Look, it would do a lot of good for you to give a little color so that when you need their support they'll be there for you."

"You know I don't play office politics. I have to do what I've been sent here to do."

"You still need friends here instead of thousands of miles away."

"The kind that burn my sources?" Whit paused for effect, "You can say I'm confident beyond doubt."

"Are you kidding me? Fifty percent? Thirty percent?"

"Absolutely certain."

"W–" Royce stopped himself again and regained his composure, "You can't say that . . ."

Whit reached into his pocket and pulled out two ID cards, handing them to Royce. "They were jail-braking a mid-grade fedayeen commander named Colonel Sadiq. He's one of the only remaining guys from the PFLP leadership after the Jordanians cornered and killed the rest of them. He's also more violent – so something is about to happen, that is certain."

Royce handled the IDs, tucking them into his pocket after reviewing them. "So they're it? Your third force?"

"No idea. But it was them at Roumieh – and if we don't stop them it's going to get out of control."

"I'm not sure it isn't already there. We're getting word of some mass rally coming in the next day or two."

"Perfect opportunity for them."

"If you weren't so good everyone would think you're crazy."

"Crazy gets real pretty quickly around here."

The two men were now about twenty yards from Royce's car. The couple had risen and was walking towards them. Royce said, "I'm heading out soon."

"Ok, is all else alright with you?"

"What do you care?"

"You're a short-timer. I would have thought you'd hunker down and wait it out."

"No. It started getting too damn interesting once you arrived."

"You making a name for yourself?"

Royce paused in thought, "To the contrary. I get roasted for the price tag you run up, but I know it's the right thing to do."

"I appreciate your editorial oversight."

"You better win a Pulitzer when we head south."

"My goals are more modest." They both laughed as Royce stepped into the street and walked towards his car. Without any further word Whit continued onward and the couple, about five feet away, approached. They were clearly engrossed in one another. The woman was looking at the man as he held his arm around her and spoke in a quiet tone. Sheepishly, she pushed his arm off.

The man smiled at Whit and winked, as if to say, "don't worry about me." As they brushed past, the man placed his arm back around her shoulder. Whit caught a glimpse of the man's watch, a red Kiple. He had seen one like it somewhere before. His mind floated into he past as he got in his car to drive.

Riding back from West Point on the same train, he noticed it for the first time. Grins had a pretty cheap watch for an Ivy League man. It was a red Kiple, refined yet not the Rolex one would expect.

"You like my watch?" he asked, smiling.

"If it does the job."

"It tells time just the same as any other." Grins started. "My father used to collect watches. Spent a fortune on them. I never understood it. They all said the same thing."

"So you're rebelling?"

"I may regret it. This one seems to be going much faster these days." Grins lamented. "So what are you planning on doing when you get done with school, Whit?"

"I don't know – I've considered the usual analyst jobs around D.C."

"No, no, you're much too smart for that. You need to get out, see the world."

"Yeah, but to what end?" Whit inquired.

"He went out," Grins spoke oddly, as if to some ghost in the ether, "not knowing where he was to go."

The memory faded from Whit's mind as quickly as the passing headlights. It had started to rain a little and he turned on the windshield wipers. He checked his watch and pressed the accelerator.

# Chapter Seventeen

Whit approached the beach bungalow several miles from the city, doused the headlights and coasted into the road in front of the building. This place had been in Martha's family for years, and Boutros had told Whit the Khourys would be here this evening. Whit could see inside that they were all moving about with various tasks. Martha was, inevitably, cooking, and Najwa was helping her. Boutros was sitting on the ground playing a game with Nadia. Khalil, who moved into view in the kitchen sink window.

Khalil stooped over the sink appearing to chop ice. Whit stood outside in the darkness and, taking a small flashlight, flashed it directly at him through the window. Khalil didn't move. Whit waited a moment, then flashed it three quick times. Khalil looked a little startled, and squinted into the night. Whit flashed the light one more time. A small grin emerged on Khalil's face, and after looking around to make sure no one inside had noticed, he gave an overly deliberate nod and wink.

"Dad," Khalil yelled, "I'm going to take this bag of trash outside." Whit could see Martha, cutting something in the next window, freeze in shock, and then look at Khalil.

"Yes, ok!" Boutros responded. Whit chuckled to himself. The two were obvious, but Whit relished that they could enjoy this together. Khalil approached the door and, as he closed it, waived into the darkness.

Whit jogged to the side of the house and Khalil embraced Whit in excitement, then went quiet. They opened the electrical box just beside the door and Khalil pulled the main breaker switch, plunging the house into darkness. They laughed quietly as the girls screamed inside; Khalil biting his closed fist to restrain his mirth. Boutros, in melodramatic fashion fit for a small town playhouse, said, "Don't be afraid! I'll go see what happened."

Boutros came to the door and as soon as he opened it, Khalil and Whit snuck in secretly. Boutros stepped outside and the door swung near closed so quickly that no one would have noticed the exchange took place. Boutros left it slightly ajar so he could watch what would happen.

Boutros waited ten seconds and flung the lights back on. The women screamed again at Whit and Khalil standing in the middle of the room. Martha in near fright, Nadia in excitement, and Najwa in otherworldly gratification. Boutros reentered and Martha ran to him, slapping him with tears in her eyes. Boutros raised his eyebrows in shock as Najwa, in a near full embrace of Whit as she had flung herself in the air upon him, was set gently back down. Whit used a free arm to grab Nadia and save Najwa from embarrassment. Martha then moved forward to hug him, as well.

"What are you DOING HERE?!" Martha screeched.

"The radios in Beirut announced there was a party for some mystery birthday woman."

"How did they know?!" Nadia yelped as she stopped her ecstatic, circular orbit.

"I don't know," Whit said, "but I was just trying to find out whose birthday it is so I could write about it."

"It's Ana's birthday!!" Nadia excitedly yelled. "She's fort—"

"Hush, child," said Martha, and the entire room, broke into laughter.

"Well, we're so glad you're here. I knew Khalil wouldn't be taking out the trash as a volunteer! Thank you for coming. I was worried you might have been near the prison today."

An icy chill spread through Whit again, though now slightly weaker. "No, I was just . . ." Whit said in a slightly shaky voice which Najwa immediately recognized as strange. "No, I just had some meetings until later in the evening."

"Who do you meet with all the time?" Najwa, unconvinced, asked. She moved over to the counter where her mom had been working. Normally, Whit would playfully remark that he had three dates with young women that night that had detained him. He sensed now that such jesting would not go over well.

"Just interviews . . ."

"Seeking the elusive mystery." Najwa said sardonically.

"Always," he said in a barely audible voice. He looked over her shoulders through the windows in search of the moonlit tide, but saw only his own reflection. He could feel Najwa staring at him.

"Ok, dinner!" Martha yelled as all grabbed an assortment of dishes, drinks, and silverware, taking them to the table.

The family all grasped hands and prayed.

Several hours later, when Nadia was asleep, Najwa, Whit and Khalil were walking along the beach. The entire beach and ocean seemed aglow under a silver fire. The night sky mixed with the liquid beauty beneath to create a seemingly surreal phosphorescence in the air, more like the setting of a dream than reality.

"Khalil, what are you doing with Marius so much, anyway?" Najwa started in, channeling the worry of a mother and trying to corner him with Whit present.

"C'mon, Najwa, can't we drop it for just a little bit?"

Whit responded, "I'm actually curious, too, Khalil."

"You're on her side?"

"I'm not on anyone's side. I just want to know how you got interested."

"Well," Khalil was pondering some way to explain his motivation, and the distant city lights, reflecting off the smooth Mediterranean surf, seemed to animate him, "remember that day when we first met you?"

"Of course." Whit noticed Najwa sheepishly looking down at her feet in the white sand, moving gracefully one in front of the other.

"I felt helpless and embarrassed. And, well with Marius's guys, I feel like we're not helpless anymore. We can do something against all the fedayeen."

"I guess I can understand that a little."

"Whit, don't encourage him," she said in disbelief.

"I don't know if there's a choice, Najwa. I don't know that Marius' crew is the best choice, but I look around this country and . . ." but Whit stopped, unsure how to express the full scope of his fearsome knowledge.

"And what, Whit?"

Whit thought, but was hesitant, and he found himself hoping more vigorously than ever before that this family could get out before it came crashing down upon them.

"I'm not even sure. I just think I understand what Khalil is saying. I'd probably feel the same if I were in his situation."

"Thanks, Whit."

"Don't let it go to your head. There's still a government and law."

"Is there? It all seems pretty bad to me. I mean, I look around and all I see is chaos."

Whit was shocked by Khalil's introspection. "I guess it can seem pretty . . . scary at times."

"Scary – it just seems hopeless."

"Didn't you ever read the Bible?"

"Which part?"

"The very beginning?"

"Not sure what you're getting at."

The wind brushed the surf more aggressively and the sound of the breeze and the tide crashed against the rocks. "Right at the start," Whit said, "there is darkness and chaos. And God creates the light."

"Yeah, well, I guess I'm still waiting for him to bring it to Lebanon." They were all silent for a few minutes.

"Alright guys, I'm pretty tired. See you tomorrow." Khalil turned and walked towards the shrubs that lined the beach just a few feet from where they were walking.

"Good night, Khalil."

"Night," he said, and disappeared.

Najwa and Whit walked a little further, and she put her arm into his. The silver glow of the moonlight animated every crevice of the beach, and all life appeared sprinkled with a nocturnal potion.

"I've got to get back to the city."

"Tonight?"

"Yeah. Too much to do."

"What are you always doing? Can a journalist really be that busy?"

"People only meet a journalist at weird times. They don't wanna be seen."

"You really like it – having no life? Do you ever have any fun?"

"Sure. I take a shower every now and then and . . ."

She giggled, and continued, "You know what I mean. You're always off to the next thing. No time for anybody or anything. Have you always been like this?"

"Like what?"

"So . . . focused?"

"Do you ever feel like you need to do something, but you don't know why?"

She thought for a moment. "Maybe. I don't know."

"I do. I guess I just listen for that."

"For what?"

"For that little voice that tells me where to go."

"You're crazy."

"Maybe. But it always seems to make sense at some point." They walked on a bit more. He put his arm around her, but she was silent as she leaned her head against his shoulder.

"You don't ever get that feeling?"

"I don't hear voices, if that's what you mean."

"But do you feel something?"

"Yeah."

"And what do you feel?"

She was silent a moment longer. "Leave this place and don't ever look back." A tear rolled down her cheek. "But now you're here," she said, stopping and looking at him.

"I am no reason to stay."

"Now I don't want to go," she cried more heavily as she tried to speak, "but . . . everything inside for so long has been telling me I have to."

"You have to go."

"I want to be where you are."

"Najwa – I'm no man for you."

"How can you say that?"

"It's too complicated."

"That's life."

"Not like this. There are things about me – it just wouldn't be fair to you."

"We've all got problems."

Whit nodded then, grabbing her hand, turned and started walking back towards the bungalow.

"Where are you going?"

"I've gotta get back to the city."

"I don't think you have anywhere to be. I think you're just running."

"Not from you."

"Then from what?"

"Time is running out for this place, Najwa. You and your family have to get out."

"You're just changing the subject. Besides," she gave an impatient huff, "what are you going to do about it?"

He remained silent, and she continued to cry softly. When they reached the steps, she said quietly, "I just hope you can figure out how to be happy." She kissed his cheek and went inside, and he heard the door lock behind her.

# The Third Force

Whit turned to the horizon and could see Beirut in the distance. The glow of the city lights, for a moment, looked like flames.

.

# CHAPTER EIGHTEEN

Several different cars were ensconced in the shadows in front of the mud brick building. A dilapidated truck was the most visible object, and a jeep sat nearest the door. In between them was a motorcycle, the lights from the building vaguely evidenced a yellowish frame, though the color was barely distinguishable in the darkness. Behind it, a man squatted, inspecting the rear tire with something in his hand.

A boy stood by and watched as the man passed a purplish light over the tire. The purple glare caused a mysterious line to reflect brightly. The man immediately stopped, put the device in his pocket, and the boy saw him write something down on a piece of paper.

The boy scurried off, and the man stood and rounded the corner into the small alley beside the building. He slouched down against the wall, removed a headset and a radio from his pocket, and leaned his head back in a somnolent pose.

"Jasim," a seasoned voice spoke, "After dawn . . . at least five men. That is just enough for . . ." Static and loud banging broke the conversation. " . . . no one can know we are bringing them here . . . " Static and then, again, clarity. "In the mean time, our friend in the south wants the first installment." Michel leaned forward and grasped the headphones to his ears. "Kasim, you . . . go south tomorrow night . . . make the exchange the next morning. Get the weapons back here in time for us to be ready for the . . . Sayyid . . . second installment . . . will go . . . bring back more . . ."

Out of the corner of his eye, Michel glimpsed a man across the street seeming to pay too much attention to him. He removed the audio set. The figure, now motioning to him to cross the street, had a brand new gun slung over his shoulder. Michel finally looked directly, unable to avoid him, and could see Salman beckoning him to cross. Cursing the friendliness, he rose and did so.

As Whit arrived across the street, Salman embraced him, "Brother, what silliness is this, sitting in dark alleys, and next to those maniacs no less."

"I go where I think people won't bother me."

Salman continued unwittingly, "Well you pick strange places. Come, let's have coffee. My uncle will be happy to see you."

As they walked, Michel looked back over his shoulder, but could see no movement from the building.

"An impressive gun, Salman. Where'd you get it?"

"I know what you think."

"That's funny," Michel responded, "I don't."

"It's not as bad as it seems, Michel." Salman said soberly, then turning almost cheerful, "This fighting can't go on forever." His eyes narrowed, "But hopefully,

Fatin will be mine soon. If I have to fight for her, then that is what I'll do."

"How long will it take, Salman?"

Salman shrugged, unknowingly, "However long it must."

Fog settled over the evening with unexpected rapidity, muffling the sounds all around them. A child's giggling was smothered by the cranking of a car engine. Whispers mixed with faint weeping. The eerie chant of a masculine choir, surging forth a bizarre Soviet hymn to scientific man, floated and faded as if with the changing of a radio dial. As ephemeral as the sounds, human figures emerged, but just as quickly disappeared. A mother's pleading voice calling for a child, and then the source of the voice materialized only feet in front of them searching wildly and desperately, before being absorbed by the unrelenting haze.

Then, in the haunting stillness, a child stood vaguely visible in the distance; face, indiscernible. The small, white-clad body was only faintly visible in the night fog. It lifted its hand towards them in a pleading gesture, as if only they could see through the murky loneliness. Though they walked closer, they never seemed to reach it, and the wind picked up, thickening the fog instead of dissipating it. The child was enmeshed and only darkness remained.

From the darkness another figure emerged, hunched and clothed in wretched tatters. Limping along in the gloom, it convulsed and stumbled every few steps, as if afflicted with some unknown curse. Unable to choose its own direction, it ambled onward, willing forward movement against an invisible weight.

Then, the figure stopped, and standing to its full height, slowly began to turn. As it turned towards him,

Michel could see the distorted and suffering face of the man he had previously seen at the entrance to the camp. The man's stained shirt was now soaked in blood, which dripped slowly down the his leg, mixing with the dirt at his feet.

Suddenly, Michel felt a hand on his right shoulder, "Michel," Salman said, and Michel turned to Salman standing in front of a door, the frame of which was clear in the hazy fog, "This is my uncle's home." When Michel turned to look back into the street, only the dark fog flowed past.

"Did you see the them?"

"What? Who? What are you talking about? No one but you and I were crazy enough to walk around in this mess. Are you ok?"

"You mean you saw nobody?"

Salman put his right hand to Michel's forehead, and Michel drew back. Salman, laughing, said, "Slow down, brother, I was checking if you have a fever. You are talking like a crazy person."

As they stood in the doorway, Michel looked back once more into the inscrutable murk. "I have to stand guard, Michel. Please go inside. Adib should be there."

Michel walked into the courtyard, where the air was clear. Adib sat alone, looking pensively at the fog that hovered over the courtyard as though it were shielded by an invisible glass dome. Into the sky, Adib was peering.

"What do you see, Adib?"

Adib started forward, seeing Michel, "Welcome, welcome." He rose slightly and motioned Michel to sit beside him, then he looked back up.

"The strangest thing—"

Suddenly, Musa Rasoul boomed an entrance, "Haha, Michel, welcome to my home. I was told you were here when I was away and rushed home to see you again." Michel wondered, of course, why the rushing might be necessary.

Adib poured coffee into cups for his father and Michel, then pursued his curiosity, "Michel, what news from the outside? What is this we hear about protests planned for this week on the campus?"

Michel wasted no time, "I have reason to believe that the PFLP is going to be there. And . . . you know, I heard a rumor that they were behind the prison attacks."

Adib responded, "That's more than a rumor. They got Col. Sadiq out – even this very moment he sits only blocks away. We think they are planning something even bigger," Adib said, and did not notice Musa Rasoul shoot him a cold, unapproving glance.

"Hush, my son, we don't know about such things."

"They must be stopped," Michel risked it.

"But how?" Musa Rasoul responded, "We are tired of fighting one another." His brow furled in contemplation of some troubling thought, which squeezed its way between his downset eyes, darted to his lips, and finally escaped in a pointed burst. "So much wasted life!"

"Whatever they do," Michel continued, "everyone knows they are based here. It would bring tragedy upon this camp if they were successful." Musa Rasoul, bombastic though he was, was sensitive to what seemed to be the tacit warning in Michel's words. He stared at Michel, who did not look away.

"We may disagree with them, but if one of us is attacked, we all are attacked."

Adib opened his mouth to speak, but perceiving the gravity of the exchange, stayed quiet.

Michel responded directly, "I'm not sure I believe that. You would rather go to destruction with a group of fanatics than live on to fight the cause you actually believe in?"

"Whatever happens between us and them, it will be on our own terms, not anybody else's. The imperialist occupiers would love to see us fighting one another."

"You really think you have more in common with a crew of bank-robbing rapists than you do with some decent citizen who is just trying to find his way through the day?"

"Ho ho!!!" Musa Rasoul exclaimed, and his excitement sent his deep voice ricocheting off the courtyard, the sound wave lifting two birds off the ground. "Strong words, Michel. A few days ago you barely knew who they were and now they are the sons of Shaytan?" But before Michel could respond, Fatin joined the group with a fresh pot of tea.

Taking a seat for herself, she asked, "What are we discussing?"

"Now here's a difference where I would agree with you about those men across the street, Michel. We'll let a woman speak at the table."

Fatin quickly chimed in, "And you'll all be better off for it. Think of everything you'd miss." The group laughed, "At any rate," she continued, "I can already tell that the three of you will bore me to tears." But she pressed the topic, "So what are we talking about?"

They all paused, thoughtfully, and Michel Rasoul responded, "We were talking about the devil." Musa and Adib exchanged curious glances. She thought for a moment.

Michel wondered aloud, "Don't you ever stop to think . . . "

"No, Michel," Musa Rasoul immediately interrupted, "that's a luxury only you have."

"Stop to think what, Michel?" Fatin's voice came softly through the still, evening air.

"Here we are, precariously balanced like history has come swirling about and come to rest right here and now."

"That is a heavy burden, young man." Musa Rasoul responded. "I look back across this century and all I see is suffering."

"I see hope," said Fatin quickly.

"Hope?" exclaimed Musa Rasoul incredulously, "Now you're sounding like a Christian." Then, as if struck with a thought that had never occurred to him, he turned to Michel.

"You're a Christian. That's all you do is hope."

"You seem to know a lot about us for thinking it's all a lot of nonsense."

"Did I say that? Anyway, what does it mean to be a Christian when all around you is suffering?"

"I don't know." Michel said quickly, but then paused for further reflection. "It's as if someone asked me a question a long time ago, and I've been searching for the answer ever since."

Fatin's eyes seemed aglow with curiosity, "What was the question?"

Quietly, almost inaudibly, Michel laughed briefly and said, "I can't remember." Shaking his head for a moment, he continued, "Maybe I was born with it." Silence followed, and then breaking the reverie, "I'm sorry, but I must go now. Thank you for your hospitality."

"So soon?!"

"I'm afraid I must beat the curfew."

"Then, good night, Michel, come back soon." Adib said, rising to shake his hand.

As Michel walked towards the door, Fatin walked to him and whispered softly, "If you see Salman, please tell him I must see him soon."

Michel nodded and said quickly, "I know he would like that." Fatin smiled, but grew serious just as Musa Rasoul had slowly risen and come to their side.

Musa Rasoul walked Michel out into the street. "You said something when we last spoke, Michel."

"Yes?"

"You said I," he paused, "we . . . didn't have to be without friends."

"Yes."

"What did you mean?"

Michel nodded with a deeply menacing look across the street and down the block where men piled into trucks from the PFLP shanty. "They will never be your friend, Musa. The day may come when you need some help against them."

"And who would that help come from?"

"They will destroy this whole place if something is not done." Down the street the cars started. They roared past in a rage, one by one, men yelling at passers by to get out of the way and swerving to and fro dangerously in the streets. Families walking in the night rushed their children out of the street. As the cars hurtled by, a yellow motorcycle sped up and Sayyid, atop it, looked at the Colonel and Michel, slowed a little as he grotesquely drew his finger across his throat. He then sped off into the dusty night.

"There may come a day when you agree with me. I will be your friend then, Musa. And I am not alone." Musa Rasoul looked on into the dust, and Michel stepped into the swirl. Within a few seconds, he was across the street and gone.

# CHAPTER NINETEEN

Whit moved through the crowded street with his eyes on the church in the distance. The two front doors were unremarkable, but their simple carvings shown brilliant against the early morning light. It was a modest entrance without stairs or other elaborations.

Across the street from the front doors Whit could see two cars filled with men. This was a little careless of Camille, as anyone looking would know that cars full of men don't simply sit around the streets without purpose. Regardless, Camille was showing up in strength.

Whit scanned the rooftops, seeing several men attempting to hide behind low walls. Perhaps Whit was wrong – Camille wasn't trying to be secretive; he was intentionally projecting force. Whoever was inside, this was serious.

Nonetheless, the attention of the gaggle on the front door was misplaced, Whit mused to himself. About two blocks from the entrance, he turned down an alley that was parallel to the church building. A butcher, a small café, and several shops lined the alley. Whit turned left and dodged some sprinting children, screaming in delight at their games. Two blocks ahead Whit could see a rear door in the church building that, in all likelihood, led into the sacristy.

Whit approached the street and could see both corners and had a clear view of the road that abutted the church in both directions. There were no cars parked here and no young milling about. Whit sat momentarily at a café on the corner. A woman drinking coffee and reading a book sat two tables away. She pretended not to see Whit, and he glanced at the title. Heavy reading for a morning coffee. It was Augustine's "Confessions;" one of his favorites.

Whit rose and crossed the street, testing the handle on the sacristy door. As he did so, he did not see the woman reach into her purse and tap the button on a walkie-talkie several times.

Inside the sacristy, a priest was unrobing from the morning Mass, and looked a little startled. In Arabic, Whit said, "Forgive me father, I chose the wrong door. I was meeting a friend here."

The young priest, who had a dark mole on the nape of his neck and hair tightly slicked across his head, was seemingly unresponsive and continued to remove his vestments. Underneath the ceremonial sticherion, he wore the garments of a Maronite clergyman. As he hung the sticherion in an aging wooden closet, without making eye contact with Whit and almost as if talking with himself, he said, "Go to St. George." Whit paused and looked at the priest, who still did not make eye contact. Whit passed through the doors and found himself just beside the front of the church. Simultaneously, the priest reached under the vestments and pressed twice on a walkie-talkie.

The door closed behind Whit, and he began moving down the side of the church. The space was dark but had light flooding in from the high-vaulted windows. Between each window were statues, each roughly two to three feet tall. Just above him and closest to the front of the church, Whit passed beneath a statute of the most venerated of Maronite monks, Charbel Makhlouf.

About fifteen rows down the wall along which he was walking he saw another statue. Between his feet, a muscular hero had lunged a spear into the neck of a wreathing dragon. The man held the spear high, flags flung behind him in picturesque triumph. He was the dragon-slayer and ubiquitous patron saint of the churches of Eastern Christianity, St. George. Whit glanced to the pews beneath it and, though his vision was partially obstructed, he caught a glimpse between two columns of a man kneeling, his face obscured in darkness.

As Whit moved closer and sought a better view through the next two columns, a figure stepped into his path. He collided with the man with a dull thud. Whit instinctively began to step back and reach into his jacket. The man put hands on both upper arms and said, "Don't, Whit." Though this side of the church was darkened and the bright lights streaming in from the windows above blurred Whit's vision, he knew immediately, and saw a split second thereafter, that it was Camille.

"Don't appear out of the masonry, then."

"C'mon Whit, calm down." Camille was an inch or two taller then Whit. He had a suit jacket and an open necked shirt. The thick gold chain hanging down from his neck held a crucified Christ, partially obscured by his shirt.

"Just watch it," Whit said, irritated.

Camille laughed, "Ok, ok. There was no need for the way you handled Nouri last night."

"That was strike one."

"Look, I'm sorry. We just didn't want anyone else listening in. Can we trust you on that?"

Whit opened his jacket and unbuttoned his shirt part way to show he was not wearing a wire, then said, "I came here so you know I'm serious. But if I'm taking risks and being serious, I need to know that you are, as well. Why did you ask me to come, Camille?"

"You know as well as I do, Whit. Personally, I want to talk with you about yesterday."

"Nothing to say."

"Did you take anything off those guys?"

"Yes."

"What?"

"Their IDs."

"Why?"

"I'm happy to give you their names – but my reasons are my own."

"Alright, we needed to meet with you because we think you can help us." Camille paused and made eye contact with Whit. Whit waited for more.

"Who do you mean by us?"

"Your people."

"My people are all back in America."

"Christians, Whit. Christians." Camille paused and when he saw Whit was waiting, he continued, "Things are getting serious."

"No doubt. But you've seen this before."

"This is different."

"How so?"

"Our alliances in Parliament are fraying; and they won't pay for the state's security operations."

"All this money in this place and they won't pay?"

"Well they barely collect on taxes, but even if they did, the political climate and this damn Arab nationalism – they think we're just out to stop the fedayeen and everyone is scared of the regional image."

"The Prime Minister?"

"No. He has the right intentions – but he's weak. He's losing the support of his own base because it's getting so bad down there. It's a matter of time before the President capitulates and makes more concessions to the fedayeen. We won't be running our own country anymore, and we can't keep it stable without the security apparatus."

"Even if that's the case, what can I do about it? Write an article?"

Camille was silent, then turned and, as he passed under the statue of St. George, motioned with his right hand into the pew without turning or stopping.

Whit stepped into the pew and knelt beside a man who was holding a rosary. Whit knew the drill. They had left the lights dimmed, picked an unlit section of the church; Whit didn't even turn to look at his face.

After a minute or so, the man said, "I come here to pray when hope seems far away." The man spoke English comfortably but with a notable accent. It was Lebanese English mixed with something that smacked of Texas.

"Is now such a time?" Whit said.

"That depends." The man said quietly.

"On what?"

"On many factors."

Whit saw the man moving the rosary beads in his fingers, and asked, "Where do you put your hope, when the desolation comes?"

"In prayer, of course." The man paused momentarily, seeming to reconsider it, "But prayer alone will not save us."

"Shouldn't it always be sufficient?"

"I had considered the seminary for a time, Mr. Whitaker."

"Whit is fine. And I don't think I got your name?

"George."

Whit laughed briefly, looking up at the statute on the wall, "Why didn't you go into the seminary?"

"Did you ever consider it?"

"Yes; but you first."

"The world is a cruel place, Whit." George lamented. "It was several years ago. I looked around at Lebanon, and thought I could do more good outside."

"I'm not sure I fully understand," Whit pretended, though he understood the dilemma completely. "How does the good you need to do correlate with the world being a cruel place?" A few moments of silence passed, as the two shared a mutual contemplation of the choices they had made, and those which still lay before them.

"What do you see, Whit, when you look around Lebanon?"

"I see a country ready to tear itself apart, but I can't fully understand why."

"I see the same thing. But is Lebanon really any different than any place else, or is it just stripped of a little decency that keeps other places going?"

"What do you mean?"

"The Lebanese are human beings, no different than any others."

"Of course."

"Why should we be any more prone to war than anyone else?"

"Maybe it isn't you, in particular. Maybe a Christian in Lebanon isn't all that different than a Christian in France, and a Muslim in Frankfurt isn't so different than one in Tyre. But the time and the place, maybe that's what really matters."

"Precisely. We didn't choose to be here. But here we are. Everyone angry and . . ." he waved his hand in disgust, ". . . waiting for their moment. In the face of that, how can I simply retreat?"

"Is it a retreat? Or better yet, before we even get to that, why are the people so angry?" A long silence followed Whit's question, and curled around the two figures as they sat, contemplating the crucified Christ in front of them and man, fallen, all around.

"I think we are angry about being displaced."

"What?" Whit did not expect that grievance, and sought more.

"The Palestinians want their homeland."

"It would seem so."

"But what is home? A place where you can be at rest? A place where you don't have to look over your shoulder? We all want to be home, Whit. You were born into yours. We have to fight for ours."

Whit fixated on the thought as he contemplated its gravity. If this was so personal, about place, why did Whit have anything to do with the fight? The question had haunted him. After another long silence, Whit finally asked, "Is this the home you're meant to have?"

"It's the one I've got. I guess, in the end, we all want the same thing. We run around like little gods with the power to create and the power to destroy. Except for one particular thing, we can't keep ourselves safe, Whit. I want safety for my people."

"Do you think Eden can be built by a gun?"

"No. But it can be destroyed by one. Let others build what they want. Someone has to man the walls."

Whit said, as he looked forward towards the altar, "Converte gladium tuum in locum suum . . ." and before he could finish, George put his hand on the pew, squeezing it as if containing some pain, and continued, ". . . omnes enim qui acceperint gladium, gladio peribunt." The two men looked at each other face to face for the first time, knowing the truth that passed between them but about which they felt helpless to do anything. Those who live by the sword, shall die by it.

George had a smooth face, almost boyish. He had spent years in the sun, but it darkened his skin without aging it. His black hair lay lazily over his forehead. The youthful look, however, was starting to show signs not of age, but strain. A tincture of dark circles had barely formed under his eyes, and the first scratch of wrinkles reached out from the outside corners of his eyes. It was not age in his face - it was the strain of someone carrying a great load.

"Whit," the man said, "my name is George Malik, and I am asking for your help. You know this can't keep going on like this. You know where it's going." He was being honest after all; laying it all on the line. He was desperate, and he must have known things of which Whit was unaware. The darkness was not far off, after all.

Whit was silent for a time, gauging this man who had so honestly exposed his identity and his intent, but cautious, Whit said, "I'm not sure what I can do."

"You won't regret it."

"I won't be the judge of that, I'm afraid." Candlelight flickered against the agony of the crucified Christ.

"We need weapons and training."

Whit was silent, but nodded slowly. "Well here's a tip for free," Whit shared, "the most beautiful woman in the Levant should not be your corner lookout. She attracts way too much attention."

George smiled. "She's my sister, and is eager to help. I thought no one would suspect a woman."

"Au contrare, mon ami, a beautiful woman is the deadliest decoy of all, but only to be used in the rarest of circumstances; and never," Whit laughed as he patted George's shoulder, "never as the lookout."

"Ok, understood," George said through laughter.

"Anyway, it shouldn't be hard to find a replacement. The guys packed into the cars out front are all ugly and very ordinary looking."

George laughed out loud and then stopped himself, looking around the church. "You're damn right about that," George uttered between smiles, "we'll look forward to working with you."

"Just a reporter, George." Whit said.

"A reporter, my friend," George said, "would have used the front door." Whit silently laughed, his head lifting slightly and a small smile passing through his lips. They would work together well, indeed. George got up from the pew, and Whit waited for a moment, then followed. They walked together towards the sacristy, and once inside, stopped. The priest, previously there, was gone.

"While I'd like to be enthusiastic, my intuition tells me it will be difficult, George. I just have to be candid."

"I appreciate the candor; but if Camille is right, I suspect you'll know just what to do."

"What I'm probably going to need is much better information, and a lot of it, about just what is going on out there." As if on cue, the door to the sacristy opened and Camille entered.

"Camille will get you what you need. But so you know, we're expecting something very significant in the coming days."

"It's time to go," Camille said. Camille, a seasoned security officer, was treating this man like the head of state. Camille had just come in from the street, checking the status and ensuring that all was in order, his demeanor was now hurried and certain, as if a window of opportunity had been presented that he did not want to lose. "Whit, I'll talk with you. Now, we must go." He opened the door and held his hand towards the light outside where two cars awaited.

George clasped Whit's hand, shaking it firmly and looking resolutely at him. He walked swiftly outside and stepped into a black BMW sedan. Camille shut his door then rushed to the passenger seat. Whit noted the license plate number through the crack in the door, which had been left slightly ajar.

Waiting a moment until the car cleared the nearest corner, and the other car went in the opposite direction, Whit looked across the street at the cafe. She was still there, pretending to read the "Confessions," eyes fixed on Whit's door, sending an explosive pulse through the heart of every man who passed within a visible radius of her. Rather than a quick death, however, this shockwave shredded their hearts, leaving them to live with the vague impression of what might have been had they only been so lucky.

When she looked towards the door with a blank stare, the shockwave hit Whit, and he was struck with an inexplicable intuition that his destiny would become intertwined with this woman's. Then he realized – it already had.

The sun was crisp against the cement buildings. The ocean breeze swam through the streets, guiding the clean, sunny air gently along. How much beauty existed amidst the gloom.

Whit focused on her as he opened the door and could see her, beneath her glasses, freeze in anticipation, preparing to move. He walked several feet to the left and watched her out of his peripheral vision. She began to rise from the table; and she was his. He immediately turned directly towards her and crossed the street. As Whit approached, she grew frantic and sat back down in a vain attempt to appear to have risen without intent. She tried to remain calm, and dug her head into the book, her chest noticeably rising with the heightened breath of an anxious novice. When he stopped just beside her table, she did not look at him.

"What book are you on?"

She waited a few moments, pretending not to hear, but Whit let the awkward silence and his looming shadow wrap itself around her. He wanted to laugh, sensing her discomfort merged with the stress of having been caught. A smile came over his face, and finally, she could no longer ignore its hold. "I'm sorry?" she said.

"It looks like you are trying to read the 'Confessions.'"

"I know how to read so I would say I'm not just trying."

"Well, judging by the way you don't seem to be able to sit still, I can't see how you're able to concentrate."

Her face turned red and she grew speechless. Her skin was like George's, smooth and clear. She also had a dark, olive tone. Her eyes, however, were an ornate blue. Against her skin, and the dark, curly hair that fell gently around her head and shoulders, her eyes were youthful and vigorous, though they had the look of having seen much.

"So which part are you reading right now?"

She glanced, dejected, towards the book. After a moment of thought and deciding there was no way out, she said "The eighth book." She looked at him, waiting for what may come next, ready also to spring forth into the warm Lebanese afternoon and flee from her shame.

"Whence is this monstrousness?" Then Whit paused, waiting for her eyes to meet his. When they did, he continued, "And to what end?" He could see her blinking in disbelief, and knew she really had read it, whether today or another time, "Let Thy mercy gleam that I may ask, if so be the secret penalties of men, and those darkest pangs of the sons of Adam, may perhaps answer me."

She opened her mouth in slight awe, her pulse quickening. He continued, "If you're actually reading it, I've been looking for someone who can explain that part to me. Perhaps next time." Then he leaned in close, "Please don't bother following me."

After he rounded the corner, she suddenly remembered her charge from her brother. Looking around to see if anyone had noticed the exchange, she rose to follow him. Only seconds after him, she turned the corner and frantically searched the street, but he was nowhere within sight.

# CHAPTER TWENTY

That night, Whit walked hurriedly towards the beach and saw several men under the moonlight holding a Zodiac rubber boat at the water's edge. As Whit approached, Royce motioned from within the boat for Whit to quicken his pace. Whit jogged the remainder of the way, and tossing a small bag to Royce, jumped over the barrier at the front of the boat. The men pushed the boat away then ran down the beach and out of sight while Royce and Whit rowed backwards and a third man, waiting for a few moments more, pulled the rip chord on a motor, reversing the boat fifteen yards before turning, and heading south adjacent to the coastline.

"We're running on schedule. Confirmed rendezvous point and itinerary." Royce said, over the initially low hum of the motor.

"Are they going to have some breakfast for us this time or make us starve all day?"

"Very funny. Somehow I think Shlomo likes us less every time we see him."

"Just you, Royce."

The boat moved seamlessly along the smooth waters, lit by moonlight so the coast and miles of Mediterranean were illuminated all around them. The palm trees along the coast swayed in the breeze, their black outlines discernible against the soft glow of the start-lit sky. The landscape, black and foreboding, rolled past in endless waves.

Half an hour later, Royce pointed ahead at a black figure bobbing in the water in the distant, murky darkness. Royce moved to a lamp on the side of the boat and flicked it twice. They watched for a moment and three quick pulses of light emerged from the watery wilderness. As they approached the boat, several figures were vaguely visible on its bow. Royce rushed to the front of the boat, and in what he had told Whit was his most favored epic gesture of international goodwill, dropped his pants, letting his buttocks reflect the full light of the moon to the occupants of the bobbing craft.

"Ah, Royce," came a strongly accented Hebrew voice from the other boat, clearly discernible as the engine in the Americans' boat had just been cut, leaving them to float the few remaining yards in silence. "Why must you always show us your best side first?"

"Up yours, Shlomo."

"You're in no position to speak." And the men in the boat laughed as Royce smiled and pulled up his pants.

As the crews held the boats together, Royce clasped Shlomo's hand and moved past. Whit jumped in behind him. Several men from Shlomo's boat hopped into the American craft.

"Hello Cordell," said the Israeli.

"It's good to see you again, Shlomo."

"What do you have for me this time?" The American boat started its engine and pushed off, slowly turning and heading back north. The Israeli boat ignited its engine, turned back south, and began heading down the coast, rapidly approaching the coastline.

Shlomo and Whit moved to the front of the boat as Royce spoke with the two other men in the back.

"Finally a reliable contact who looks primed to build a strong Christian militia."

"No kidding? If you are interested than this must be seerious my friend."

"You probably know better than I do, Shlomo. The coalition is fraying. The politicos can hold it together for a while longer, but it's not clear how much. If they lose Wael in the South, then the whole thing falls apart. What's the latest with this maniac I've been hearing so much about who is at war with Wael?"

"Funny you ask. I'm taking you to see him today."

# CHAPTER TWENTY-ONE

Qustantin sat in the passenger seat as the young private, Stephen, looked to the left before turning the corner. Stephen looked at his map and list while driving. The list was lengthy, sketching out the morning patrol. Over two dozen lines down, still an hour or so worth of driving remained.

"Lieutenant," Stephen said to Qustantin, tapping the page, "why is this one circled?"

"Ah, some intelligence this morning just said we should be a little cautious on that road."

"Why?"

"Are you kidding? We're lucky just to get a hint. I have no idea." Qustantin cursed the lazy analysts in his mind. Someone probably risked their life to get information that got translated into a single circle; all because some guy didn't have time to think before getting his cup of coffee.

"Well, I think we have to be cautious on every road, sir."

Qustantin laughed. "That's why you'll make a good soldier, Private."

"Thank you, sir." The youth said smiling, and looking at Qustantin.

"Watch the road, soldier."

"Yes, sir," he said, as the smile evaporated quickly.

"You have family, private?"

"Just my mother and two sisters."

"Ah, a quiet household." Stephen laughed and shook his head. Qustantin was scanning the road and the side streets for anything abnormal, and didn't notice Stephen's laugh turn sober quickly.

"Lieutenant look at these guys over here," Stephen nodded to the left where two young men sat on a curb and a third got up and went inside a store.

"Alright, it's your turn." Qustantin said. "I'll stand back ready. You go talk to them."

Stephen looked at Qustantin somewhat fearfully, and Qustantin raised his eyebrows in an unspoken, "Why are you waiting?"

"Yes sir," said Stephen. He pulled the car over and closed the door behind him.

"This is Falcon 1, we're stopping to check out a crew."

"Tamam."

"We may need back up."

"Negative, lieutenant. All the extra back-up is being pulled for the protests. You guys are on your own today." Qustantin threw the walkie talkie onto the dashboard and looked behind him where the other car in the patrol had stopped. There were three men in it – all the support he had. He rolled down the window. Though early morning, the day was already showing hot. When he turned back to look at Stephen, the private was almost at the car door.

Opening it and hopping in, he said, "They're just shopkeepers taking a break."

"See, that wasn't so bad, was it?"

"Yeah, not until they actually pull something."

He shifted the car into gear, drove two more blocks, checked the third line off his list, and turned right.

As day broke across Lebanon the people lived in joy and pain, in complacency and impatience, in silence and outrage. Across Lebanon the people lived their lives half certain that they were about to change forever; yet normally as if nothing different were to come. Their emotions and their thoughts were woven together into an inextricable marriage of human love and anguish.

In an empty parliament building, the Prime Minister, Wael Ghanem, sat on a chair at the head of a room with a couch and several chairs around it. Kadir paced a worn path into the tiled flooring. The men in the room shouted back and forth, " . . .must stop him or he'll destroy the entire region . . .", ". . . people are terrified and looking to us to do something . . .", ". . . can't invite the army south now or we'll be at war with the fedayeen."

In a small, dusty camp near the border with Israel, Jawad Keswani, draped in black, walked through the early morning hours, crossed an empty lot, and entered the oldest building in the complex. It was a mansion, fortified with stone walls and timbered trestles that supported a small second floor. As he approached the door, a bearded guard opened it, but didn't make eye contact. Keswani passed through the space and the darkness followed him inside. Walking down a short hallway, he paused to whisper something to another guard. He climbed a short staircase and warned a man sitting in a chair not to let anyone past at the top. He stood in the doorway as the guard turned his face towards the ground in shame. Inside a young woman sat crying with her hands tied to a bedpost.

From the campus of AUB, Najwa held a pay phone up to her ear as the other end rang continuously, but Whit did not answer. Najwa hung up the phone, her eyes now fully streaming. She wiped her face as she got up to leave. Exiting the building, she did not notice a man follow her, walking roughly twenty yards away behind her. She turned to look behind her, but seeing nothing, continued towards her dorm. The man followed her there, writing something in a notebook before walking across the lawn to the University gates. He moved a motorcycle to a space across the street in an alley, and then walked into a coffee shop across from the gates. Strolling to the back of the coffee shop, he opened a door in the rear where a group of men were feverishly talking. One of them was drawing on a chalk board, "The protest will start here," he said as he tapped the bottom part of the drawing, "and come past the front gates at about 1:00 p.m."

Several miles from Tal Za'atar, two cars slowly pulled onto opposite ends of a large street and parked. An old man walking along the sidewalk thought he could make out the forms of four or five men in each, and hurried further, not turning to see what would happen. Another car crept along and, pulling at an angle across the road, slowed to a stall. The driver got out, lifted the front hatch, and began inspecting the engine. The men in the other two cars simultaneously got out and walked into several different buildings on either side of the road.

The individual whose car had broken down reached into his jacket, pulled out a handgun, and nestled it in between the carburetor and the drive shaft. He checked his watch, and waited.

# CHAPTER TWENTY-TWO

The sun rose slowly over the borderlands. It rose the same over those who slept and those who toiled. It rose the same over those south of the border and those to its north. The sun rose and shed light evenly; but different shadows fell across the land.

As the sun rose, Whit saw seated next to him a haggard, smallish man, bags under his eyes and morning stubble on his chin. An Israeli army cap hung on the back of his head. Small tufts of sandy hair poked forward form a receding hairline under the hat. Whit saw a man he knew had been at war for most of his life, whether with guns or without. Whit saw a man whose eyes, wizened by the sun and his own experience, saw through Whit, as well.

"How old are you now, Shlomo? Aren't you ever going to get out and just become a kibbutznik?"

"What?! It's too early to be philosophical, and my English isn't so good." Shlomo responded.

"Seriously – you could be fighting wars the rest of your life. Isn't it time to just let someone else stand watch?"

"I don't know how to do anything else. But you don't have any border here, so I should be asking you, Whit, what are you doing?"

"Fair enough," Whit said, "I think I'd be scared to live in a world where America just looked the other way."

"Ahh, yes!" Shlomo almost screamed. The underbrush slipped past more quickly as he pressed hard on the accelerator and said melodramatically, "The idealist American come to save the day! Look, there he is, the hero of our little war – he stood between the dead and the living, and God's wrath ceased!"

"Not like that. But seriously – there are plenty of guys waiting in line to fill the vacuum."

Shlomo sobered a little, the smile growing serious as the creases emerging from his eyes smoothed and the upturned corners of his mouth slackened, "I know Whit. But do you really think it matters? You're one man, and this isn't your home. They're going to draw you into a fight that isn't yours."

"It matters enough to you to be here."

Shlomo thought a bit. "It's our history. What else can I do?" Whit didn't have an answer, and Shlomo looked at him for a moment, then back at the road. "You know in 1967 I was down in the south." Whit braced himself. Israel's war with the Arab states just a five years before had been short, but the Sinai action in the south had been fairly intense. "It was already over, and both sides knew it, but we were going through and clearing out some villages of Egyptians, fighting to the end, I guess." Shlomo looked over the rims of his glasses, and Whit couldn't tell if he was telling him or if there was somewhat of a question in his description.

"Anyway, we got to this one building, one room, just sitting out there in the desert. We knew they were in there and we normally just would have blown the thing up. The Egyptians were still fighting, I don't know maybe out of pride more than any hope, you know. It was towards the end of the day and we were just tired. Tired of fighting. None of it seemed to matter at that point, it just seemed like, shadow boxing, like we used to do in training. You dance around the ring and you throw a few punches, maybe you land one, maybe you don't. At any rate, there we were. It was late in the day. We could see two or three of them in there. Maybe eight or ten of us with a tank outside this craphole. We called back – what do we do? They won't come out."

"'Blow it.' The commander said on the radio. We all just looked at one another. Commander said our job was still to clear out the area. It was purple out, you know the way it gets in the desert in the evening. Everything starts to turn cool. Then it happened. We had the, oh what do you call it, the thing . . . on the tank," motioning with his hand the shape of a cannon, "anyway it was pointing right at the doorway, which had no door. And then, one of the Egyptians just appeared in the doorway. Motionless. No gun. He just stood there with his uniform pants and a ripped shirt hanging off him. Soaked through, it looked like he'd been there for days. We just stood there, silent. 'What do we do?' a guy asked. 'Lieutenant says blow 'em,' one of the other knuckleheads said."

"'If the lieutnenant wants to blow it, he can come down here himself and do it,' another guy says. So there we wait. I'm staring at this guy, and he stares back, but not at me. Just, I don't know, at us. All of us at the same time. Then he steps out, hands hanging down at his side, makes this one last long gaze – I'll never forget it. Then he turns, walks in front of the building and around its corner. Then walks out, straight out into the desert."

"Just like that? Out into the desert?"

"Just straight out – ziiip!" Shlomo motioned with his hand directly over the dashboard and leaning forward, then looked back at Whit over his shoulder, nodding.

"After a few minutes, another two, they come out too. They step out of the doorway, and the one guy was clearly sick or injured, had his arm over the other guy's shoulder." Shlomo paused, placing his hand over Whit's shoulder, and nodding again, as he guided the car with his left hand, paying more attention to Whit's reaction than the road ahead.

"So what'd you do?"

"They leaned back against the wall, so I just told my guy to turn the gun away. After he did, I walked up, and handed them my canteen. The one guy, carrying the other one, he nodded. I said we're supposed to kill you guys if we find you. You better get the hell out of here."

"What did he say?"

"Man, he just nodded. He didn't say anything. Then they went off after the first guy, just walked off into the desert. Which by then, was all dark. I looked inside. No guns. No rations, not even trash. They were just out there with nothing."

"Why didn't you kill them?"

Shlomo paused for a long time. "They didn't want to be there. They were just kids. Well, then that lieutenant shouted over the radio, 'Did you kill them? I didn't hear you shoot.' All the guys looked at me. One or two were smoking. One or two just sat on the ground leaning up against the tank. So we fired the cannon once and the building just turned into ash and sand. 'They're gone, lieutenant.'"

"'Good. Anyway, congratulations, we just got word there's a cease fire. Come on back we're putting up camp here.' I turned to look, could see the two guys just barely."

"What about the third?" Whit looked at Shlomo, and thought he captured, in the morning sun, a softening of his eyes that almost looked like they had moistened.

"That's the real story, Whit. We went out on patrol the next morning. Setting out the boundaries, you know," Shlomo motioned in a circular fashion with his hand. "Anyway, we come up on some low hills in the distance and there they are, these two Egyptians."

"Just the two?!"

Shlomo squinted his eyes and motioned for Whit to calm down, "Hold on, hold on I'm getting to it." Whit moved uneasily in his seat, he could see the guard house that he knew to be their destination in the distance.

"So one of the loud mouths in the group says, 'here we are again, you two, now you're ours,' or something like that. And I walked up to the two with my hand on my gun. They looked up, exhausted. 'Are you going to kill us?' they asked. Everyone looked around again and the loud mouth started loading his chamber and walking up. They wriggled, but it was . . . they couldn't even . . . barely move."

Whit was quiet. He looked out the front window, and then across the border into Southern Lebanon. In the distance he could see a small camp that appeared to be under construction. He could see a car leaving, evidenced only by a dirt trail rising up into the air.

"So they were laying there, and looking up at me as he's cocking his gun." Shlomo continued. "I said, 'No, we're not going to kill you, just take you as prisoners. Can you walk?' I asked. They looked even more scared than if we told them we were going to kill them. One guy didn't think they could walk, so we told them someone would be along to pick them up, and, as we were walking away, one of my guys reminded me about the third guy, the first one who came out of the building and just . . . stared. I went back, 'Hey, what happened to your friend?' They looked . . . shocked. 'What are you talking about?' they asked. "You know, the first guy that came out of the building?" They just stared blankly at me, like my Arabic was bad or something. 'There was nobody else.' Me and my men, we all just sat there, confused."

"They were just lying to cover him."

"Yeaahh, that's what some of my guys thought. I just didn't care. But two of the younger guys came back, when we were back near the place on break. They said they had gone around the house and up a ways into the desert. They only could find the one set of tracks – the guy and his buddy limping alongside him. No tracks for a third guy."

"C'mon – there had to have been something."

"Nothing. And those two could have tracked a gnat all the way to Cairo." Shlomo said, shaking his head.

"What did you make of it?"

"What?"

"I mean, what did you think then?"

Shlomo stopped the car behind a small brick building that was sitting on top of a platform and shrugged as he leaned over the steering wheel, his forearms against the tops and bottom of the wheel and his chin hanging slightly over, looking through the windshield.

"The guys couldn't stop talking about it. They even gave him a name – yetzer. They thought he was some kind of ghost."

"Yetzer?"

"I don't know some religious thing. Comes from 'yetzer hara' – I don't know how to explain it. It's from – what do you guys call it – Genez?"

"Genesis?"

"Yeah. 'Yetzer hara'. It basically means man has this tendency towards evil that he can't shake. You know – it's with him just like the good, too – and the two of them, they are constantly fighting."

"Maybe I should have studied some more Torah." Whit shook his head curiously, "but why yetzer?"

"Huh?"

"Why yetzer for this guy that disappeared?"

"Oh, yeah. Well – we had some of the best trackers, but" Shlomo wiped his hands together, as though brushing them of dirt, "no tracks. That means for sure, no guy."

"You mean, you really thought he was some sort of phantom?"

"They thought – well we could have killed those two, or they could have killed one or two of us – but they didn't shoot and we just let them go. So – it was like yetzer just up and left. Heck those guys talked about it all the way to the end and up til now. Where's yetzer now? Have you seen yetzer lately? That kinda stuff."

Whit paused, rolling the thought around, "and what did you think?"

"It's war, Whit," he said, looking somberly, "I guess I didn't think about it. Or at least, I didn't then," turning and smiling.

Whit took the cue, "But now?"

Shlomo nodded silently, then grabbed the handle and opened his door.

"C'mon. You're not going to believe this."

# CHAPTER TWENTY-THREE

Stephen squinted and rubbed his eyes as the sun broke over the buildings. He checked the map again as they ground to a halt behind the morning rush hour traffic. The cars loosened again, and at the next intersection, he turned right.

"So is it always like this, sir?"

"Like what?" Qustantin asked, sleepily.

"You know, doing patrols in the streets, like we're gendarmes."

"You'd rather be down south dodging mortars?"

"No, sir. I just didn't expect, well, I just thought, with everything going on, we'd be seeing more action."

"Be careful what you wish for, private. The day may come when we get more of it than we want."

"Yes, sir."

"So why have you stayed in, sir, all this time? If you don't mind me asking?"

"Nothing heroic. I wasn't ready to go back to the village and wasn't sure what I'd do next."

"Have you heard the rumors, sir?"

"What rumors, private?"

"About Colonel Hadad. That he's going to leave and take a bunch of Shi'a with him?"

Qustantin stared at Stephen. "You just worry about your job, private. Let the generals worry about Hadad."

"Yes, sir." But the private couldn't let it go. "Well, it's just, they said he's going to fight with the fedayeen."

"Who said?"

"You know, the guys, talking."

"Well that's all it is, private. I was in the academy with Hadad. He hates the Palestinians."

"Yes, sir."

"Hold up – what's this?" Qustantin asked. As they drove down the street, he could see a car blocking a lane of traffic with its hood open.

"What do you want to do, sir?"

"Pull up to the side here about 10 yards away. I suppose it's my turn."

As they drifted towards the side of the street, the car behind them pulled to a stop, as well. Qustantin got out, and began walking down the street. He looked around, and did not see anything out of the ordinary. Several empty cars were parked. People rushed to and fro. The traffic had generally cleared up. Though his angle was bad, Qustantin could see a man hunched over the hood working on the engine. To get a clearer angle, he'd have to walk into the middle of the road, so he stayed to the side.

"What seems to be the problem?" Qustantin asked as he neared. A burly man with a scar running down the side of his face looked up at him.

"I can't tell. Something down in here," he said, pointing, as Qustantin walked up beside him, slightly to the front of the car's left corner.

Stephen watched from inside the car, he had forgotten to step out and cover Qustantin. Over his radio, one of the members from behind said,

"Private aren't you going to get out and c-" and Stephen saw Qustantin lean over to look, but couldn't react quickly enough as the man lifted a pipe and brought it down over the base of Qustantin's skull, knocking him over forward. Immediately, fire erupted from the buildings on both sides of the road.

Stephen tried to get out to run forward, but the gunfire raked his door and he shut it again. He grabbed the walkie talkie and yelled "We're under attack, we're under attack!"

"Where are you?!" The line went dead as he was about the respond.

Stephen began to open the door, but bullets again ripped against it like iron rain. About mid-way between where Qustantin lay and his car, he saw several men emerge from a building, firing towards him and the car behind him. In the rear view, he could see his fellow soldiers emerging from their car, firing straight ahead and towards the opposite side of the street, where he saw additional men rushing out of two doors. One of the soldiers behind fell to the ground as the other two sprinted behind his armored vehicle. He tried opening the door again, but again a volley of fire spread across the ground, sparks flying as the line ascended the side of the car, and he heard the left front tire explode.

Several miles away, a man burst into Col. Chartouni's office, "Qustantin's patrol is getting hit."

Rising quickly, "Send an emergency platoon,"

"We can't," the man, sweating and indecisive yelled, "they're all allocated to the protest route."

"Get a helicopter up there; break one away from the protests!"

Back in the streets, fire exploded over the front of the hood, and Stephen could see his two compatriots firing from behind his car. Fedayeen made their way around and to the right of Stephen's position, down the street. Others had moved behind his car, as well. One of the two soldiers suddenly ran around the left of his vehicle seeming to try to grab his door handle, and was shot, the fire slamming him up against the side of the truck. In the distance, Stephen could see Qustantin being pulled into the car that had been blocking traffic, it's hood now down.

He heard an additional thud against the back of the car, and looking, saw no one left. The firing stopped, and as he looked around, he saw fedayeen closing in all around, guns pointed.

"Get out of the car," one man yelled, shaking his gun towards the side. "Get out now or we'll shoot. Lift your hands up."

But before he could even move, two fedayeen rushed to the side, grabbed the door, and ripping it open, yanked him out of the car by his shoulders and threw him on the ground. They began hitting and kicking him, and the left side of his head exploded in pain as he felt immense pressure and liquid flooding out of his eye and down his cheek. He groped around for his weapon, but felt only an empty holster.

"Enough, get him into the car," he heard someone yell. He couldn't see out of his left eye, but could feel the painful grate of the gravel on the back of his neck as he was drug, lifted and thrown into another vehicle. Laying on the floor he heard several doors slam.

"Go, go, go!" They lunged forward. Dizzily, he saw the tops of buildings racing past.

"They're already here."

"Just police," another man yelled, "follow Jasim, left left left!" The car swung as a few pieces of metal rang out across the car. He felt the car accelerate.

"Is that a helicopter?!"

"Yeah, but it doesn't have any guns, look." As the car sped, the men all peered out the windows.

"They can follow us back."

"It doesn't matter just get back!"

Stephen grew woozy as the car accelerated and hit several bumps.

"He's conscious," another man said, looking down at him, "put a hood on him dammit." He felt a sharp pain as a hand struck the left side of his head, and the hood was pulled down over him. Everything went black.

# CHAPTER TWENTY-FOUR

Royce was talking with several of the Israelis in a building down towards the bottom of the hill. Whit sat with Shlomo inside the guardhouse. It was dark inside, and covered with brush so that from the other side it would have been indiscernible.

Shlomo explained, "The fedayeen don't come around here too often, but if they caught sight of this shitbox they'd try to blow it back to biblical times."

"You have a way with words, Shlomo."

"Thank you."

"Why don't they come around here too often?" Whit inquired.

Shlomo smiled, handing a pair of large binoculars to Whit, gently nudging the IDF guard looking out the window out of the way, and pointing towards the distant set of buildings Whit had seen as they drove to this site, he said, "They don't want to mess with him." Whit pulled back from the binoculars, looked curiously towards Shlomo, who nodded and motioned to look. Whit returned to staring in the distance.

Five buildings, three older and two newer, sat ring-fenced by high barbed wire and metal mesh, almost as if it was a prison. Men in black clothing walked the fence line as sentinels. The fences were roughly fifty yards across. The compound's outside rims were laid out in a square, but the buildings inside were structured in a u-shape surrounding an empty, dirt-ridden courtyard. The U shape of the buildings faced to the west. From Whit's vantage point, it opened up to the left. The southernmost buildings, closest to him, blocked the view of half the courtyard. A large gate sat along the western fence, so that those entering and exiting could go directly into the courtyard. On the south, east, and north, the fence appeared to sit only twenty feet or so away from the building's walls.

"It looks like you're going to get to see a show," Shlomo said. "Now maybe your bosses will believe what we've been telling you guys about this sick bastard."

In the distance a caravan of three cars was rumbling towards the western gate, kicking up dirt in its wake.

"Why haven't you guys done anything?" Whit asked.

"We have too many targets down here. This one is smarter than the rest. We can't tie him to any direct threat."

"Do you have something to record this with?" Shlomo nodded to the soldier, who flipped a dial on a separate scope.

"Have you figured out the MO?" By that time, Royce had entered the room.

"We're talking about your friend down here, Keswani, the next MP from the Arqoub." He turned back to Whit, "The caravans come sporadically with no pattern. They come, stay for about fifteen minutes, then leave."

"Who is in the cars?"

"We don't recognize the guys coming in, and we know everyone in the south, so they've gotta be from further north."

"What if they're fedayeen? That's a link enough to go in?"

"Whit, dammit, that's why I'm sitting here going crazy. They won't let me do a thing without evidence that they're harming us. And as Royce knows well, your guys don't believe us. That's why we invited you down."

"Well, what the hell are they coming in here for?" Royce said, perturbed at Shlomo's sideswipe.

"Watch."

The three cars slowed to a halt before the gate. The dust, enswirling them, rising in a slow, circular motion, lifted like stage curtains to reveal an armed guard speaking with a man outside the first car. After some wild gesticulating, the small convoy entered and pulled to a stop just inside the fence, still within full view. The curtains of dust again enfolded them and, when they raised a few moments later Royce let out a gasp. From the second car men were pulling three young women.

"What the . . ." then a silent pause.

"Now you know."

"I don't understand." Royce said. Whit was silent and angry.

They tugged the women along by their hands, bound in front of them, aggressively.

"Why are they doing it out in the open?" Royce asked.

"We haven't been able to figure it out. Unless they're just giving us the finger."

Whit responded, "They didn't really inspect the cars too closely outside the gates, so perhaps they don't want to offend these guys. But they don't trust them enough to let them pull all the way in next to the buildings, and potentially blow the whole thing up with a car bomb. I bet they're feeling out whether this is a crew they can trust and work with. The strange thing is that there is no exchange. They get these women, but what does – whoever these transporters work for – get in return? Something is going on outside of this exchange that we're not seeing."

"Why do we care if we're not seeing the impact?" Royce said.

"First of all, there are clearly women down there against their. . ."

"Hey," Royce interrupted, "I don't like it any more than you do, but we can't go in playing Robin Hood against every common criminal."

"Neither can we, Whit. Look, I know what you're saying, but we'd have to kill half the twenty year olds in southern Lebanon."

"I get that – but there's more to it. We can't see the impact now, but what if we don't see the result until it's too late?"

"What do you mean?"

"These guys aren't running some criminal network just for fun. They're taking risks to buy this guy off; and he's hiding all this from his constituency further north and west. He'd rather you guys see it than his own people."

"Yeah – but if he's in so deep – why do it so boldly in front of us?" The men watched while the soldier panned the fence line with his Galil sniper rifle that Whit stood to admire. Noticing Whit's attention, the soldier leaned back and offered a look in the scope. Whit leaned into the gun and peered for a second, then leaned back, turning to Shlomo.

"Maybe it's because he doesn't consider you his primary threat." Shlomo's head pumped briefly up and down as he exhaled sharply. It was a sign of both his being impressed, but also his disbelief at the possibility.

"If that's the case, then we may have even more serious problems on our hands."

"Exactly." Whit responded, turning back to peer through the scope, scanning the compound. He turned to the soldier, "Could you hit a target in that compound from here?"

The soldier look at Shlomo, not understanding. Shlomo translated into Hebrew, and the soldier leaned down to peer out the window. The man answered in Hebrew, and Shlomo translated back, "He says if the conditions were right. Low winds, clear air, he could hit a target in very limited parts of the compound that aren't obstructed."

Whit looked again, two tall figures, clad in black and with AK-47's slung over their shoulders were taking control of the women. They disappeared into the southernmost building. "What parts of the compound?" Whit asked.

"Whit, c'mon why are you asking? We can't do..."

"Just curious, Shlomo." Shlomo didn't notice that Royce had left the guardhouse. Shlomo turned to the soldier and spoke in Hebrew again. The soldier panned the horizon and then turned to Shlomo, still leaning into the window, and said something in Hebrew over his shoulder.

Shlomo waited until he was done, then said, "He says the tops of the roof and the area in between the southern wall and fence, obviously..." the soldier interrupted him and said something again. "Ah," Shlomo said, and asked the soldier something in Hebrew. "But he says the best shot is probably just a few feet south of where the cars are now leaving from." The cars were turning to exit through the gate, giving rise to more dust as they did so. "He says basically right there off the western corner of the southern building. The building gives him a distance gauge and blocks the wind so there isn't a swirl at the contact point. He would then basically just need to calculate for the west winds, and if it's calm," Shlomo nodded, pursing the corners of his lips, "he could pull it off."

"If it's windy?" Whit asked.

Shlomo spoke in Hebrew again, and the soldier responded. Shlomo said, "Then it could be pretty difficult, but this is a confident man, and he's done it in worse conditions, he says."

"Alright, Shlomo, another word." The men walked down the short ladder of the guard station and leaned against the berm from which the tower extended. From their vantage point, they could see no portion of the Lebanese side, and could in turn not be seen from any part of it.

"Back to our Christian friends. If we wanted your assistance to start training them, how difficult would it be?"

"That's a policy question. And its high level so we'll talk to R—"

"Don't talk to Royce, I'm just trying to get a feel for how hard it would be logistically before I propose it to them. Just your assistance – all we may need is some land. How hard might it be to get them in here so we can do our work?"

"Ah – if it's approved by the right people, not hard at all. If it's not approved by the right people, but only the wrong people," Shlomo smiled and shrugged his shoulders, "a little more difficult."

"How quickly would it take to find out more?" Whit asked.

"Is this an authorized request?"

"Not yet, but it will be."

Shlomo stared at Whit soberly, and then, as he slapped him on the shoulder, screamed "Dammit, I love you, kid!" After a moment, and looking out across Israel with admiration, he turned back to Whit, "Give me a couple days." He held out his hand, and they shook just as Royce arrived.

"I don't know what that's all about, but we gotta get back." Royce interrupted, approaching. "Whit – just got a call – it's finally hitting the fan in Beirut. Camille wants you at some field headquarters ASAP."

"Field headquarters?"

"That's the message."

"Whatsup there?" Shlomo wanted to get the word back to his bosses before anyone else.

"Unclear – someone kidnapped some Lebanese soldiers and may have killed a couple of them. Shlomo, we need to get across the border. Someone will be waiting for us there. He'll drive us to a spot where an army helo is going to pick us up."

"If you don't have permits you'll never g–"

"We're fine. Just get us to a good spot."

"No problem."

# CHAPTER TWENTY-FIVE

Najwa was nervous and scared. As she looked down onto the main gate, she saw a protester smash a street sign outside. She noticed a young man who seemed to be looking up at her, but thought she was being paranoid.

As more protesters streamed onto the campus, she heard them beginning a chant and throwing their arms into the air in unison. The herd was growing wild.

"Death to Israel! Death to the West!" The chant grew louder and sounds in the distance, like explosions, seemed to rise.

Her roommate read a magazine and laid on her bed, seemingly oblivious to it all.

"Aren't you seeing this?"

Her roommate shrugged, "My dad said to just stay inside." Najwa watched for a few minutes more.

"Oh I forgot," her roommate intoned absent mindedly, "your brother called earlier."

"What?! What did he say?"

"I think he said to meet him down by the gate at one or something. Your dad wanted you to come home or something."

"What?" Najwa said, "Thanks for telling me." Her roommate shrugged. She checked her watch, it was 12:50. She began grabbing some things to go.

"Hey what are you doing?" Her roommate said, "You're crazy if you go-"

A rock suddenly cracked her window, sending Najwa screaming and fleeing to the back of her room. She could hear people yelling in the hallways as men started to smash things out in the courtyard.

She sped down the stairway into what had suddenly erupted into a frenzied madness behind the building. People were running in every direction, screaming with fear and rage. She heard loud, tremulous bursts. Looking towards the center of campus, she saw a pillar of smoke. Turning to the entry gate, she thought she could see her brother in the distance. The space between them seemed to stretch into a violent infinity. Shaking and nauseous, she closed her eyes for a moment, inhaled deeply, and began to run.

The earth shook as she ran. Her legs felt weak. Protesters burned a tire in one portion of the campus and were pulling on a statue in the other direction. She did not see the young man, once standing calmly, now sprinting roughly twenty yards behind her. Another few seconds, and she rounded the main gate pillar and saw her brother ducking, though looking around.

"Najwa, what are you doing, why did you call me?!"

"What are talking about?" She ducked beside him. "You called me," she screamed frantically.

For a moment, they stared at one another, and for that long, ceaseless moment, they realized something dark had crept into their lives. Even as the gunfire rang out around them, it was not as sickening as the sudden realization that someone had drawn them into a horrible trap. Just as the realization dawned on them, two men appeared and knocked Khalil out. Najwa stepped forward and was grabbed and yanked from behind. Someone bound her feet. As she struggled to kick and tried to break free, a scarf fell from one man's face. Her heart fell to the pit of her stomach. She had seen him before.

They dragged her and threw her into a car. Her brother landed on top of her. Suddenly, someone opened the other door and she felt a blunt force on the top of her head. Before she passed out, his name crept through her mind – what had Whit called him? Sayyid.

# CHAPTER TWENTY-SIX

Camille was leaning up against a post in a makeshift tent that had been set up fifty yards outside the Tal Za'atar camp. There were tanks and other armored vehicles lining the streets, encircling the camp. Sporadic gunfire burst forth between the army lines and the camp. Camille's shirt was soaked in sweat and there was an uncharacteristic paleness in his face.

"This could be it, Whit. I'm not sure the army will hold."

"Any defections so far?"

"No, but we've barely started responding."

"What's happening right now?"

"What do you think?" Camille uttered in disgust. "We're waiting for the generals to work things out with the parliamentarians. I've got hundreds of men out there who are ready to tear that camp to shreds, and I'm just trying my best to hold them back and plan for this to happen in an orderly way."

"Why did you call me?"

"I need your help."

"How?"

"Look, Whit, I know you've been after the PFLP for some time. You know we've been blocked out of the camps and we've lost visibility on what it looks like in there. I'm hoping you know the inside so we can do this right."

"You don't have a source in there?"

"We don't . . . we don't know how to contact him. He . . . he only contacts us."

Whit waited for a moment, looking out the tent towards the camp. "I'd have to get authorization if we're assisting a military action. I haven't seen you sweat this much before, Camille. Are you feeling ok?"

"This could be the end of it all."

Whit sympathized with his anxiety, but experienced a strange, detached comfort, as if he was a spectator to the storm. That's how he thought he felt, but knowing oneself is perhaps more difficult than knowing another. One can fool himself for a long time about his own interests and desires in ways that he cannot be fooled by another. "I thought you've been preparing for that all along?"

"Dammit, Whit," Camille moved in close with a marked earnestness, "we're not ready. Besides, you think we actually want that? Hell no – we just don't have a choice."

A volley of gunfire broke out again somewhere in the distance. It was now late in the day and the sun hung low over the ocean; bathing the camp in an orange hue like a fiery oracle of days to come. How was it that nature, Whit wondered, seemingly neutral, could simultaneously drench a man's surroundings in unrelenting judgment. The gunfire calmed as the red deepened.

"Do you think the fact that you're all hastily arranging for the fall makes it more likely to happen?"

"I can't afford to worry about that. I've gotta live this while you philosophize. I've gotta think about a wife, my kids, and my community. If the state won't protect that, then I have to find a way to do so." Camille was visibly disturbed, and that disturbance seemed to be reaching a crescendo; but Whit felt he was on the verge of knowing something essential, though he was uncertain of what that might be.

"And that's why you're behind him?"

"You say it with disdain, but I know you understand."

Whit contemplated for a moment. "I think I do, Camille, but . . ." Whit wasn't sure how to articulate the tension he was experiencing.

"But this isn't your country," Camille said in a somber, hushed tone.

"No," Whit said, "I suppose it's not. And frankly, I feel this almost surreal . . . perspective. Like I'm in the audience, watching something play out in slow motion. And being part of the audience and part of the show, I'm not certain what role I'm supposed to play."

"Your role is to help our military while you prepare our Christian militias for total military failure."

Whit was silent for a few moments, feeling the guns in the distance reverberate through his body, his muscles and sinews vibrating like strings in a violent refrain. "Get your men together, Camille. I need to make a call."

Camille put his hands on Whit's shoulder. "You're making the right choice."

Whit stepped out of the tent. The sentry's stood guard over the eerie silence between explosions. Whit walked a block away from the camps into the city, and spotted a pay phone on the street corner. Approaching it, he thought momentarily, and picking up the receiver, dialed the number.

Whit took it, and said in Arabic, "Connect me to the following number." The phone rang.

"Jerome's Bakery, what can I do for you?" came the answer.

"Hello, is this Jerome?" Whit asked, recognizing Royce's voice.

"Yes."

"Good," Whit said. "I'm here at the party. It's become clear to me that I have to serve up the bread."

"Will you be just giving the bread or participating in its distribution?" Royce asked.

"Yes, it seems I'll have to help distribute as well."

"Give me one second to check whether the baker has enough bread to fill the order."

"Ok." Whit's envisioned himself stepping out of the audience and onto a stage. It was dark, and he could barely make out the dimly lit expressions of those watching. He couldn't tell if they were laughing, crying, or indifferent.

"Hello sir," Whit was shaken out of this thoughts, "the baker says the bread will be ready and you can serve it up. But you're on your own, as usual."

"Of course." Whit hung up the phone, then picked it up again, dialing.

"Alo?" Came a terrified sounding voice on the other end. "Alo?"

"Salman," Whit said.

"Yes."

"This is Michel." All he heard on the other end of the line was a pained cry.

Then, a rushed flurry, "Michel, oh my God thank God I don't know what to do I need your help."

"What happened Salman?"

"I can't . . . I need help. I need help."

"Salman I can't get in right now. What do you need my help with."

"They came. They . . . they killed Adib. And they took Fatin and Musa."

"What?!"

"I, I tried to stop them but I got knocked out somehow. I don't even know what happened. I think something blew up and knocked me out. When I woke up they were dragging uncle towards a car he was bloody and he just yelled, call your friend, call your friend, and then they began beating me and I could hear Fatin screaming. Ah Michel! I don't know what to do! I didn't know how to call you."

"Ok, calm down for a second. Who was it?"

"Who do you think? I don't know what to do . . . I'm going to go over there myself."

"No," Whit said emphatically, "don't do that. Wait for me. Salman listen to me carefully."

"Oh I can't . . ."

"Salman, if you want to get Fatin back and your uncle, listen carefully to me. Don't go there now – they'll kill you. You have to wait for me."

Salman was quiet at first, then said, "Yes, ok."

"There's going to be a lot of shelling in the next hour – stay inside and I'll come to you."

Salman was silent. "Ok, Michel. Ok. I am waiting."

Whit hung up and walked the block back to the line. Entering the tent and seeing Camille, Colonel Chartouni, and a group of others around a map, he took the center spot on the table. Before he began speaking, he looked down at the map in astonishment. It contained the rough outlines of the camp, but it was outdated, and it certainly could not be used for targeted shelling.

"Colonel, do you have a helo in the air?"

"Yes. He will be calling in their blockade positions to us shortly, then we can commence. We will enter from all four gates around the camp."

"They'll expect that and may have multiple blockades, making it difficult to get through. I recommend these two," Whit said, pointing to a northern and southern side, "but then blowing the walls here and here," and he pointed at opposite ends of the respective sides of the camp from where the other two gates stood.

"It will present a surprise," the Colonel said.

"Right, and you can hopefully get around behind whatever they have set up, allowing your forces to both squeeze from behind and get another group straight to their central headquarters more quickly."

"What will we find there? Why can't we just blow it from here?"

Camille chimed in, "We want as many of them alive as possible. Something bigger is going on here and we need to get out of them who they are connected with and what may be coming next."

"We may have high casualties if we can't just go in and blow it up," the Colonel blurted with frustration.

"We're going to have higher casualties," Camille responded, "if all we do is kill a bunch of them today and leave more fighting to tomorrow."

"We may already be there," Shehadi, who had just entered the tent, said. "The protest down at AUB is turning violent." Whit grew visibly attentive. "There's a lot of gunfire and torching of buildings. It's starting to spread and move towards parliament."

"Ok," Whit said, needing now to move fast, "you're here now to take care of this, and the longer you wait they may slip out. They also have hostages not only from the army, but some Fatah." Chartouni and Camille exchanged curious glances. "Your saving both from them and getting the publicity about infighting could be a huge public relations success." The other men nodded, and Whit continued, "The headquarters is located in this tight section of buildings," as he spoke, Whit drew a square towards the middle of the camp, "there is a small meeting room here," pointing to a lower corner of the building, "the leadership moves around a bit, but the hostages are likely in this adjacent building," he directed, circling the map again.

Colonel Chartouni chimed in, looking towards an artillery officer. "I want you to start putting shells down at the blockades first, then the road leading towards the headquaters." The man nodded in assent.

Whit continued, "I have some men on the inside who know the buildings and recognize the key hostages. I'm going to have to go in with them to get the Fatah commander out of there before they can kill him; if he's still alive."

"How will we know them?"

Whit thought for a second, then looked at a scarf on one of the younger troops. "They'll tie scarves around their left arm. As soon as you start covering fire I'll go in – so we'll probably be inside getting them out by the time you are getting inside. If you see them on the way out – you just let them go." The Colonel and Camille nodded, understanding Whit's discretion.

"Ok." Colonel Chartouni said, "Let's get started."

# CHAPTER TWENTY-SEVEN

Whit knelt inside the camp as the earth in front of him lifted out of its dry bed, erupting like volcanic ash, shards of dirt and rocks spraying in every direction. Were an observer capable of slowing down time, he would see – before any debris made visible the devastating trail of the explosion – the impact the shockwave had, vaporizing entire bodies, ripping limbs apart, tearing flesh from the bones it covered, and knocking people to the ground as it weakened and dissipated.

Those nearest the center of the explosion bore its wrath most directly. A young man sprinting across the street when it hit was the closest. He was wearing jeans and an orange shirt. Whit, running to find Salman, had been looking straight towards the man when it happened. As Whit lay on the ground regaining consciousness, the image in his mind played like an old film ribbon flapping the same few frames chaotically upon a dark screen.

191

A man wearing an orange shirt was in mid-stride, fear cementing his features, attempting to flee the rapidly approaching cacophony of mortar fire. Back and forth, the image fled as quickly as had the man, who then returned, who disappeared again. The image flashed continuously, orange shirted anxiety in motion, a completely empty space, orange anxiety, empty space, anxiety, emptiness. Whit's vision cleared and the deafening shock wore off as loud bursts and screams became increasingly audible. The frames stopped repeating and the man was gone. A small piece of orange cloth, blackened, lay with seared edges on the ground before him.

Others were not so fortunate as Whit. The coincidence of their distance and proximity rendered them far enough from the explosion to avoid immediate death, but close enough to suffer the wickedness in extremis. Whit stumbled to his feet and saw a man, abdomen cut open, lying on the ground and slowly turning his head to look at Whit. There was a look of bewilderment on his face.

Whit was ten feet away, the man held out his hand. Whit stumbled too him. Another explosion half a block down sent Whit crouching. Then he saw the man begging him with his eyes and his outstretched hand. Whit grasped the man's hand. His beseeching eyes closed, and Whit thought he saw him smile slightly.

Whit laid the man's hand on his chest, and looked up towards Salman's apartment door.

The carnage diminished with distance from the blast core, now evident in a four foot sink-hole in the ground. Whit ran around it, and ducked again as an explosion, now a block away, landed directly on a small car, sending metal and glass hurtling in all directions. Up and down the street Whit could hear the shrieks. He sprinted across the street and pounded on Salman's door.

"Who is it?!"

"Salman it's W – it's Michel, open the door!" Whit heard the unlatching of the door and Salman opened it, staring at Whit.

"Michel!" Salman exclaimed, "Oh my God, get in here before you get killed."

Diving inside, Whit urged, "Salman there is not much time. The Lebanese Army is coming and they are going to destroy everything in their way. Where is your uncle?"

"How do you know? What is happening?!" Salman screamed.

"The PFLP killed several soldiers and kidnapped two more. The army chased them here. They are mortaring the hell out of the camp before they come in after them."

Salman rocked back and forth on his haunches like a man half crazed. "Oh my, God, Michel, what will we do?! What will we do?! They have uncle. They killed Adib. They have Fatin!" Salman screamed, grabbing Whit's arms and shaking him.

"Salman – enough! We have to go after your uncle and Fatin." Salman continued to scream uncontrollably and Whit slapped him across the face, shaking Salman out of his delirium. Explosions sounded closer again outside and Salman flinched. Whit did not move and spoke in a low, calm voice.

"Salman, we have to go now if we want any chance to get them out. Who else from your uncle's unit is around?"

"I don't know! They attacked the house and everybody fled."

"Time is running out. Do you have your gun?" Salman got up and walked over behind the couch and picked it up.

"Alright – we have to get to the headquarters."

"The headquarters?! They'll. . . they'll kill us."

"Do you want to get Fatin back?"

Salman was silent. He looked down at his AK-47, and with a new resolve cocked the chamber, looking back up at Whit and nodding.

"Salman, is there anyone we can get to help us?"

"Two guys liv. . ." an explosion rang out nearby shaking Salman's apartment, and the shower of debris rained down upon the door, sending both Salman and Whit instinctively crouching as dust fell from the light fixtures and the ceiling trembled.

"Ok – they'll get further away for a minute. We have to go now. Lead me to where they live."

Whit opened the door and Salman timidly stepped out. Flames and rubble lined the street. People limped along in disbelief. One man's arm was on fire as he beat it relentlessly on the ground. A woman ran by screaming. The burnt-out shell of a car sat charred across the road.

"Yalla, yalla," Whit shouted above the roar – urging Salman to hurry. Salman jogged along slowly until Whit grabbed him and screamed over the cacophony, "Hurry!" The earth shook beneath them as mortars dropped a block in front and half a block behind. Whit had the bizarre sensation that a dull-footed giant was stomping indiscriminately around Tal Za'atar.

Salman pointed as the men hurtled forward, his finger indicating some spot near the most immediate explosion. "They're there?"

Salman nodded as he winced his eyes and they continued to run. Silence reigned for a moment as they ran to the door and Salman pounded it, yelling for the men to let him in. They did so.

Inside were two brothers, both large, and looking nervous amidst the madness. "Who is this?" One of them said.

"This is Michel," Salman said, looking down at the ground.

"What do you want, Michel?" said the older brother. The man had greying hair and a pronounced nose and mole on his left cheek. His bloodshot eyes were set closely together, and his voice, deepened over the years from smoke, revealed a shaky apprehension about what was to come.

"I'm here to help you get Musa Rasoul out of the PFLP buildings." Michel said in less proficient Arabic then he normally used. The two brothers looked at one another, they grabbed Salman and pulled him to the side of the room.

The older spoke, "How can we trust him? He could get us all killed."

"Fahim," the younger man said, "what choice do we have?"

"Shutup, Ahmed. I'm talking to Salman." Ahmed was about four inches taller than Fahim, his elder brother, and had an additional two inches on Salman, the smallest of the three. Both Fahim and Ahmed were thick-set and darkened by the sun. Ahmed's hair spread out from his head wildly in every direction.

"You can trust me because I'm risking my life to do this, rather than running away when the firing starts." All three stared at Michel across the room. "Salman, I don't have time for this. If they're too scared to do this, I'm going in alone."

"I'm going with you," Ahmed said and took a step.

"Ahmed, you're not doing anything until I say." Then turning to Whit, "Just who are you and why are you so interested in helping?"

"Does it really matter?" Whit said with impatient disbelief. "Salman, the Lebanese army will be here any minute, if we don't get Musa Rasoul out of there now, he'll be killed. I'm leaving."

"Wait, I'm going with you." Salman hurried to Whit's side as he walked out the door. Ahmed joined them, pushing Fahim away as he went.

As they stepped outside, the men could hear distant gunfire. Roughly two blocks ahead, Whit could see the PFLP headquarters. Men were running back and forth, most away from the large building in the distance. The explosions grew more distant. Whit took out three sheaths of cloth, tying one around his arm just above his elbow. "Here," he said, handing the two other pieces to Ahmed and Salman. "Tie it on."

"Why?"

"The army will know not to shoot you." Salman and Ahmed exchanged an incredulous glance.

"Whose side are you on?" Salman said, confused.

After a few moments, Whit said softly, "My own." He motioned them across the street, and began jogging along himself. By the time they arrived at the headquarters thirty seconds later, the explosions had again grown close. Men were scrambling to load weapons and documents into trucks.

As they rushed towards the grouping of trucks, with the buildings behind, over Whit's shoulder a thin line of smoke whisked past and he instinctively yelled to the other two men to get down. The truck closest to the men, which sat roughly twenty yards away, had a driver and three PFLP foot-soldiers who were frantically loading weapons. They did not even see the rocket-powered grenade that Whit felt whisk past his shoulder. It impacted directly in the center of the truck, lifting it off the ground slightly and breaking it into two pieces in a fiery roar.

Whit looked over his shoulder and a little less than a football field away, the Lebanese military was approaching. One of them had certainly shot the RPG. That was amazing accuracy for the distance, so Whit knew it must have been Colonel Chartouni's special forces group. In other words, he knew they had only a minute or two left to get in, find the captured Lebanese soldiers and Musa and Fatin, and get out. Over the roar, he shouted across the street, pointing back behind himself to the army, "Army – we gotta go in now!"

PFLP fedayeen were lying around the destruction; others had fled. Whit rounded the burning remains of the truck to see one man standing in the doorway. He slowed to a walk and held out his hand in a friendly "Don't shoot" gesture.

"Where's Sayyid?" Whit said in Arabic.

The man looked stunned, and stammered, "He's getting the prisoners out the ba . . ." the man suddenly looked up over Whit's shoulder, where Salman and Ahmed were rounding the car. The man lifted his gun to shoot and Whit, dropping to a knee, fired one shot directly into the man's chest. Sucking for air, the man looked on, perplexed. Whit approached him slowly, reached down, tossed the man's gun aside and slowly drew his eyelids closed. By the time Salman and Ahmed had reached Whit, the man had stopped breathing.

Salman and Ahmed came to his side and momentarily stared down at the man. Suddenly, the pitter-patter of small-arms fire began to impact the façade of the building. The army was closing in. "C'mon, we have to go. He said Sayyid is out back with them."

They lunged inside as the firing grew more intense. The doorway opened into a dimly lit hallway that ran left to right, adjacent to the front wall. "You guys go left and I'll head this way," Whit said, pointing right. Ahmed and Salman nodded. "We gotta find our way to the back before they get out."

"I was in here once before," Ahmed said, "This goes around a courtyard in the middle and there is a hill behind the building. The road is about 20 meters behind, so we'll have some open territory to cover once we get out back."

"Ok," Whit said, nodding. "Don't move until we both get back there. When we do, you guys cover me with fire and I'll make my way down to get a better shot to stop any cars." They broke. Looking around the hall, Whit spotted two fedayeen at the other end. They both opened fire immediately upon seeing him. He returned fire, but heard nothing further.

When he looked again, they were gone. He sprinted down the hall and ran directly into a man stepping out of a side room. They tumbled together onto the floor, and as they rose, their eyes met. The man was unarmed, older, and clearly exhausted and fearful. Whit raised his gun towards him, but the man lifted his arms, dispirited.

"Where did they take the prisoners?"

"You won't shoot?"

"No, dammit, just tell me."

"Some place down south."

Whit was confused and surprised, "What? Where?"

"I don't know."

"Why?"

"I don't know. Some guy down there they have a deal with."

Whit held his gun up, "No please, I just cook for the prisoners."

"How many?"

"One man and his daughter, and then there are two Christians, a boy and his sister." Whit grimaced, but as he spoke a roar erupted just out in front of the building. The army had arrived.

"Get out of here – the army is coming in." Whit urged the man, and turned back down the hallway. Whit sprinted down the hallway and stopped at a muddy window, through which he saw a hazy line of black and green splotches moving down to the base of a hill. He could barely make out the figures, and looked around frantically for some exit. Finally, he saw, just to his right, a door heading outside. He heard gunfire to the left, and thought it must be Salman and Ahmed. He sprinted for the door.

Breaking outside, Whit made it two paces before gunfire erupted from somewhere below. There was a rock and sand strewn hill, at the top of which Whit knelt, that was pocked with small bushes. At its base was a road that ran perpendicular to Whit's approach and which held a caravan of Land Rovers. On the other side were trees dusted by the dry, granular surroundings. Whit did not have time to look in the other direction.

The gunfire seemed to be directed at the opposite end of the building Whit had just exited. There, Ahmed was firing wildly. Whit squinted and could barely see Salman's smallish figured crouched behind the barrier, his hands on his ears. Ahmed pulled Salman's shoulder as he fired and yelled at him to get up.

Whit turned and began sprinting down the hill. Almost immediately, the figures near the caravan of cars became more discernible. The closest armed fedayeen looked to be pushing Musa Rasoul into a car. Whit stopped, momentarily aimed at the man, and fired. The captor dropped to his knees. Whit could barely make out Musa grabbing the man's gun and turning to fire further ahead of him, drawing Whit's attention towards four cars, and, in particular the front car which a large group of people convulsively approached, but which was partially obstructed by a tree.

Whit ran a few steps further and his heart stopped. There, being pushed by Sayyid and two other gunmen, were Najwa and Khalil.

The world condensed into this one, tight space. On this hill and block, the sweep of Whit's constant search for meaning seemed to come to a rest. Time, suspended, collapsing along with it. There was no before and no after. Past and future were erased. Geography was eviscerated. The moment became the focal point of all of Whit's experience. There was good. There was evil. He was the vengeance of God against the twisted part of humanity.

Najwa looked over her shoulder and up the hill. Just behind her, a driver was entering the front door. Sayyid was pushing her towards the open door behind Fatin, who had already been shoved in. Najwa screamed, "WHIIIIT!!!!" She would have only seen the muzzle flash and felt the whish of the bullet, hearing nothing. The bullet sliced a wisp of her hair as it rushed within inches of her head and struck the soldier behind her directly between his shoulder blades. Sayyid pushed

Najwa into the car, then turned to fire up towards the hill.

Whit pulled the gun again to his shoulder as he dropped to his knee, aimed at Sayyid, and fired. The bullet ripped the ammunition belt apart at Sayyid's upper right shoulder and knocked him to the ground. Whit took careful aim at Sayyid's torso, and moved his finger to the trigger for one last shot. A thunderous roar erupted behind Whit so forceful it threw him to the ground. He stumbled to his knees and turned to see a helicopter hovering only ten feet overhead and maybe twenty feet behind him. He cursed the gunman who was letting loose indiscriminate fire from a heavy-caliber machine gun mounted on thick brackets aside the helicopter compartment.

When Whit turned back, he could see bullets impacting the earth all around the cars, and Sayyid pulling his left leg inside the driver's side door as he shut it. Whit took aim at the driver's side window as the tires spun and the car jerked forward, but he had no clean shot. He started sprinting down the hill.

The helicopter hovered overhead as its gunner rained fire down upon the earth as Whit hurtled forward. The rear car in the caravan had been disabled and Musa was at the car just in front of it. Whit withheld fire and the front cars sped off.

Several fedayeen jumped out from behind bushes when the firing from the helicopter ceased. Whit found himself in the open road alone between four fedayeen. He turned and fired at one just as gunfire burst from across the road, killing two others. The fourth threw down his gun and began running up the street. Across the street, to Whit's surprise, was Fahim with two other men. They took aim and gunned down the final fleeing

PFLP foot soldier as Whit sprinted to the nearest car. He pulled a dead man from the driver's seat, quickly got in, and tried to start the car. Nothing happened. Then he realized that the engine block had been pulverized by the helicopter gun. Getting out, he thrust the door shut. When he turned around, Ahmed and Salman were coming to his side from one part of the road; Fahim and two men from the other.

Musa Rasoul walked up and embraced Salman and Ahmed. As they all began to speak, Whit looked up towards the hill and saw Colonel Chartouni step out the back door of the building. He could see the man speak into the walkie-talkie and the rest of the soldiers held momentarily.

Musa Rasoul walked to his side and embraced Whit. "Michel, they have my daughter."

Whit "The army," nodding, "will be down here any minute and it's best for you all to get out of here." Musa nodded and waved the young men on.

"Michel, what can we do? There were others. They have my Fatin."

From the house, Whit could see the soldiers start to move again.

Whit refocused his attention. "For now, get back to your homes and make sure all are ok. I'll come to you in a few hours and we'll make plans."

"That may be too late. We need to go after them now!" Musa was visibly shaken and angry.

"Do you know where they're going?"

"No!"

"There is fighting all around this place. They are going to be slowed down. We need to figure out where they may head. You do some checking around the camps, and I'll check as well. But for now – I have to deal with the army.

"How do you. . ." Musa begin to ask, but stopped short as Whit shook his head no.

"Tonight. Now you must go."

Musa turned to walk, and the other men walked more quickly up ahead.

"Musa."

"Yes," Musa paused, turning to look.

"I'm sorry about Adib."

Musa was stoic, but responded, "We don't have much time." Whit nodded.

They walked quickly away and Whit opened the back seat to the Land Rover. He had not even noticed the bruised bodies of the two kidnapped soldiers, bound and tied up. Whit checked their pulses; they were unconscious, but alive. He leaned out of the car and saw the soldiers still a hundred yards away, too far to see his face in detail. Whit leaned back in and patted the cheeks of the two soldiers, cutting loose the ties that were binding their arms and legs. As one of them came to, Whit said, "Do you know your name?"

The man's face was so bruised and swollen that any emotion was barely detectable. The man seemed to swallow something, and said in a whisper, "Qus-Qustantin."

"You're going to be ok. Your friends are here now – they'll get you some help, ok?" Qustantin only nodded. He turned to Stephen, who moved slightly upon Qustantin's nudge.

Whit marveled at them, at that vast, inexplicable urge within each man to survive. Whit suddenly heard someone clearing his throat, and saw Camille standing on the side of the road behind Colonel Chartouni and several soldiers. Whit stepped away from the car as two younger medics rushed in to assist. Whit walked over to Camille and the Colonel placed his hand on Whit's shoulder.

"I was wrong to doubt you. I won't forget it."

Whit gave curt recognition to the gratitude before hastily proceeding, "I have a serious problem. The car in front has two Christians and a Palestinian female." The Colonel and Camille exchanged a glance.

"I assume your dragnet is going to stop them. Can we check on where they are? I need to get to them and get them out of here as quickly as possible."

"Hadad was guarding the route they would have taken." Chartouni said as Whit noticed Camille look notably crestfallen. "He should have stopped them by now," he continued, "Radio!" As the Colonel turned away, Whit looked at Camille. Camille spoke first.

"All hell is breaking loose, Whit. The parliament is ref . . ." Whit wasn't listening, though, as Colonel Chartouni was yelling into the radio angrily and then threw it down.

"The imbecile let them through already." Chartouni yelled as Whit's heart began to race.

"What?! He couldn't have, it was one car with . . . he probably has sixty to eighty men. What do you mean?"

"He thought they were civilians."

Whit implored them, "I have to track them down. It's going to be too late. I need resources before it's too late." Camille was shocked by Whit's uncharacteristic frustration.

"Whit, I wish we could help," Camille complained, "but we can't even get enough resources to deal with Beirut. The city is on the verge of collapse after just one day of these fights. The fighting is spilling out of the camps into the streets." Whit was in a daze. Najwa, Fatin, and Khalil raced through his mind as quickly as they moved towards the outskirts of town and into the unknown.

"I have to get them. A man inside said something about their going south."

"Whit, it's a suicide mission down there," the Colonel spoke. "You know damn well the whole region is controlled by the fedayeen. You can't . . ."

"I'm going," Whit said with stoic certainty. He tried to think of what would justify it to these men. He tried to find some way to explain that this wasn't about an ulterior motive or twisted self-interest. He wanted so badly to make clear the base simplicity of it all, but wasn't sure they would understand. He loved the Khourys because they represented one of those few, pure things left; and he couldn't let that be extinguished.

"Camille," Whit pulled Camille aside so they could speak privately. "George said you could help me with some things, and I do need one other thing from you for now."

"Anything I can provide, I will."

"I need to know about the weapons shipments in the Port. Who is bringing them all in and how are they paying? Who is picking them up?"

"Ok, I'll work on it."

Two minutes later Whit was holding the receiver to a pay phone.

"Jerome's bakery."

"I need to get a bread delivery within the next fifteen minutes." There was silence on the other end.

"Can we get more detail about the order?" The answer finally came.

"I'll have to meet you for a glass of water."

"Ok."

—

Twenty minutes later Whit spotted Royce strolling along the coastline where they had agreed to meet. He thought Royce had a dejected look, like a man who was about to deliver bad news to a friend.

"They've taken the kids, Royce."

"What?"

"They've taken Najwa and I have to go get her back."

"Alright, calm down a second."

"And her brother. They have him, too."

"Ok, wait a minute, Whit. You know this isn't how we do things. We can't get involved in a conflict because you fell in love with some co-ed. And we. . . "

Whit grabbed Royce by the collar in rage, "You know that's not what this is! They crossed the line. It's not about this civil war and it's not about . . ."

"Whit, I've gone to the mat for you, multiple times," Royce shouted. "You're out there pushing the limits and leaving me to justify it. I get it. You bring in better information than we've had here for years. But you're getting too close to them dammit. And you've gotten nothing out of that guy. You have me chasing visas, and you've been working him for months. What do you have to show for it?"

Whit stared coldly and waited for Royce to calm down. "I'm almost there with him, but this could ruin everything."

"Alright. Alright. Hold on." Royce could see Whit was incensed. "I'm not trying to crap on your relationships. But you could end up losing the edge here. You know the game."

"Got it, Royce. And you have done more for me than anybody. I am not going to forget it. But I need this one cleared."

Whit looked out towards the sea, rolling in aggressive waves and crashing on the shore. He dipped his head angrily forward, recognizing the quandary and wondering if he was going too far. In the distance dark clouds were gathering themselves in anticipation. A cool ocean breeze made abrupt landfall, brushing across his spine with the serrated, salty edge of the mysterious deep.

"Whit, whatever you are doing, it's working. If you tell me this makes sense, if you tell me this isn't just emotion, then I'll do what I can, but you've got to give me something more to work with then just the potential that this guy is going to start talking."

Whit thought through his options, staring at the darkness in the distance. He thought through his conversations, arrayed in his mind like puzzle-pieces on an otherwise empty table. Suddenly, a few of the pieces seemed to match, and the wind picked up as lightning in the distance lit the sea beneath. He remembered listening in on the PFLP about taking gifts to the South. He grew sick recalling that Keswani was receiving women in exchange for something. Then he recalled the bevy of weapons the PFLP were unloading. That was it. They were kidnapping women and using them and potentially other resources to pay Keswani to smuggle weapons. And that explained Keswani's growing wealth and ability to challenge Ghanem. "I think there is a way."

"Talk to me."

"Can we get Shlomo on the line?" Royce raised his eyebrows and looked at Whit closely.

207

"I can try, but he'll need a damn good reason."

"I have one. Tell him . . . just tell him I think I found yetzer."

"What is that crap?"

"Just tell him."

"Ok. So what's the target?"

"Do you remember the compound we saw from the guard tower when we were down there?"

"Whit, you've lost your mind. You'll never make it out alive."

"I think he's been running guns to the PFLP; and they're using the weapons to kill Lebanese soldiers and drive the state to collapse."

"Maybe we can cut off the flow and by Wael some time?" Whit nodded his assent.

"It can't be tied to us. I know they'll draw a line there. No material assistance, no communications."

A silence passed between them, and Royce, frustrated, asked what he'd been dying to know, "Why do you care so much?"

Whit looked directly at Royce, who continued. "All these people – what are they to you? They want to destroy themselves – what can we do about it? There is no end in sight. You going to play hero in every crisis we send you to? Today Lebanon. Tomorrow maybe Jordan, or hell, even Vietnam. On and on until you end up crazy or dead."

Whit looked at Royce and again at the sea. "Please get me the green light, Royce, if you can. Call me at this number," Whit said, handing a piece of paper to Royce.

Royce glared at Whit, shaking his head. The storm was swiftly fighting its way to the coast. Lightning charged the sky. A single streak hurtled downward through the air, electrifying each atom in its path and stretching forth in every direction so that, as it reached the water, it spread like an inverted, glowing elm. The sound of thunder, from a distance rushing towards Beirut, crashed against the rocky shore atop the expanding waves.

"You've got too much talent, Whit. Don't hang it all up for these people." Royce extended his hand as a gesture of friendship, but also commitment.

Whit shook, then pulled his hand out of Royce's and turned away, walking down the path as the wind picked up. Royce watched for another second or two, then jogged towards his car.

# CHAPTER TWENTY-EIGHT

The flash of lightning set the apartment momentarily aglow. Its sobering, silverish-blue hue overwhelmed the flickering orange of the candlelight. The power had been out for about half an hour, having gone dark at roughly the same time Whit arrived.

Whit leaned against the kitchen counter, watching the candlelight meld shadows across Boutros' haunted, waxen face. The wax shifted with the light, revealing various parts of his visage like puzzle pieces that must be remembered to make sense of the whole. Soft whispers and sobbing emerged between the dull rumblings of thunder. Mona was inconsolably weeping. She sat on the couch, surrounded by three women and a coterie of relatives vacantly circulating like phantoms.

"All these people," Boutros spoke softly, "but still so alone."

Whit looked into the doorway. Nadia was leaning, choking down a louder sob than she thought appropriate and seeking comfort from someone. Whit held out his arms and she rushed into them, squeezing him around the hips. Lightning again filled the room. Gazing out the window, gently stroking Nadia's hair, Whit saw a thousand slivers of light, but the liquid silver rushing along the windows could not wash away the crime that hovered over their home.

Kadir walked into the room and leaned up against the wall. Nadia ran off to her father, who had left the kitchen to speak with a relative. Kadir and Whit were alone.

"What does the Prime Minister make of all this?"

"What would you?" Kadir said angrily. "It's slipping away. The military is already fraying. We're getting word that Colonel Hadad may be ready to break off with his men."

"Can't you arrest him?"

"We don't have enough evidence for one thing. Second, it's a, what do you Americans call it, when you can't win?"

"Catch 22."

Kadir nodded. "If we make a move he'll break off and we'll have both sides of the army in a civil war."

"And if you don't?"

"We hope that Colonel Chartouni and our officers," he was speaking of the Sunnis aligned with the Prime Minister, "can hold things together long enough to stamp out this fedayeen explosion."

"How are things in the south?"

Kadir stared, "I should be asking you."

"Your friend Keswani seems to be involved in some serious stuff."

"Tell me something I don't know."

"This is the kind of stuff that could ruin him if it gets out."

"What are you . . ."

Boutros re-entered the kitchen like a cool breeze, extinguishing the conversation. Outside, thunder gave way to a deeper roar. The sudden burst of warm, Mediterranean rain had doused the fires burning throughout the city, though it failed to quench the broader conflagration. Tank cannons and explosions punctuated the hushed vigil.

The flash of the lightning and explosions, it wasn't clear which at any given time, coursed through the Khoury household like an inscrutable omen. Good and evil took irreducible form and were washed by the waters. Light, cradling the edge of the rational, rushing across its margins, illuminated the borderlands of the unknown. What awful glory lay just beyond in the vast, unfathomable spaces?

Together the lightning, rain, and thunder wove into a naturally orchestrated canticle of sorrow. Arythmic gunfire shattered the chorus. The sounds, echoing through the rain, drove Mona to the verge of madness. "Make them stop! Make them stop! Bring my babies back to me!" Emin sat beside her holding her.

Suddenly, shattering the discordant symphony, three distinct raps burst through the Khoury's door and recoiled off the walls of the apartment. For a moment all were silent, but when the knocking repeated, one of Boutros's relatives went to the door and opened it. The candlelight cast a shadow across George's youthful countenance, turned grim. The lightning and thunder seemed timed to announce this surprising arrival.

Boutros moved towards the door as George stepped inside. Then, Whit felt momentarily deprived of his breath as George's sister entered quietly and scanned the room for familiar faces. When her eyes came to rest on

Whit, she let out a small gasp and stared back, her lips slightly pursed.

George went immediately to Boutros and embraced him; but Boutros returned the gesture only half-heartedly. Partly sullen, partly out of a conviction that this man was part of the problem. Had he known Whit's truth, perhaps Whit would receive the same partial dismissal. Time would tell, Whit thought.

In the mean time, whether as a nervous escape or genuine hospitality, it didn't matter which, Boutros said, "George, I want you to meet our friend, Cordell Whitaker." George stood for a second, not having seen Whit immediately, and after a moment extended his hand, "It's a pleasure meeting you, Mr. Whitaker," he said, this time in impeccable English.

"And that is George's sister, Rafqa," Boutros said, pointing at Najwa who was embracing Mona and exchanging familiar words with Emin. "Rafqa is a doctor at the American University hospital."

"Yes," George said, "she's much smarter than me."

"This is true," Boutros said, "but enough."

"Boutros, I am sickened to hear of what's happened. We cannot stand for it. What can we do?"

"I've spoken with the police and a friend in the military. They say with all the fighting that is going on, they cannot provide the resources to focus on it. I don't know what we'll do."

"They will be no help, Boutros, and you know it."

"Now is not the time for your politics."

"I know how you feel, Boutros. I would also not capitalize on such a horrific event-"

"Then don't."

"But Boutros, there isn't much time. Please let me do something."

"How can I know it won't make things worse?"

"It won't be worse! I can try to . . ."

"You know we already got a call from them." Both Whit and George raised their eyes.

"What?" Whit said, "Who?" George looked at Whit out of the corner of his eyes.

"Of course, they say nothing. They just say they'll give us Khalil back for a price."

"And Najwa?" Whit said.

Boutros became visibly emotional. "I ask . . ." he began to choke down tears, and George looked at Whit and then put a gentle hand on Boutros' shoulder. "I said you have our daughter, too. And they laughed."

"They said nothing?"

"No."

George continued, "Boutros, I will do nothing to hurt your children. But we must try something. The police will do nothing."

"What can you do?"

"I can at least try to find out who, and get that information to the right people."

"Yes, of course, please. I would be willing to do anything. I would pay all I could, but I have nothing."

Whit's rage boiled over. He was tired of the life of darkness that seemed to thrive all around. Tired of humanity turning on itself in grotesque acts of futile dominance. He was tired of the weak feigning strength and getting away with it.

"They will be paid back, Boutros." Boutros looked at Whit, stunned, but unlike his resistance to George, he said nothing. Some part of him wanted to believe that this man, who had helped him before, could do so once more.

In that moment, the phone rang. Boutros, answering it, paused, and turned to Whit, and in a confused voice, said, "It's . . . it's for you." Whit grabbed the receiver, and putting his ear to it said, "Yes."

"Your order from the bakery has been approved." Whit sat in silence for a few moments.

Boutros, Kadir, and George all stared blankly at Whit, who hung up the receiver and looked back at Boutros. "I'm afraid I have to go."

"Wai...what, what will we do?" Boutros questioned.

Without another word, Whit embraced Boutros and walked into the living room. He walked straight to Mona, grabbed her hand, and kissing it, said, "You will see your children again, Mona." She stared at him and as she looked at Boutros, Whit turned and walked out the door.

# CHAPTER TWENTY-NINE

As he exited the Khoury's building into the light rain, Whit heard from behind a soft, yet confident, "Wait." He turned to look, and saw Rafqa walking towards him. The distant lightning faintly lit her face, which seemed to hold the glow after the darkness returned. The breeze lifted her hair and small beads formed on her brow from what was now more a mist and thick fog than a falling shower.

"Can we talk?"

"I'm afraid that I'm late for something."

"Our car is there. Get in. I'll drive."

She swept her hand under the steering wheel, and Whit smiled, his head nodding a bit in amusement.

"What?" she asked nervously.

"Nothing. I'm Cordell by the way, but you can call me Whit."

"I'm Rafqa." She looked through the windshield as she pulled into the empty road. "I almost forgot to ask where we're going."

"You can drop me off near the Mkalles roundabout."

"Don't be crazy, that's right by Tal Za'atar. There's fighting all around there, we can't even get close."

"Then as close as we can get, doctor."

She looked at him curiously.

"What are you going to do?"

He watched Beirut seem to lift and fall around them like waves in a storm. Pursing his lips, he said, "The PFLP has them down south. I'll do whatever I can."

"What can you do?" she said, incredulously. "You're one man. You need our help."

"You can't be there. It'd be civil war."

"Oh, but an American getting killed down there would be ok?"

He simply squinted through the windshield, and after pausing, she said, "Look, I'm sorry, it's just that – it's as risky for you as it is for us. Just let me go, at least."

"Rafqa, I barely know you and I already admire your spirit," she blushed, but under the darkness, he couldn't see it. "But it would make the situation even worse if you were discovered down there."

"I disagree. It's time, anyway, Whit. If not now, then when? It will just keep happening, over and over. Us, on the brink like this – what way is that to live?" Whit sensed the sincerity and frustration beneath her passion. "We need to stop them – it is madness what they are doing to my country."

"Right now, I'm just trying to get Rafqa and Khalil back."

Rafqa was silent for a moment. "Is it because you love her?"

Whit thought for a moment, "Yes," he thought he may have seen a hint of disappointment, "but not in the way you mean it." Her face was emotionless.

"What do you mean?"

"There's something in her – in the whole family – that I just feel. . . I don't' know. . . compelled to . . ."

"Defend?"

"Yes."

"Then we do have more in common than you think."

The rain smoothly patted the car as they drove. It gradually picked up its pace, as if protesting their attempts to approach the fighting. Rafqa's weak headlights shone only a few feet into the distance. The street was empty of any other cars or souls, inhabited only by the rain and Rafqa and Whit. Whit jerked around as he saw a sudden movement to the right of the car, and as he turned, Rafqa screamed and slammed on the breaks. Five feet in front of the car, a child-sized figure with a hood was crumpled like a small mound of mud in the rain.

"Oh my God," Rafqa said, and started to reach for the door.

Whit grabbed her wrist and said, "No, wait."

She looked at Whit, horrified, and started to speak, "Where's its mother?"

"Just a second." Whit got out of the car and approached the figure. The rain's pace had quickened and he felt water trickling through his jacket to his shirt. Lightning flashed and blinded him for a second as it simultaneously illuminated the entire empty street and, in the instant before the white flash covered his vision, seared an image of his surroundings into Whit's memory. Roughly twenty feet ahead, a lamppost, broken. Two stores on the left of the street, shuttered. On the right, a cement wall and a closed door. A white Toyota sat roughly forty feet ahead on the right, a figure may have been in it, or it could have just been the seat. Otherwise the street was empty – no people except this child, frozen in time by the white-hot flash of the lightning.

"Hello little one, where is your mother?" Whit questioned, beneath the quickening rain, but the child continued to look away. The image seared in Whit's head replayed and something else popped out at him, the feet of the child were the only visible part of its body, protruding awkwardly from beneath the jacket that descended like a triangular tent from its head. The feet loomed strangely large beneath the tent. The rain hardened and Whit took a step closer and began reaching for the child when he suddenly saw toes, filthy and blackened, sticking through man-sized shoes at the base of what he thought were the child's legs.

As lightning flashed again, the figure turned quickly and the grotesque, almost animalistic face of the possessed man glared viciously at him. Whit stepped back in horror, but could not look away. The eyes seemed to glow faintly like red embers, and snot dripped from his nose. His face was caked with dirt and dried blood at one corner of his mouth. The face had taken on some combination of vacancy and other-worldly aggression.

The man's hood fell, his sweatshirt opened fully on one side, showing the left half of an indiscernible, bloody symbol. The man, staring directly at Whit and laughing, drew his finger across his throat, and in an unnatural jolt skipped to the side of the road and disappeared down an alley.

After a few moments, Whit regained his composure, and turned to walk back to the car.

Whit re-entered the car in a half daze. "What happened?" But Whit did not hear her. Through his head flashed the image of the man outside the camps and then in Gaspar Vartabed's church. The shape he had noticed in the church emerged, like a still photograph before his eye; a different shape was there outside the camp, too. And then there was the shape in the fog before entering Musa Rasoul's home. The distinct and bloody images repeatedly flashed through his head.

"Quick," he said, "something to write with . . ." Pulling paper from his pocket, he closed his eyes. It was as if the white-hot lightning, burning the street's image in his head, had triggered a dormant chamber of his senses. Whit was still shaking from the encounter, and his attempts to jot down the images tremulously mixed with rainwater leaving a nearly indiscernible imprint. Rafqa stared at the imprint, but could make nothing of it. It seemed to be random dashes combined together in some formless and inexplicable fashion.

"What . . . who was that?" she asked, placing her hand on his wrist.

Whit squinted. He rubbed his right hand viciously against his pants to try to dry it, then tried writing again.

"I don't understand."

"There isn't enough time tonight," Whit said, finishing the scrawls on the paper. Rafqa sensed Whit was downplaying a deeper sense of unease. They looked at one another for a second, until she realized she was holding his wrist, and she quickly let go. She turned back to the road, putting both hands on the wheel and the car lurched forward under her direction.

After a long silence, she said, "So how are you going to do it?"

"There's only one way. I don't have any options."

"We never have only one option, Whit."

"No? Then why are you guys ready to bring the whole deck down?"

She said, "That's different. Still – we have options. We could continue to live like this – our children with no future."

"You have children?"

"No, I have no time for children."

"But you have time for war?"

"I have time for our future."

"No time for your own future?"

She was silent, then began, "That quote, from the book."

"Augustine?"

She nodded. "I've thought about it a lot, since we . . . since you mentioned it."

"Any conclusions?"

"I don't know. I feel trapped here. Like all of us are being punished for choices we did not make."

"Sons of Adam."

"What?"

"All the children of Adam." Whit swept his hand over the city. "This side of paradise anyway. There's no escape."

"I don't know," she said, turning it over in her mind seriously. "I mean, there has to be some place where it doesn't seem like we are faced with such impossible choices. I'm a doctor, Whit, I want to heal people. But I can't heal Lebanon without fighting for it. And I really don't want to fight." She shook her head. "So what do we do?"

"I'm not sure I know anymore." He spoke with a somberness that broke her heart. She could sense a profound exhaustion in him that was far too significant for their shared youth. She wanted to heal him, too.

She pulled over to the side of the road. The rain stopped falling and the glowing clouds moved swiftly over the city. She leaned forward and kissed Whit on the cheek. He lifted his hand and stroked her hair and searched her eyes. In their unknowing largess, they balanced love and hate, birth and death. Reflecting some primordial touch of the fall, they balanced the manifold tensions of human nature. She smiled and closed her eyes as he leaned in to kiss her, but opened them suddenly when an explosion rattled just a few blocks away. He grasped her and placed her forehead to his as they both looked down. He turned away placing his hand on the door.

"Wait," she grabbed the paper on which he had written and scrawled a name. "This is a friend we have down in the Arqoub . . . a village called Yanta. Whit, if it is the PFLP . . . you may only have a day at the most to get to them before it's too late. And you'll need friends to help you out. I'm sorry to tell you, but George said I must."

Whit looked at the name, Naim.

"Thank you." He opened the door, stepping out into the night as gunfire reverberated down the alleys into which he had to walk.

Rafqa held her hands to her mouth and a tear ran down her face, "Whit," she said, as he turned, his hand on the door, to look at her. "Come back."

He nodded and stepped out of the car. She watched him walk down the street. A flash in the near distance sent dirt flying, but he was unmoved. The low-hung, ashen cloud seemed to freeze in the air and then drifted towards them. In the moment before it engulfed him, Whit stopped and turned to look at her.

Across Beirut, people loved and people hated. People dined together and people killed together. Some people prayed and some people smoked and some people did nothing at all. Colonel Chartouni was reporting in front of a parliamentary committee to describe the fighting and explain why the army had no choice but to take the offensive. The Prime Minister somberly nodded his head. Rafqa sobbed in her car and, regaining her composure after some time, pulled off to drive away from the fighting. Boutros and Martha held one another in the darkness, as Nadia looked out the window into the rainy night, candles flickering in the occasional home. Khalil, tied to a chair, spit out blood as Sayyid stood over him, yelling at him that his parents must think he's worthless. Najwa and Fatin embraced in fear in a corner, as a man stepped in and yelled at Sayyid to stop and that they had to move again. Gaspar Vartabed stood beside a bed of an elderly woman, placing oil on her forehead as the family surrounded them in tears. Michel held a map on a table, drew a line down a winding mountain highway and circled a spot low down in the Arqoub region near the Israeli border. Musa Rasoul pointed at several points along the map, and all the men, Salman, Ahmed, Fahim, and others watched intently. Musa checked his watch, "Let's go." All of them finished loading weapons and moved towards a truck with a covered bed behind Musa's house. Shutting the doors, they sped off into the night.

# CHAPTER THIRTY

Under the shimmer of a half lit moon, they slipped through the mountain roads, moving towards their destination with languid hesitation. How like life's journeys were these lonely massif ways, winding and unwinding in infinite approach.

In any other circumstances it would have been a drive of the sort Whit loved. When scenery slid past, presenting a natural votive to the imagination and fueling expansive conversation. The passengers could explore the terrain between their minds where their experiences, beliefs, and aspirations met in the fluid, interstitial borderlands of human contact.

The shaking jarred Whit, and he looked around at the accidental crew of passengers sitting in the back of the truck in silence. Musa was staring straight at Whit. Whit could tell he was working on a thought, but wasn't in the mood for conversation and so left it dormant.

Fahim, too, was staring at Whit, but with no valuable thought in mind. He seemed angry, and Whit was concerned about his anger. He could do nothing about it, however, and had little choice but to go through it with these men.

Ahmed slept, unique amongst the group, perhaps lacking the depth to reflect on what was to come, but endearing in his simple willingness to fight when his sense of justice was violated. There was something Whit loved in this simplicity. Ahmed was in no danger of overthinking life; nor was his a simplicity devoid of moral substance.

Three other men that they had brought, Farouk, Jasr, and Yusef, sat checking their weapons or merely staring at their feet. They were Musa's men for life, and Whit was not concerned about them. They would point their rifles in the direction that Musa told them.

Salman, however, hunched tremulously in the corner. He clinched the barrel of his gun as if it were a lifeline that might pull him from the terror of potential death. Whit admired him too. Fear, he thought, was an emotion derided only by those who had never truly experienced it. Every man was afraid in his own fashion. The question was not whether he feared, but what he did in spite of it. Here Salman sat, voluntarily riding into the heart of an impenetrable horror where the only certainty left was that men would be seeking to kill him.

So they moved on through the night together and each still alone. A dull knock came from the front cabin. Whit felt the truck bounce off the road and could feel and hear the sound of gravel being crushed beneath the wheels.

"What's going on?" Whit asked.

Musa answered, "The first checkpoint is about three miles ahead. It's one of ours, but we need to call and check if the PFLP guys already went through."

"You think they are ahead of us?"

"I'm not sure. If they had a rough time getting out of Beirut there is some chance they are not. But given how easily they got out of the camp, I think they are far ahead."

Whit grimaced, "I don't understand why the checkpoints can't stop them?"

"Abou Ammar doesn't want to be involved in the fight, so it has to be the regular policy for the other militias."

"The regular policy?" Whit enquired.

"Yeah – as long as they keep paying the local commanders from their proceeds, they can get through any checkpoint they want, no questions."

"So . . ." Whit started to ask the next question, but thought better of it in front of Musa's men. The fact that the PFLP could openly kill the son of a Fatah commander and still move freely in the South showed not only how weak Musa was, but how weak Abou Ammar was over the loose confederation of different power players in the south. The truth, Whit realized, was not that Abou Ammar was letting them through, but that there was nothing the supposed central command in Beirut could do to control things in the Arqoub. Man against man; at one another's throats for the spoils and without security unless it came at the tip of a blood-soaked barrel. It was the ungoverned and lawless place. It was the Hobbesian inferno. It was the portent of what all of Lebanon could soon become.

The car ground to a halt. "Ok, I have to go make the call." Musa stepped out; Fahim had the moment he sought.

"So you think you're going to do something great? Some hero riding in to the rescue going to get us all killed?"

"Do you think I care whether you hate me or not? You're not here for me." Whit had seen this type of hard case before; and he began to wield the art that had made him legendary in the halls of the CIA. "Answer me – are you here for me?"

"Of course not, you're a Zionist."

Whit shook his head incredulously, "Neither of us is here for the other. But when this goes down, we're both going to be trying to kill the same people, and trying to keep from getting killed by the same people." Fahim swallowed deeply.

"Yeah, well what do you bring here anyway. The way I see it, we're all risking our lives just for Fatin, and your two friends. So all you've got is you and all of us."

"Fahim, if you're with Musa, you can't be as bad as you seem. What I bring is between me and Musa, but I can promise you this, without me you would have let them drag Musa's dead body through the streets."

Fahim began to speak, and Whit interrupted, "And without me you guys wouldn't even have a clue where Fatin was."

"Maybe that would be better."

Salman suddenly emerged from his dormancy and let loose a perfectly-timed state of vitriol. "What do you think, Fahim, that it's not worth it? To save Fatin? I agree with Michel – you don't want to do this, then get out. But next week it will be one of our other families, maybe the week after that Ahmed," Salman said, nodding, "or your sister or mother."

Fahim angrily grabbed Salman's shirt and reared back to hit him. Whit lunged forward, pinning his retracted arm against the cabin of the truck and simultaneously grabbing his throat around the Adam's apple. Fahim initially made a sound, but was silenced by Whit's grasp. Ahmed awoke suddenly, and moved towards Whit, but Salman put his arm across Ahmed's chest. "Fahim started this." Ahmed sat back down, knowing his brother's tendencies, "Ok, guys let's calm down."

At that moment Musa opened the rear door, "What is going on here?!" Musa exclaimed.

Whit let go of Fahim, who gasped for air and struggled out of the car.

Whit turned and slid out, as well, standing face to face with Musa. "Nothing, Musa; just a little discussion."

"Cut it out. Given the news I just heard, I have no time to referee schoolyard fights. I spoke with our guy at the second checkpoint, it sounds like we're about two hours behind them."

Whit began breathing more deeply and pacing, "Can any of your checkpoints delay them long enough for us to catch up with them?"

"Not on the highway. Pretty soon they'll hit Keswani's territory, and we will have to go on foot from there because there is no way we'd get through on their roads. The sun is going to be coming up soon, so our main hope is that they won't make the final stage during the day to meet with him. Hopefully they'll prefer to do that at night. If so, we can get in position outside the camp by nightfall."

"At the camp?!" Fahim said in derision, "Are we going to just walk right in and ta. . ."

"Fahim, I am your commander. Whatever I decide will happen, is going to happen. I don't have any idea what has happened here, but if you don't like what's going on, you stay here."

"But you listen . . ."

"And I can listen to whomever I know has better information than us. Got it? Have you done anything to understand what the PFLP is doing down there? Do you know what Keswani's camp looks like? How many men with guns there are? How long it may take other reinforcements to come? Do you know anything?"

Fahim was shamed and said nothing more. Musa Rasoul continued, "I want all of you to listen to me. We're going down there because they took my daughter and killed my son. Because they're taking over Tal Za'atar and because they are turning the fedayeen into a criminal gang. And it's better that we fight them there than in the camps. None of you had to come, but I'm grateful that you did. You can turn around, but even if it's just me and this Zionist, I'm going in to get my daughter."

Ahmed stepped forward, "We are prepared to die for you, Colonel Musa." As Fahim stared angrily at Ahmed, all the men nodded their heads, and Musa looked each man in the eyes, with only Fahim resisting the gaze.

"Ok," Whit said. "It sounds like they will beat us down, so I've got to make a call."

Whit walked to the side of the empty gas station and picked up the phone. It rang several times before Whit heard an answer.

"Shalom?"

"Shalom, it's yetzer," Whit said.

"Ok, ok. Here's the deal, I can give you info, but they are still trying to decide whether to authorize."

Whit was silent, and Shlomo, after pausing for a moment, continued.

"If you do end up down there, look for a sign at roughly 2100."

"What kind of sign?"

"The simplest. Red light, green light. And so you know, there has been a lot of activity at the camp. They brought in two trucks of something, which we've never seen them do. But there's also been fighting with some of Wael Ghanem's men an hour or so north and west of the compound, so you're in luck. Usually they have thirty to forty guys, but it looks like only ten or so stayed around. Word is that the fighting is going to continue for another day or so. You saw one exchange during the day, but that was rare. Usually it happens at night, so if your exchange happens tomorrow night, you should be in a good position. Ok, goodb. . ."

"Wait . . ."

"Yeah . . ."

"Thank you." There was a fuzziness on the other end of the line, and after a moment, it went silent.

When Whit returned to the van, all the men were inside. He closed the door and sat down, and Ahmed hit the wall twice. The truck jerked forward and the men shook simultaneously. As they hit the highway and smoothed out, Whit knelt down in the middle of the group and spread out a map.

"Ok, here it is." Another forty-five minutes passed as Whit and Mousa further described the operation. The car stopped several times without incident. Whit assumed these were the Fatah checkpoints. The last stop, however, brought the familiar knocking on the wall of the cabin. Ahmed turned to Whit and nodded towards the door. Whit turned the knob, and the men all shielded their eyes as the morning sun burst into the tiny space.

They got out one by one, while Whit looked into the distance with a scope. As Musa approached him, Whit handed over the scope and pointed in the distance. It's off down that valley.

"Ok, we're going to take this northern route to the left of the highway, Michel, you and your team will go to the south and so you are closest to that southern fence by nightfall." Whit looked around the group and nodded. Musa continued, "Then, we just wait until they come for the exchange."

"See you guys down there." Ahmed said. The men, except Whit, all embraced one another, and each group walked away in separate directions.

The hills from which they would emerge dropped gradually into a flat plain of dry land. There were a variety of trees, stretching down the hillside that looked like battalions of alien soldiers preparing for battle. Instead of a battalion, however, Whit had seven men.

As they walked, he began to see the evidence of the fighting that had forced the inhabitants away from this country. Giant craters were visible, the scars of Israeli reprisal bombings for fedayeen incursions and attacks in Israeli territory.

They walked on for another hour or so before Jasr finally broke the silence. "Michel, I know you are an American."

Whit continued walking for a few moments, and said, "That's right."

"So, what do you Americans want here with us, anyway?"

"You know, I was just asking myself that question."

"Why do you always help the Israelis?"

A moment of silence passed as the breeze brushed over the trees and bushes. "Sons of Isaac, I guess."

"What?" Ahmed said, hurrying a few steps forward to try and be part of the conversation. But Jasr and Whit ignored him

Instead, Jasr engaged, "Ah, yes. And we, sons of Ishmael – we must stay banished to the desert? Is that it?"

The men walked quietly for a few moments, until Whit responded, "We're all sons of Adam."

"You know, I studied at the madrasa," Jasr said. "Not like these fanatics down there," Jasr said, tossing his hand towards the base of the valley.

"Yeah, how was it different?"

"We read the Bible, too." Now this, Whit was interested in.

"So how did you end up here, instead of as a cleric?"

"I guess I lost faith. I looked at my people. We are supposed to be a people. We are supposed to have a land and grow olive trees and watch our children dance in between them and have weddings and bury our family in some place we call our own."

"I don't know what to tell you. It happened; and it's never going to go back to the way it was before."

"What?"

"You said you read the Bible?"

"Yeah."

"Do you remember Isaiah?"

"A little."

"Well I remember this, 'And Lebanon is not sufficient to burn.'"

But before he could finish, Jasr continued. "Ah yes, 'and all nations before him are as nothing; and they are counted to him less than nothing, and vanity.'"

All the men were quiet.

Whit broke the silence, "Do you believe it?"

"Believe what?"

"That Lebanon is not enough? You'll burn the whole thing down and then you still won't have a home."

"Frankly, I'm not fighting for Lebanon or Palestine. All these years and it's just been a bunch of Palestinians fighting each other, too."

"Then why are you fighting?"

"For dignity."

The men walked on and the day lumbered aimlessly towards sunset. The land and the sky, bathed in an orangeish-blue kaleidoscope, was an image of fire and water settled inexplicably beside one another. The land was aflame; and the water rushed over it, pushing the fire to the horizon until it was, at last, extinguished. The land grew still, darker and darker, and the night set in.

The crackle of the walkie talkie broke the silence. Salman said in a hushed town, "We are in position." Whit grabbed the walkie-talkie from Yusef, who had been playing with it, "So are we. No more talking unless you have to." Whit checked his watch, it was 8:30.

# CHAPTER THIRTY-ONE

The four men moved down behind a rocky outcropping only twenty yards from the southern fence. From this position, they could see into several windows along the nearest wall of the compound's buildings. Whit could also see a guard moving back and forth between the fence closest to them and the wall. The walk took him about fifteen seconds to complete. From a bag, Whit pulled out four pieces of a rifle. He assembled the portions together and placed a silencer on the end of it. The rifle was compact and had a scope.

Whit panned the horizon with the scope, watched the guard walk, and looked in the distance where he thought Shlomo's guard tower sat. Removing from his bag a set of small night-vision binoculars, Whit looked again into the distance and, through the green lens, could see the tower just across the border. He marked a low-slung tree, its trunk splitting in two as it rose, which was at the base of his vision of the tower. He then switched back to the rifle scope, so he could tell the difference between green and red, and stared in the darkness just above the tree. It was 8:55 p.m.

Whit waited. Then, it came. One. Brief. Flash. One momentary blink, at the sight of which, his heart felt as if it had dropped to his stomach. For some reason, he had thought that Shlomo would come through. Now, seeing the brief red flash, he seriously thought that this plan may not work. He may never get out of this place with Najwa and Khalil alive.

For several hours the men sat, pondering their lives at brief intervals. Whit tried to distract himself from the distant memories of those things from which he now stood so far. Memories surged forth from the darkness like ephemeral phantoms, gone just as they were glimpsed.

Static broke caustically over the radio, "Here they come." Whit swung around and pointed his gun towards the gate as his heart raced. From his vantage point, he could see only the left side of the compound.

Squeezing the walkie-talkie, he said, "What do you see inside the gate?"

"Two large trucks." Now the voice was Fahim's. "There are eight men waiting inside . . . all about fifteen feet inside the gate."

"Ok, we'll wait for the gate to open, then we'll move." Whit looked at the guard, who had started his return path from the side of the wall on which the gate stood. He headed back south, towards the Israeli side of the compound.

The gate began to open, and the man was about half way along the fence. Whit brought him cleanly into the crosshairs. The man stopped at the furthest edge of the compound, out of sight of all of his comrades. Just as he turned, Whit pulled the trigger and the man dropped like a load of rocks, straight to the ground, unmoving. Whit sprinted with the three others to the fence, and removed a device they had never seen and at which they looked curiously. He swiped it quickly in an inverted u-shape and it cut silently through the links. He then removed the fence and motioned each man through.

A lump rose in his throat as he heard screaming. All this time and Najwa was still fighting. "Khalil!" he heard her scream, "Khalil!"

Over the walkie-talkie he heard, "They are splitting up the hostages, the women to the left. They are dragging the boy towards your building. He looks barely alive." A moment or two later a light flipped on in a room about thirty feet away from Whit's location. Whit handed a small package of C-4 to Yusef, and pointed at the wall straight across from him. He then tapped his own two eyes, and pointed at the window. Yusef nodded, and ran to the wall, as Whit broke south to get a better look into the lit room.

Whit was concealed by the darkness, and could see two burly men drag Khalil inside and hook his arms to a dangling chain hanging from the ceiling about four inches behind an exposed light bulb. They had positioned Khalil so he was facing the window. Whit turned and motioned to Jasr, who ran to his side. "Keep your gun on the one on the left, and I'll take the one on the right." Jasr nodded and aimed. They waited, but heard no gunfire from the front. Whit looked over his shoulder, Yusef was holding the detonator and had rushed twenty feet further north, so he and Ahmed could see the gate and be clear of the blast.

Whit looked back through the window. "Now we get to kill you, Nasrani," said the man to Khalil, and then struck Khalil across the face, blood flying through the air. Whit pulled a flashlight out of his bag, as the men took turns hitting Khalil.

Khalil's face was swollen. For a moment, Whit saw Khalil lift his eyes, and Whit flashed the light briefly. He felt a palpable pride at the determined look that seemed to pass over Khalil's face, who, barely visible under the swelling, seemed to stare out the window in indefatigable hope. Whit flashed the light once more, and could see a faint smile at the left corner of Khalil's mouth.

Khalil looked up at the light, dangling from the ceiling, and began swinging towards it wildly. Whit's gaze widened as Sayyid suddenly entered the room, and he trained his scope on Sayyid, then back on the interrogator on the right. The man on the right let a blow fly on Khalil's back, and an explosion rang out in the front of the compound. Simultaneously, the strike pushed Khalil forward just far enough that he cracked the light bulb. Immediately, the room went dark, and Whit and Jasr fired in unison. Gunfire erupted from the front of the compound.

Yusef tripped the explosion, sending brick and mortar bursting forth from the south wall as the earth shook. Whit rushed towards the smoking hole and lunged through it into an empty room. From there he opened a door into a dimly lit hallway. He turned right towards Khalil's room, ignoring the two men coming from the opposite direction. Someone behind him must have fired as the two men slumped over against both walls.

As Whit neared the room, he saw Sayyid emerge from it, coughing and confused. Whit jumped upon him just as Sayyid saw him at the last instant. They rolled over one another, Whit punching Sayyid in the face and Sayyid cursing as he tried to choke Whit. Sayyid broke free after slamming Whit's diaphragm with his knee. Whit regained his breath in enough time to grab Sayyid's ankle, who then kicked him in the face. As Sayyid got up to run, Whit saw Khalil swinging in the darkened room out of his peripheral vision. Sayyid was several feet down the hallway. Whit gritted his teeth and turned towards Khalil, rushing in to lift the boy off the hooks.

Towards the front, Musa and Fahim fired from both sides of the road. They had shot the driver of the first truck, which rolled to a stop a few feet from them. They had disabled the second truck by firing into the engine block. It sat, smoking, in the middle of the gate, prohibiting it from closing. Black fumes billowed forth and several men fired wildly in their direction from behind the truck.

Musa motioned to Fahim to close in, and as they did, Farouk sprayed the truck with bullets. Salman slumped beside a rock, started to break out, and then slumped again as gunfire riddled the pathway beside him. As Musa and Fahim closed in on the smoking mass, they shot two men who had popped up. A heavy round of gunfire exploded forth from the northern arm of the building, sending Farouk ducking for cover as Musa and Fahim dove behind the smoldering truck. Suddenly, adding to the cacophony of explosions and chaos all around, a motorcycle burst forth and was fifteen feet down the path before they could react. Fahim shot at the motorcyclist, but its red taillight, already small, disappeared in the distance. "Who the hell was that?!" he yelled.

Musa yelled back, "I don't know. We've gotta get some fire on that building. I'll head right, you go from under the left side." They each moved around and began firing again.

Inside, Jasr, Yusef and Ahmed rushed ahead of Whit, who had Khalil slung over his shoulder. The men reached the next corner, and Whit saw them firing around it at unknown targets. They all rounded the corner together, firing, and Whit leaned Khalil against the wall "Ahmed, stay with him," Whit turned up a short set of stairs and shot a guard at the top. He kicked open the door and beheld a bed with Fatin tied to it screaming wildly. When she recognized Michel, she began to sob uncontrollably. He ran to her, and told her to lean away as he shot the chain on the bed post. "Can you run?"

"Yes."

"Where is Najwa?"

"I don't know, they took her in the other direction," she cried.

They ran back down stairs as intense fire forced the group back around the corner they had just rounded. Whit yelled, "Let's regroup at the front!"

Outside, Musa fired on the northeastern most building. The men could now tell that all of the remaining fighters were shooting from there. Someone leaned out of the doorway at the center of that building and fired a rocket-propelled gun towards the front gate. As it exploded, it flung Musa several feet into the air and he went limp upon hitting the ground. Salman broke out from behind the rock and ran to Musa's side.

Whit, Khalil, Yusef, Jasr, Fatin, and Ahmed emerged from the door of the southern building. Fire ripped towards them. Whit knelt and fired at the building while the rest of the group ran behind the truck. Salman dragged Musa behind the truck, and Fatin, rounding the corner and seeing her father, immediately flung herself on top of him. "Abi, Abi!"

At that moment, Whit could see Farouk backing up the other truck through gunfire towards the group. When he arrived he leaned out and yelled over the spray of fire, "C'mon we have to go!" Fahim ran to the group and yelled over the gunfire, "We gotta get out of here, there are too many of them. Did you get the other girl?!"

Jasr yelled, "We had to back out, there was too much fire from the north building."

Whit screamed over the maelstrom, "I can't leave without her." Khalil was leaning, bloody, against the tire of the disabled truck.

Fahim answered vengefully, "We got Fatin. We're going."

"No," Salman yelled, "we have to help..." Fahim struck him across the face. Without speaking further he yelled at Ahmed and Yusef to help him get Musa in the truck. He then lifted Fatin in, and the rest of the group, except Salman, loaded behind.

"We can't leave him," Salman yelled with frustration. Ahmed stepped out, bear hugged Salman, and threw him in the back of the truck. He turned and looked at Whit, yelling, "Just come – there are too many."

"I can't leave her," Whit yelled, "but take Khalil."

"You're on your own," Fahim yelled, as the truck started to pull away. Whit stared in disbelief as the truck pulled away, and the gunfire grew quiet. He could see Fatin, Ahmed, and Salman's faces glowing softly from the compound's floodlights. Their glowing faces grew small in the distance along with the red lights of the truck, until they were gone.

Whit heard men yelling in the background, but no more gunfire. He looked up over the truck, and saw no one. Silence wrapped around the compound. Few things were quiet like the silence following a fight. A hole had been ripped in the moment, creating a hollow vacuum where life had once been. The quiet was deafening.

So this is how it would be. It wasn't as he had expected – this way of dying; but nothing in life ever seemed to happen the way he expected. Why would this be any different, he wondered, momentarily, in the milky-white stillness of the flood-lit evening. A pang grew in the pit of Whit's stomach.

"Khalil, can you move?" Khalil had only the energy to shake his head no just once. Whit thought for a moment. It could never work. He looked out, and saw bodies littering the compound. There were probably at least six or seven more men alive inside. Then, he heard her scream, a scream so visceral and so desperate that he knew he had no choice. "Khalil, listen to me. Here is a gun. I have to go in after your sister. If anyone comes around the corner of that truck, you shoot, ok?" Khalil nodded. Whit had too many thoughts running through his head, but no time to consider them.

He could see Khalil, courageous and abused, look at him with pride. Then, he saw a tear break across his bloodied and bruised face. Whit grabbed him and kissed his forehead, then nodded as he looked in his eyes. Najwa screamed again, and Khalil pushed Whit.

Whit ran around the truck and toward the door of the southern building. Gunfire erupted as he ran across the open distance. As he neared the door, he stopped abruptly. A man was standing in the doorway pointing a gun at him. The man yelled something in Arabic, then yelled again. Whit dropped his weapon and held his hands up.

So this is how it would be.

"Yalla, step towards the fence," the voice echoed through the silence. The man walked behind him and pushed him. The compound's floodlights lit the landscape for several dozen yards around. Bleached in the colors of midnight and this artificial light, the surrounding land appeared like a harsh, lunar landscape. Whit imagined that the moon would be just as silent. Darkness lay beyond its rim. The vast, untamed distance of eternity stretched away infinitely.

So this is how it would be. Executed on the border of the promised land, in a fight he didn't choose, for a woman and her brother whom he had only come to know of late. This is how it would be.

Then, from the deep darkness of eternity, Whit thought he saw a brief glimmer. Instead of one step toward the fence, Whit took two, coming adjacent with the southern edge of the building.

"Stop," the man shouted. Whit squinted to the distant ridge, and as he heard the man behind him say, "Goodbye, American," he saw it again - one faint, green flash.

"Wait."

"What?"

"At least let me die kneeling to my God." The soldier kicked Whit's legs so he fell to his knees, and the next light Whit saw was a quick orange burst. He felt the splash of warm blood against the back of his neck, and only a second later heard the report of the sniper rifle in Shlomo's tower. Turning to the man, he saw that the power of the shot had crushed his entire face. Whit grabbed a grenade from the man's vest, and ran to grab his rifle again. The sound of helicopter rotors emerged from the distance. Looking over his shoulder, Whit saw two choppers coming from the Israeli side, and relief washed over him.

Whit turned back, and began firing at the northern building. Several men fired from two windows and a doorway. He heard Najwa scream again, and threw a grenade, which exploded directly beneath one of the windows just as a man leaned out to fire.

Whit ran and as he neared the building, a rage of gunfire from behind him spattered across its wall. He hurled himself through the doorway and was trapped behind the next door as several men fired from down the hallway. The next second, he turned to see Israeli commandoes bursting into the room, led by Shlomo.

"Howdy partner!"

Whit just shook his head in disbelief. "You're late." Shlomo laughed. "All that's left are a handful of guys in this building." The firing continued. "Several of your guys should go around from the center, and I can come with you from this side." Shlomo motioned to four others, who ran out.

Moments later Whit heard gunfire erupt in the center building, and he and Shlomo fired and ran down the hallway. He followed her scream. He kicked open a door in the last room on the left, and found himself face to face with a man, bedecked in black garb head to toe, whom he took to be Keswani, holding a knife to Najwa's neck.

Najwa yelled "Whi…" as the man pulled her tightly and she was silenced. Tears streamed down her face. Keswani was far less impressive than he expected. A full beard hid his youth and fear. Whatever he lacked in appearances he must have compensated for with charisma.

Whit could hear gunfire and screaming in Arabic and Hebrew in both hallways. Then the gunfire stopped, and he only heard Hebrew.

"Do you hear that?"

"I hear nothing." Keswani said impetuously.

Whit pointed his gun at the man. "It's over, Jawad."

Then Keswani looked around, desperate, and Whit could feel the presence of several men behind him.

"We'd prefer him alive." Whit recognized Shlomo's voice.

Then Shlomo said, "Drop the knife now, and we won't torture you to death." Keswani relented after a mere second or two of thought. He dropped the knife and held up his hands, as Najwa screamed something indecipherable and sprinted towards Whit, crashing into his body with her arms and legs around him. "I knew you'd come." He could barely discern her words, ushering forth between sobs, her face buried in his shoulder. "I knew you'd come, Whit." She cried uncontrollably as the Israeli commandoes shoved Keswani to the ground and tied his hands and legs together.

As they took the man out, he spit at Whit and said ominously, "I remember." Shlomo hit him across the face and said in perfect Arabic, "You'll have plenty of time to remember where you're going." Then Shlomo spoke in Hebrew to the men, who responded and then left.

Shlomo turned to Whit, "I hope you don't mind, we'll help ourselves to any paperwork and other souvenirs."

"I owe you a lot more than that, Shlomo." The three walked out of the room and then outside into the courtyard.

"What about Khalil?" Najwa asked.

Whit turned to Najwa and nodded towards the gate, "Behind the truck. You can go and check on him, just – before you round the corner, just yell out that it's you and not to shoot." She looked strangely at him, and then sprinted off.

Whit turned to Shlomo, and said, "I don't understand - why?"

"Ahh," Shlomo smiled and shrugged his shoulders, "you know our policy, we can retaliate if they are firing at one of our own." He winked and an impish grin broke across his face. Several of the commandoes came up and said something in Hebrew, saluting Shlomo, who returned the salute.

"We gotta get back to our side, enough tourism for one night. Now Whit, I'm sorry, but we can't help you from here."

Whit nodded. A man emerged from the building and handed something to Shlomo, speaking in Hebrew and pointing at Whit. Shlomo took a look, and looked up at Whit.

"What?"

"Looks like we were just in time," Shlomo said, handing the documents to Whit, "Ghanem's lucky you were here." Whit grabbed the documents, looking at them, "You better take those back to Beirut." After a moment, Whit looked back up at Shlomo with the same surprised look Shlomo had just given to Whit, but Shlomo was now on a walkie talkie.

"Ok, Whit. Intell just reported that there are a group of these guys on their way back down the highway. I'd take one of those jeeps near the gate, and, what do you Americans say, high-tail it up the road that goes northeast towards Hermon and veers into the mountains towards Bekaa. There's a Druze town there."

"I'm familiar with it," Whit said knowingly.

Shlomo nodded, assuming he would be, "If you can make it there ok, you should be able to get in touch with your people and be good from there."

"Thank you, Shlomo." Whit turned, then stopped. "Oh, Shlomo, one more thing."

"Yeah."

"Does this mean anything to you?" Whit pulled the piece of paper out of his pocket on which he scrawled the symbols from the possessed man.

Shlomo squinted at it, "Well, it's not Hebrew. Where did you see it?"

"Hard to explain. Any ideas?"

"I don't actually know – it doesn't really make sense, Ahh wait," Shlomo said, tapping the paper, "I've seen this." Shlomo said something in Hebrew to one of the men, who yelled at a soldier in the doorway. Moments later another man came running out. Shlomo handed the man the paper, saying something in Hebrew, and said to Whit, "This guy is a rabbi, believe it or not." The man immediately handed it back to Shlomo and said, "Dan-yell" to Whit, in a thick English accent. Then turned and ran back inside yelling something over his shoulder in Hebrew.

"What?" Whit said.

"Daniel. He's saying it's from what you call Daniel. Whit, I'd love to stick around for a Bible study, but we gotta go." The two helicopters were beginning to slightly lift as all the troops but Shlomo had loaded.

Whit turned to run, but heard Shlomo yell quickly over the rotors' noise, "Hey Whit –"

Whit turned back around, "Yeah?"

"Did you find yetzer?"

Whit shook his head – "I think he got away."

Shlomo smiled and squinted, "Funny how he always seems to do that." Whit nodded as the two exchanged a smile.

"Yeah – but I'm going to find him."

"Not if I find him first, you bastard," Shlomo smiled and made a faux salute to the American.

Whit turned and ran towards the gate. Najwa was caressing Khalil. He picked up Khalil and carried him to the back seat of a nearby jeep. Najwa stood beside the car and Whit, for the first time really, made eye contact with her.

"Get in, sweetie, we have to get out of here."

She got in and grabbed his hand, kissing it as she squeezed it to her lips and began to cry. Whit started the car, pulling onto the mountain road as the helicopters lifted off in the background. In the rear view mirror he could see dust thrown in every direction and, only moments later, when the Israelis were fully airborne, the buildings exploded. The landscape went dark except for the warm flicker of the burning debris.

The fire diminished in the distance until they were driving alone in a darkness lit only by the distant stars and the faint headlights of the jeep. They sped forward towards the mountains.

# CHAPTER THIRTY-TWO

As the morning sun, just beneath the horizon, emitted a soft glow that began to animate the land, they arrived to the outskirts of Yanta. An old man walked along the side of the road with a small herd of goats. Whit slowed the car and pulled over.

"What are you going to do?" Najwa asked.

"Get directions," Whit said and got out of the car. Najwa watched him walk up to the man. She watched the way he moved, confidently and with purpose. She saw the old man gesticulating wildly and pointing to the left and then the right. They shook hands and she watched as he walked back to the car.

Whit was a stranger in this land; but to her he had mastered it all, and had saved her in the process. And now he was going to do whatever he could to get them home. For the first time in days, she felt a sense of comfort even in the face of uncertainty. That, she thought, was what love must be. In that moment, her heart also broke. In her heart this memory would never cease, the mountains and the morning and Whit. Wherever she would go, whatever she would do, she would love him forever more, just like this, under a red sun rising full of hope.

The door opened, jarring her out of her thoughts, and Whit hopped in. Whit turned down a series of streets, and as they passed him, Whit made eye contact with a man in a velvet colored jacket standing on the side of the road. He was middle-aged, but had the look of a man without purpose. Such men – the bored and the unscrupulous – were the most dangerous men of all. Even those busy with evil had a logic to their misdeeds – and the logic could be fought. It was the illogic of totally vacuous indifference that posed the greatest threat in a place like this. Whit broke eye contact and drove on as if he knew his way around; but watched in the rear view mirror as the man continued to stare.

Moving through Yanta, Whit could see potholes and destroyed buildings spotting the village. He turned the wheel once more as the sunlight, now occluded in part by the high cliffs surrounding this section of the village, only gradually engorged the streets. A grey, one-story building emerged around the corner that had a fading, bluish garage. "There it is." He pulled in close to the gate, "Stay here for a sec." He jogged the few short steps to the door and rapped on it.

There was fumbling in the background. After a moment the door handle shook and the door slowly opened just a crack. A head hovered four inches above Whit's, eyes squinting from the light.

"Naim?" Whit asked. The man looked shocked, and rubbed his face several times as though he was trying to understand what he was seeing.

"Who are you? What do you want?" The man responded in rapid succession.

"Some friends from Beirut told me that I could stop here on my way through." Naim's eyes expanded quickly and he swung the door open.

"Of course, forgive me, we have to get you to a different house immediately," he said motioning.

"Naim, we probably should hide my jeep around the side of your house where that driveway goes. We can talk more in a moment, but can we get it inside?"

"Yes, yes, my brother took the car last night, I don't know where he went, but let me open it and you pull it in." Naim walked around behind the gate and paused for a moment as he saw Najwa holding Khalil's head. Naim opened the gate and looked around the block as Whit pulled the car into it. Naim approached as Whit stepped out. "Don't come out front with him. Go through that back door," Naim said, pointing around the back. "I'll meet you in back." Naim went to the front and looked around again, stopping as his eyes fell on the velvet-jacketed man leaning against a wall in the distance. A chill ran up his spine.

"Sir, there is an individual . . ." Naim said as he met them out back.

"Velvet coat?"

"You saw him?"

Whit nodded. "He spotted us on the way in initially, and I now see him just a block or two away, clearly watching your house. Is he a problem?"

"There are some rumors around town that he's involved with . . . them. But, if he were to bring them here, it could get bad for you very quickly."

"I can imagine. Right now I'm just thinking about how quickly we can move on to avoid problems for you and get Khalil some help."

"Ok, wait here and I'll go make a call." After what seemed like an eternity, Naim emerged and opened a back gate. He walked to a small white Nissan waiting outside the gate with an old man in the driver's seat. Whit stepped out into the street, and looking both ways, saw no sign of the velvet man, or anyone else, watching. They hopped in, and Naim patted the hood and stepped back inside, nodding to Whit as they pulled away.

Down another labyrinth of streets they wound. Whit tried to keep track of landmarks at each turn; but after too many quick turns around non-descript corners, he realized he wasn't going to remember it all. It was the worst position in which one could find himself, without signposts in a strange land. He cursed himself for letting them get so exposed, but also knew that they had no choice. If he didn't have Naim and this old man he had summoned, they would be finished anyway.

Whit was silent as the car slowed to a halt down a narrow alley. No one was around as the old man opened a gate into a small courtyard and ushered the three through it into a tiny, one room shack. It appeared to be some sort of storage hut, which abutted steep hills. The man walked Whit and Najwa to a grimy rear window after they laid Khalil on a makeshift cot. He pointed behind the shack where an opening between two trees had been surreptitiously cut.

The man spoke again in loud tones as he patted Whit's shoulder and smiled. Whit could understand nothing of what he was saying except the words Joub Jannin. From some of the things Najwa had said, Whit clearly recognized that as a village of some Christians who were friendly to George's militia.

Najwa explained, "There is a path that leads through those trees and the hills behind. He said it is an old shepherd's path that spills out on the other side of the hills and leads to the town Joub Jannin, in the Bekaa. He said that it can only be passed on foot, and it would be a safe way for us to get to Joub Jannin, if it came to it. What did he mean, Whit?"

"I'm not sure, but they must think the roads are going to be too dangerous to pass. Someone was watching us on the way into the town, and if we can't get out by road, these guys must think we can walk to Joub Jannin. How far did he say it was?"

"I think he said a couple of hours, but it was difficult to understand."

The old man continued talking and motioning to the hills. "He wants to tell you that," Najwa gasped, and then laboriously continued, "that he killed a man who had tried to attack the woman he loved," Najwa continued to translate. "But, no one believed him so he had to hide out in those mountains," Najwa nodded her head towards the mountains beyond, "for an entire year."

The old man began speaking fervently again, and Najwa said, "He wants us to know that we'll probably need some time at night to sleep. We can make a fire, he said, just on the other side of the mountains." She asked him a question, of which Whit only understood she was asking for more specific directions. When the old man began responding again, Najwa translated, "There are a series of caves – I don't know what he's talking about – but he claims there are a series of caves with fresh water and we can make a fire that no one will see."

"What happened?" Whit asked.

"What?" the old man responded, looking at Najwa.

"What do you want, Whit?"

"How did he end up coming back – out of the mountains?" Najwa translated to the man again, who smiled.

"Ah" the man smiled, waving his hands, "the truth went back down before me," as he started walking away. "I just followed it home," he laughed and walked out towards his car.

"What are we going to do, Whit? How can Khalil make it?"

"Well – we'll worry about that if it comes to it. For now, let's try and get some food into him and get his strength up."

Whit looked at the map as Najwa heated soup on an old stove and fed Khalil. He was now in a semi-conscience state, but not speaking. Whit unfolded a map and noted the hills between Yanta and Joub Jannin. The pathways through the mountains were not marked, so this was clearly an old trail known only to a few locals. Even allowing for some winding through the hills and plains beneath, Whit guessed they would be eight to ten hours on the road to Joub Jannin if they had to take it.

Whit noticed a phone in the corner, and decided he was running out of options. Naim seemed trustworthy, but he couldn't know if the Druze would defend him – why would they fight and risk their lives for a couple of strangers if the fedayeen showed? Whit picked up the phone and when an operator answered, he asked to be put through to a number that masked his actual call to Royce. A second operator answered, also under the name of the Lebanese telecom, and asked how to direct the call. "Jerome's Bakery, please."

The phone rang for what seemed to Whit an interminable period. "Hello, Jerome's Bakery." But it wasn't Royce's voice. Whit immediately had a sense of foreboding. Something serious had to be going on for this change.

"I'd like to put in an order for a huge delivery." There was a long pause on the other end.

"I'm sorry, sir, you must not have heard, Beirut is completely shut down."

"No . . . no, I'm not in Beirut and have been . . . traveling. I need – "

"The fighting has spread throughout the city, sir. The Syrians have closed the border, the docks have been closed because of the chaos. It's quite bad, sir. People are actually beginning to run out of food. The bakery can't deliver any of our products anywhere in the country, I'm afraid."

Whit's sense of foreboding turned to a sickening feeling. He feared Keswani's men and the fedayeen had probably regrouped and were scouring the countryside, searching for Keswani as much as for Whit and probably assuming both were together. He could not move with Khalil at the moment, but Whit knew from experience that the line between discomfort and desperation could be crossed very quickly. He could see the events forming so that he and the Khourys probably only had a matter of hours before that point would be reached.

"I just want to be very clear, you are my only," he emphasized the word with a starkness, pausing to let its severity be imprinted on the listener, "option, and the situation here is very, very bad."

"Sir, I am really very sorry – but the situation here is worse than it has ever been. The bakery is cl . . ." then there was some scuffling on the other end, and Whit heard two people arguing. Royce came on, "Sir, sir, I'm so very sorry. You . . . your business is so very important to us," Whit could tell Royce, now on the line, had understood that Whit was near the end of his choices. The sound of sporadic gunfire suddenly tapped through the airwaves. He saw Najwa come to attention, and Khalil was beginning to stir. At first muffled, it rather quickly grew louder.

"My friend, this may be my last order."

"I . . . sir, I am," his voice broke, "so sorry. There is nothing I can do." Whit held the receiver against his forehead for a moment, then hung up the phone. The gunfire grew regular and intense, creeping more closely towards them from the outskirts of the village.

# CHAPTER THIRTY-THREE

"Najwa." She looked at him. Whit grabbed his handgun and checked the small machine gun he still had in a bag. He grabbed an additional gun and handed it to her. "Do you know how to use one of these?" She shook her head no. "We're . . . if something happens to me, you just flip this switch here," he said, indicating the lock, "and aim and pull. If you need to reload, you take one of these," he said, dropping the magazine out of the gun and showing her another one in the bag, "and slide it in like this." She began to cry and shook her head slowly from side to side. Whit set the gun down and placed his hands on both sides of her head, putting his forehead against hers.

"It isn't fair," she whispered, "it isn't fair." She continued to cry as Whit held her. He heard a braying sound behind the shed. He went to the window and saw the old man tying a donkey to a post. The old man looked at the window, and seeing Whit's face, nodded, and thrust his arm twice, finger pointing, to the path between the trees. Whit rushed back to Najwa and said, "If we have to go, do you think Khalil could ride a donkey?"

"What?!" she said in disbelief.

"Najwa, we can't get out of here by car. The people who. . . took you, they're going to be all over on the highways. We have to try to make it down into the Bekaa and Joub Jannin. Do you think he could make it?" They both looked at him, Khalil's eyes were open, and he lifted himself to his elbows.

"Whit, I can. I can go."

Whit turned and shifted himself under Khalil's arm, lifting him. "Khalil, there is a donkey out back. We have to walk to Joub Jannin. It's the only way."

"How . . ." he coughed slightly, "how long?"

"It is going to take through the night." He turned to Najwa, "Can you scrounge around for any food in here and put it in the bag?" She jumped up and got to work, loading bread and filling a canteen with a small hand pump in the corner of the shed. Whit looked again out back, and flinched as the gunfire seemed to grow closer. At that moment, the door burst open, and Whit lunged for his gun.

"Don't shoot! Don't shoot!" Naim yelled as he held his hands up, "They've come for you guys. He must have tipped them."

"Velvet jacket?"

"Yeah."

"You've gotta get out of here. You can't take the roads."

"I figured. What's the gunfire?"

"We have our own militia."

Najwa worked frantically, grabbing food, as Whit started towards the door with Khalil.

"Uncle Tarik showed you the mountain route, I'm sorry, but it's the only way."

Whit began to move with Khalil, turning to Naim, "Thank you, so much. I'm sorry we've brought this on you."

"This has been a long time coming. Just get to Joub Jannin."

Whit moved and opened the door, then turned back to Naim, "One more favor."

"Anything, of course."

"Can you call our friends in Beirut. Tell them, we may . . . we'll need them in Joub Jannin." Whit realized the full gravity of what he was saying. He felt himself crossing some transparent threshold. He was relying on them. In his head, there had always been a line between himself and them. He was separate. He needed no one. He could operate on his own without their – that is, anyone's – help.

Naim nodded. Whit went outside and they turned into the shaded forest.

Gradually, the gunfire grew into a muffled mixture of distant reports and echoes. Exhausted and without sleep now for two nights, Whit's legs felt heavy and increasingly useless as the ground beneath them rose towards the mountains. They walked on silently, and the light grew brighter at the end of the forest path where, once free of the trees, they beheld a winding trail just wide enough for a donkey and humans to walk. It rose up into the mountains, which closed high on either side. It was the type of place where they could be easily trapped, but they were out of options.

After some time climbing, the trail leveled and they hit a steady pace. The cliffs rose in a kaleidoscope of limestone hues around them. Whites, yellows and pale oranges were stacked by the hands of time on top of one another. Only an occasional tree grew from the stoney soil, and brush clung tightly every fifty feet to the sides of the trail, but the dry ravine through which they moved was otherwise devoid of vegetation. Sunlight seemed available here only for the brief time that it passed between the cliffs towering overhead.

The gaps had been carved by the waters, waters that had washed day after day, month after month, year after year across the mountains. Carving, insistently, they had run their course until their course had been its own signature, a natural monument to persistence and patience. Whit marveled at the natural beauty, and was shaken out of his contemplation by Najwa's soft voice.

"Who are you?"

Why was it that people you cared for had a habit of asking the most difficult questions? Who was he? Who did he want to be? As a boy he had read T.E. Lawrence and become enthralled with the magic of the Middle East. It was a dangerous, uncharted vastness where honor held sway. Like Lawrence, he dreamt the dreams of dangerous men – the dreams of the day. The dreams of the day were all the more tangible, chanting in mellifluous harmony that coaxed one towards the unrealized ambitions of his future. A young man was he, but he had come to this land of daydream ambitions to find humanity interrupting the rhapsody. He felt his dreams slipping through his fingers like the gravel skating down the ledges of this lost trail. He tried to focus on the path forward.

"Who do you want to be, man?" Whit thought about the question as Grins sat across from him, lifting the coffee mug to his mouth. "You want the white picket fence and the nine to five? I'm not seeing it. We're giving you a chance here."

"I recognize that," Whit, impatient with Grins's semi-threatening undertone, assured him.

"If you're going to go through with this, then we gotta go. They'll be waiting." Grins counted change and left it on the counter, getting up to leave. Whit rose and followed. They walked outside to Grins' car. As they got in and pulled out of the parking lot, Grins continued, "So the big graduate. You're probably juggling plenty of family this weekend."

"To say the least."

"Not going well?" Grins left the door open.

"No. I'm just saying goodbye to a lot."

It had been a year since their first meeting in New York, and Whit had seen progressively more of Grins since that time. Over that time, Whit had learned Grins was someone far different than he first thought. "You still ready to do this?"

"Of course."

"I promise you, you'll never look back."

"You haven't?"

"I haven't had time. I've been too busy serving my country." Whit was still too young and – he thought in retrospect – perhaps too naïve to grasp the way Grins was manipulating his convictions. "Look, we've talked about it. I never said it was going to be easy. But you're going to be part of a small group of elite. How many Americans can really be out there fighting for their country the way we're offering you the chance to do?"

Whit nodded and they were silent for the remainder of the drive. Eventually, the car shook wildly as Grins pulled off onto a gravel path. The path headed into the woods, where suddenly, seemingly from nowhere, a guard house stood overlooking the road. Grins slowed to a stop, showing his ID to the man who emerged. Whit looked at the small plaque on the guard's door, which read "Central Intelligence Agency."

"Whit," he felt a gentle hand on his shoulder, "Whit are you ok?" Recognizing again where they were, he looked upon Najwa.

"I'm sorry Najwa, I was . . . what did you say?"

"You said, last night when we were driving, you said you're not who we think you are. So I want to know, dammit, who are you?"

"Woa!" he exclaimed, laughing, "Maybe you should walk in front of me, it may not be safe to have my back to you."

She giggled, "Don't try to change the subject. You know what I mean. Who are you? You sweep in to some . . . horrible place. You have God knows who helping you, they come and go. You – you stay. Whit, are you an angel?" He laughed at the ridiculousness of it, until he realized that she believed in such things, a thought which sobered him.

"I wish I was, Najwa. I think I would have done some things differently."

"Well, I don't know what that means. All we've got is what we are. We can't change that."

"Certainly we can be better."

"Why do you always speak in puzzles?"

"What do you mean?"

"Every question you answer with some vague, I don't even know how to describe, some . . . what do you call it when you just miss getting hit by something?"

He laughed at her insight – grasping the concept – stripping him down to his elemental defenses without even knowing the word in English for it. "Dodge?" he said.

"Yes – exactly. You dodge. You think I don't notice, because you always ask mom how she's doing and she gets distracted when you complement her hummos. And you talk with dad about politics and he gets pissed about the Palestinians. You can play with Nadia and you can wrestle with Khalil. But me – me you can't dodge. I see it, every time you're at our house I watch you, Whit. It's like, I don't know, it's like you're always running."

There it was. The first time anyone had gotten to the core. Anyone, he realized, including himself. He was always running, and he didn't even know why.

"You want the truth, Najwa?"

"That's what I'm asking for."

"I'm in the CIA." She stopped. The donkey moved ahead and he turned to look at her, she stared at him in shock, and her chest slowly rose and dipped more rapidly. As she stood silently in the trail, he said, "Najwa, we can discuss this more – but we have to keep moving now." He turned to catch up with the donkey and Khalil, who still had not stirred.

For a time, they walked on, thoughts racing through their imagination like sparks jumping through dry chaff. The flames seared the cluttered madness so that only a few sturdy questions seemed to remain. For Whit it was a matter of survival. How would they make it to Joub Jannin by the morning? For Najwa, it was wonderment at what type of man walked this trail before her; and how he had lived so long in their midst as someone different than he seemed to be.

"So was any of it true?" she said. He stopped for a moment again and turned to her. "You, I mean. Any part of it true?"

"Certainly all of it that pertains to you and your family."

They walked on in silence. The occasional muffled sound would echo through the canyons, as the limestone burned a deep orange with the sun's repose lower on the horizon. The canyon grew cool, and they stopped briefly to eat and take a drink. Najwa was exhausted, and Khalil had awakened and began to speak. They took him off the donkey and sat him against a boulder. He ate on his own, but silently. Whit took out his map and reviewing it, said, "We're nearing the end of the canyon, which should drop us out on the Bekaa below. It's growing late – so I think we'll need to look for a place to sleep out the night and keep going early in the morning."

Khalil spoke first, "I think I want to walk. I can't ride this donkey any more."

"I'm so tired, Whit." Najwa said, "Can we stop here?"

"It's going to get cold and we'll need a fire, I'm afraid. If we stop, we could be trapped if anyone," Whit stopped for a second and continued, "if there is anyone coming from either direction. We also need to find a place where no one can see the fire."

Najwa perked up, "The caves – the caves the old man said, can we find them?" Whit raised his eyebrows at the thought.

"We'll have to try. Najwa, maybe you can ride the donkey for a while?"

She didn't hesitate, "Ok."

They continued onward for a while longer, and the canyon began to drop steeply, but Najwa said, "Look, it looks like it opens up just up there." Whit and Khalil couldn't see the opening from their lower vantage point until they reached the spot where Najwa sat atop the donkey. A devastating, primordial beauty broke upon them. The sun, low on the horizon, flooded a vast, rich plain with a warm light. Water snaking through the plane reflected in electric shimmers as far as they could see. Green rows unfurled from the mountains like a fertile blanket. Even the donkey seemed to strike an inexplicably reverent pose. Together, they beheld the glory.

"You know," Khalil spoke first, "my dad always says Bekaa was the Garden of Eden."

"Yeah?" Whit said.

"Yeah. He says Eve ruined it. But it sure looks amazing to me."

"Imagine it," Whit said, "if this is the ruined version – what a sight the real thing must have been."

After a few more minutes, Najwa started, "So, guys, how are we going to find this cave?" They looked to the left and right at a range of hills marked with various holes. Suddenly, as if he had understood, the donkey began moving, and turned left down a path they would not even have seen.

"Whiiit?" Najwa said hesitantly.

"No, let him go, let him go." Khalil said laughing.

"Heck," Whit said, "I guess he's been here before." They all laughed together as the donkey stepped around various crags and boulders confidently. After twenty minutes of walking, he turned left again down a decline that even Whit and Khalil had a hard time navigating.

Najwa leaned far back and nervously turned to Whit, but Khalil waived her on. Then, Whit saw a massive olive tree, and the donkey made a sharp right behind it, dropping a few feet and stopping where thick brush grew all about.

"Well, so much for his memory." Khalil shrugged. The donkey snorted.

"What do we do now?" Khalil said. Najwa jumped down as the donkey snorted again, and Khalil threw a rock. All stood bewildered as to their next move.

"Khalil," Najwa said.

"What?" Khalil said absent-mindedly, frustrated and scared.

As darkness finally ended the dusk's slow retreat, Najwa said, "Throw another rock where you threw the last one." He threw another rock into the brush, and they heard a small echoing sound. Whit shined a light on the brush, seeing a black hole large enough for the donkey and each of them to fit through. Whit grabbed the brush and pulled it back.

"I'll be damned," Whit said, "the old man was right. I'll go first." Whit shined his light in, and as he walked through, he spied a cluster of little spaces, probably three or four. At the back, there was a blackened wall and ceiling, and an opening in the ceiling. Whit ran back to the top.

"Let's get inside – it'll work for tonight. Khalil, can you grab some of that wood?" The donkey instinctively went to a place he had known and the three sat down in the farthest space. Whit began to pile the wood.

"No, no, that's not how you do it." Khalil stacked the wood in a teepee shape. He grabbed the lighter out of Whit's hand, and a small fire burst forth, illuminating the room. Najwa laughed profusely.

As they looked on at Khalil in disbelief, he said, "I've seen the westerns." They all laughed again, and leaned back against the rocks. Najwa was the first to fall asleep, and Khalil and Whit sat, looking at the fire. Whit tuned into the noises outside, but heard nothing but the wind. He hoped it would stay that way.

"You know, Whit, I think I've been pretty stupid."

"What do you mean?"

"Well, all this time, fighting with dad about the militia. After this . . . you know these last couple days, I think I see now what he has been trying to say all this time. I mean, I can't live like these guys. They, I mean, not just cause I'm scared. It's just, you know, I can't . . ."

He grew silent, and Whit sought to pull out his answer, hoping to solidify his reservations. "You can't what?"

"Well, it's just that, these guys . . . I mean, to do what they do . . . they just have to, they just have to live so . . . I don't know so pissed off all the time." The donkey stirred momentarily in the corner, and Whit focused on whether he could hear anything further outside. He couldn't.

"You were born in a rough country." Whit said, staring into the fire. Khalil was silent. "And Beirut is in a really bad situation right now."

"Really?"

"Fighting all over. Unless they can broker some sort of ceasefire," Whit shook his head, "this is going to descend into total chaos."

"So I guess he was right."

"Who?"

"Marius."

"About what?"

"Marius said it was coming. He said either we kill them or they kill us."

"Why do you hang out with his guys?"

Khalil shrugged. "He's right, isn't he?"

"Marius is a thug, Khalil. You know it. He's got guys selling drugs an-"

"I don't get involved with that."

"Yeah, not yet. But at some point he won't give you a choice." Silence again. The fire crackled in between their thoughts.

Khalil said softly, "We just need to get out of here." Whit saw Najwa's lips purse in a smile, though her eyes were closed. "But then I feel also like we'd just be running."

"You're not running away if you're meant to be somewhere better."

"Yeah. I guess so."

"Promise me something, Khalil." Khalil looked up at Whit, sensing the sobriety in the request.

"Of course. Anything."

"When we get back to Beirut, you make sure you help your dad get everyone out of here to the States."

"Well," Khalil paused, surprise registering upon his visage, "I don't know how we're going to do that. He's been trying for ye—"

"He'll find a way. After all this, he'll find a way. No matter what happens. You help him get everyone out." Khalil was frozen by a deep stare that Whit held, "Promise."

"Ok, Whit, I promise, I promise." They were silent a bit longer. Whit continued to stare. "Hey," Khalil said, laughing slightly, "if it does turn into chaos, I don't want to be here for it. You know something, Whit?"

"What?"

"I was thinking about what you said the other day, about the Bible and all."

Whit's eyebrows lifted involuntarily in surprise. He saw Najwa's eyes open, and was about to say something, but just barely out of the blanket, pulled to her chin, she slowly nudged her index finger to her mouth to silence him. Whit turned back to Khalil.

"Whaddaya you thinkin'?"

"Well, I went back and took a look at it." Khalil seemed to contemplate something in silence. In the distance, Whit thought he heard a helicopter, but could not tell the direction from which the sound came. He said nothing.

"Well the thing is, those first couple of lines. You told me about the other night – that there is darkness and chaos and then God creates the light and separates heaven and earth."

"Yeah?"

"Well, the thing is, it doesn't say it was good."

"What?" Whit was confused. "I could have sworn he saw that the light was good."

"No, he did. But . . ." Khalil held up his hands, as though trying to form a point. His brow furled as he looked through them into the fire. Najwa seemed to concentrate, as well.

"The second day, he separates heaven and earth. Every other day, he does something and sees that it was good. But that day, the second day when he separates them – it doesn't say it was good."

Whit leaned forward against his knees, forgetting the helicopter, forgetting the fedayeen and Sayyid, forgetting he was in Lebanon, or even in a place so foreign. On the precipice of Eden, outside, looking in.

"You know, I – I can't say I've ever read it closely enough to notice. I can't believe it," was all he could muster. Khalil leaned back against the rock and pulled his jacket over him. Whit stayed poised on his knees.

"Thank you for coming for us." Khalil choked up a little bit, but his eyes were closed. "I don't know how you did it, but thank you."

"Of course, brother."

"Man, when I saw you flash that light and knew it was you, I can't even tell you how I . . ." Khalil caught himself, then covered his face with his hands and started to cry.

"Well, buddy, no need to think about that now. Let's try and get some sleep."

Khalil quickly fell asleep. Whit stared into the flames. Najwa watched him as he looked into the light, wondering what it was that always kept him awake. He didn't notice that she watched as he rose and walked out towards the entrance to the cave, looking now into the darkness. Comfortable as she was, she drifted off to sleep.

--

Some time later, Khalil was shaken awake by Whit, who immediately held his fingers to his lips. The fire was extinguished, and Whit said, "I've gotta wake up your sister. I think there are fedayeen outside in the canyon. I heard someone yelling. Let's stay quiet." He handed Khalil a gun.

Whit moved over towards Najwa. Voices echoed through the canyon. She was stunned awake, and just as she almost yelled out, Whit covered her mouth and lay down next to her, pulling her to his side. She began to shudder with terror, and tears welled up in her eyes.

"We're going to be alright," he whispered, "but we gotta stay quiet." She had grown hysterical. He took his hand off her mouth and pulled his gun closer, but as he did so she began to sob, and he had to cover her mouth again and whispered forcefully, "Najwa, please." She calmed down, and they could see the occasional flashlight beam as they heard voices yelling back and forth. Whit could make out nothing specific.

Minutes seemed like hours as the lights swept across the foliage that masked their cave and then moved away. Voices were closer and then further away. The donkey rustled, and a light seemed to stop right on the cave's entrance. They all froze, including, somehow, the donkey, and were silent. Whit heard a hushed voice saying something, but he couldn't make it out, and a second light came towards the cave. Whit cocked his gun, and pointed it at the opening. He looked back at Khalil and nodded, who did the same.

Footsteps slowly scraped against the outer room.

Then, a loud whisper in English, "Whit? Whit? Are you there?" Whit looked back at Khalil, shocked, holding his hand up to stop any action by Khalil.

"Who is it or we'll shoot," Whit responded.

"Save it for later, brother, it's George!" Whit struck a match and saw the cherub looking face peek through the doorway with a huge smile. Najwa began to cry as Camille came through next.

"Well I never thought I'd be so glad to see you hooligans!" The group laughed and embraced.

"C'mon, we gotta get out of here before daylight," George said. "We've got a helicopter in Joub Jennin, but the fedayeen are patrolling the roads. We'll make it back fine through the fields, if we do it in the dark."

As they walked, Camille separated Whit from the group. "I know now is not the time, but wanted you to know in case we can piece this together quickly."

"What?"

"You asked me about the Port."

"Yeah. Find anything out?"

"There some sort of shell game going on down there with various accounts. I've never seen anything so sophisticated."

"What are you thinking?"

"I'm not sure yet, but no one here bothers covering their tracks this extensively. The money for the transfers traces back to an account at the Banque du Liban."

"The central bank?"

"Yeah - but no name associated with it. And it's quite the process to get from there to the final disbursement account that goes to the shipping company and we lose the trail there. Not the kind of thing we normally see here. You guys are going to have to get involved if you want any more."

"Ok, ok. We'll work on it when we get back."

Two hours later, a Huey lifted off the ground on the outskirts of Joub Jannin. From his spot near the open side, Whit could see the Bekaa stretching forth into the quiescent distance. He turned to watch Rafqa, who had come with George to help, on the opposite side of the helicopter. Khalil was leaning, semi-conscious against the rear wall of the passenger compartment. A long, black strand of Rafqa's hair danced gently in the breeze across her forehead and cheek as she knelt before Khalil, holding a cold compress against his face. She turned to look at Whit and shook her head in disbelief.

The moonlit Mediterranean and the Lebanese countryside, glowing silver, drifted past behind Rafqa. Her eyes settled not upon Whit, but within him, as though she was looking deep into his soul from a place similarly profound and sacred within hers. Her eyes communicated a vastness in which, just for an instant, he was lost. For that long moment, her eyes open and aglow, her hair drifting in the breeze, the mountains and the ocean flowing past, it seemed they were far removed from anything that could cause pain or anguish. They were far removed from Beirut. They were far from the conflict to which they were resolutely returning.

# CHAPTER THIRTY-FOUR

"How could you have let this happen?!"

"There were too many of them, Colonel, and they came from all sides." Sadiq looked suspiciously at Sayyid.

"And you were the only one of my men who survived?" Sayyid was silent in the face of Sadiq's hatred and disbelief.

"So we lost all the money and didn't get any of the guns?"

"They . . . there were too many of them. They took one of the trucks and the other one was destroyed."

"Who was it?"

"Some American spy was helping Musa. And there were others!"

"Who?"

"I don't know, Colonel. But we can go back and get . . ."

"Go back and what?"

"We can regroup with Keswani's men and find . . ."

"Have you not heard?!" Sadiq spoke with raised disdain. "Keswani has disappeared. You must not have stuck around to find out what happened to him. His men followed your American friend to Yanta. They think he has Keswani, but the Druze militia there fought them out of the town," Sadiq let the comment fester in Sayyid's bitterness. "They've got bigger problems now than helping us." Sadiq contemplated his options, "at least it is still chaos here. We may not need the guns right now. We'll find a way to get them back."

"What are we going to do, sir?"

"You mean what are you going to do?" Sayyid swallowed hard.

"The fighting is everywhere. They are going to have to reach out to Abou Ammar, if they haven't already, to try and make peace. We wait for that."

"How will we know?"

"The way we know everything you fool. Get in touch with Karim in the Deuxieme Bureau. Tell him we need to know as soon as he does. Once they set a place and we know the Prime Minister and the Generals are there – you'll take our men in there and we'll hit it with everything we've got."

Sayyid looked down, then back up, nodded and saluted, "Yes, sir," and began to leave.

"Oh, and Sayyid."

"Yes, sir."

"Don't ever fail me again."

# CHAPTER THIRTY-FIVE

Lining the streets, the women of Ayn al-Roummaneh ululated in piercing intervals. Signaling no coherent words, and formed when they made a high-pitched howl and beat their tongues rapidly against the roofs of their mouths, the noise was usually reserved for the spontaneous outburst of joy at a wedding or lamentation at a funeral. As the late afternoon crawled across the city, there was no shortage of joy and pain suitable for both.

George, at the head of the group traipsing down the middle of Ayn al-Roummaneh, held both Najwa and Khalil close. Boutros and Martha had come down from their apartment at the sound of the noise, and even from two blocks away could see their children and began running. The crowd embraced the family, the sound and their presence perfecting a simultaneous auditory and physical cocoon. The cocoon moved through the streets as people danced and clapped, rolling their way to a makeshift square that, out of nowhere, seemed to produce musicians and tables.

The streets simmered under the afternoon heat. The joy threw into sharp relief the suffering throughout the city, writhing now under a fifth consecutive day of conflict.

Whit sat drinking coffee in a second story café that overlooked the celebration. Across from him, nervously, sat Royce. He spoke quickly, like a man worried about the future, and the unwitting role he had played in this form of its arrival.

"What's he doing taking the credit?"

"It's not like we can, Royce. Besides, we're going to need friends. This is a down payment."

"Ok, whatever. We've got bigger things to worry about. It's all falling apart. Washington has called for us to evacuate all Americans." Whit's attention was drawn from the celebration to Royce's face.

"When?"

"The Marines are pulling in tonight. We're already getting the word out that people need to be down in the port by tomorrow."

"What's the situation in the city?"

"The fighting has completely closed the port, which means nothing is getting in or out . . ."

"What?!" Whit exclaimed, "If we can bring in the Marines, can't we provide security there?"

"We are not yet ready to engage, apparently. Vietnam. They aren't going to commit troops to anything except the most basic security operations for Americans." Whit nodded, understanding the quandary, though frustrated. "The city hasn't gotten any staples for nearly a week. But it gets worse – all public utilities have basically shutdown. In most of the city, no running water, no working sewage – hell, the UN thinks they've identified typhoid starting to spread in the camps."

"I can't see how we sit this out."

"That's where you come in, buddy. We won't pursue anything publicly, but we've been given the green light for . . . alternatives."

"What do they have in mind?"

"Well," Royce shifted uneasily, "we kind of thought, at this stage, you might know best."

Whit was stunned. It was his job to provide information, not ideas, but he had developed the latter. "Before we do anything drastic, we need to make one last attempt to settle this thing down and get the goods flowing again."

"How can we do it?"

Whit thought for a moment. "Through the Prime Minister – I . . . we did him a favor. And I can't imagine a scenario where he wants the fighting to continue, either."

"Favor? You mean taking out his competition?" Whit nodded. "What happened down there?"

"No time now. In any case – Kadir is probably down there somewhere in the crowd. I'll corner him. Tell him if he can get Ghanem to the table, we'll deliver Abou Ammar and the Army. Can you get both of them?"

"Yeah, I think so. We're getting word that even Abou Ammar thinks it has gotten out of control, and more importantly, he's not ready for an all out civil war." Royce had a sardonic smile, "I think he needs more time to arm. Also, too close to Jordan. They don't have the funds. Morale is bad. You name it. So I think we can get him."

"Maybe it's the perfect time to finish them off?"

"Yeah, we talked about it. You know as well as I do that it won't be that easy. If the military disintegrates, it's anybody's game."

"Yeah, yeah, I know."

"Oh, and you asked about the visas."

"I know, I know, couldn't do it."

"No, but I need something in exchange."

"I don't have anything that'll buy those."

"He's given you nothing?"

"We've got a strong lead down in the Port. It seems someone is funneling cash from an unmarked account at the central bank to a shipping company?"

"Seriously? Do we have details?"

"I've got sufficient leads to start working them, but we're going to have to work it on our own. They're insight is limited."

"How much money are we talking?"

"Enough to arm three-quarters of the militias."

"Jesus - how do we shut it down?"

"That's the easy part. The question is if we want to right now, or if that's going to just push them into a darker hole."

"Who is it?"

"Don't know yet. We've got more work to do."

Royce thought for a few moments, then slid an envelop across the table, Whit opened it to see the Khoury family's passports with U.S. visas, fully approved.

Whit looked confused, "I didn't think that would fit the bill."

"After...what happened yesterday, I told them I had to get these."

Royce leaned into the table, "Hey man, about yesterday . . ."

Whit shook him off before he even got started, "You don't need to explain, I understand."

"I know, it's just that, I want you to know I tried everything. I knew you'd be calling. It was . . . I don't know what to say."

"It's the game we're in, Royce. I knew that when I started."

They both took a drink and watched the dancers, Royce turning again, "Ok, well, there won't be much future here if we can't get them all to the table. So let me know when you get word."

"Got it."

"And your friends," Royce said, tapping the envelope, "get them down to the Port with the rest of the Americans and we'll get them out." Whit picked up the envelope, nodded and rose.

"Thanks, Royce." They exited the coffee shop and the music and dancing flooded across their senses. Whit worked his way through the crowd, looking for a familiar face. Grabbed intermittently by various women, then men, and spun about, the bright afternoon sun shown on faces laughing, sad, and both simultaneously. They laughed and danced through their pain. Maybe Najwa wasn't all that far off, Whit thought; maybe they still had to dance.

He passed a table with food and noted a few pieces of pita bread and a dish with hummos. He thought about eating. His body was confused by exhaustion. Then he noticed that no one was eating and no one was drinking the one bottle of wine on the table. He stepped away from the table back into the crowd. He saw Najwa and Khalil, sitting at different tables and talking with their friends.

Scanning the various groupings, Whit finally saw Kadir. Emin was next to him, looking miserable. Whit thought she must be ready to give birth any day. Then, as a few revelers moved and the music pounded, Whit felt a sudden burning in his chest. Rafqa sat at the table with them, speaking with Emin. Whit could not speak with Kadir in front of Emin and Rafqa, and hovered in the crowd until he caught Kadir's eye, nodding briefly to him. After a minute, Kadir appeared.

"I suppose I owe you, now?" Kadir's voice dripped with ironic frustration.

"I don't know what you're talking about."

"Yeah, well, you disappear from Boutros's house and within a couple of days my boss has a clear path to re-election and Boutros's kids miraculously return."

"Funny how life works like that sometimes."

"I don't get you, Whit."

"I've been hearing that a lot lately." Kadir looked back towards the table where Emin and Rafqa spoke, and noticed Rafqa was watching them.

"So what do you want?"

"I'm not coming for any favors." Whit looked across the dancing crowd as the shadows interrupted the light shimmering in his eyes. In his peripheral vision, he could see Kadir shift his weight.

"Your chances of re-election are golden, but then you need to get re-appointed as Prime Minister. I can help you improve those chances, too." Whit waited, watching the crowd, and as Kadir hesitated, Whit forced his hand by starting to walk away.

"Why is it that every time you come to me with something, I feel like I'm getting into a deeper hole?" Kadir asked.

Whit thought it was an appropriate question, but now was not the time for contemplation. They had no choices. "I guess I'm the guy who shows up when you've already run out of options."

"I'm not sure if that makes you good or bad."

"Does it really matter to you at this point?" Kadir said nothing, and Whit started again to walk away.

"No, wait." Kadir grimaced. "Let me hear it."

"It's time to get together and talk this thing through with Abou Ammar and the military."

"What makes you think Abou Ammar wants to do it?"

"He's not ready for war."

"So what? Maybe we'll just finish him off while we can."

"The military's on the verge of collapse, you told me yourself the other night."

Kadir turned this over in his head. "If we can do it in secret until it's over, I might be able to convince him to meet. We can't afford any public failures."

"I'll try, but you know with Abou Ammar that everything hits the press."

"This one we'll have to spin as our victory, not his."

"That depends on what you guys can negotiate – all we can do is get you to the table."

"If we can keep them on the status quo, then we can spin it as a win."

Whit grimaced. "You know where that heads. I know you have to do whatever it takes right now. I just think that Lebanon has given too much up already. We're seeing it now, the status quo is unsustainable."

"Maybe we can hang on while we find a way to work something out."

"Maybe – but where else do they have left to go?"

"I'm bringing a child into this mess, Whit. Believe me, it is the only thing I think about these days. When and where?"

"We'll get word to you. My guess is you'll have only a matter of hours to close it before others converge on wherever you do this – so you better tell your boss to be prepared to talk fast."

"Who do we think we'll be up against?"

"Hard to say . . ."

"Ah, your mysterious third force."

Whit shook his head. "We know the PFLP will show up for the party. Given the general spread of the fighting, it's not clear how many others will be willing to take it all the way." They both watched the revelers silently for a moment. "Oh, Kadir, it doesn't matter much now, but . . ." Whit removed the set of documents Shlomo had given him in the Arqoub. Kadir, unfolding them, perused them for a few moments, then looked at Whit, stunned.

"Where did you get these, these are highly secret. . ."

"Where do you think?"

"Oh my God. They have his whole schedule. Every day. Every place he'll be. Who he'll be with. Security details. Everything. How could they get this?"

"Someone's gotta be on the inside." Kadir nodded, folded the documents and put them in his pocket. Kadir extended his hand to Whit, who took it and shook it in turn.

"Now if you'll excuse me, there is a beautiful doctor who owes me a dance." Kadir smiled and let go of Whit's hand. He waited as Whit walked over to the table. He watched as Whit greeted Emin and Rafqa, and Rafqa jumped up to hug him so excitedly that Kadir was taken aback by her display of emotion. He watched as the two walked out onto the dance floor as a slower song started, and Rafqa held her arms over Whit's shoulders, clasping her hands behind Whit's neck. He watched the way Whit looked at her, and held his arms around the small of her back. He watched the two move gently to the music, and realized that Whit had given something to her that no one else in Beirut had received: his trust. He watched.

# CHAPTER THIRTY-SIX

Hours later, Whit was sitting in Gaspar Vartabed's church, leafing through the Book of Daniel. It was a Latin translation of the Bible, so Whit could make out little of what it said. He searched for the strange words, but found them nowhere. After five minutes or so, he set the Bible down, but open, and closed his eyes.

"I don't mean to interrupt." Gaspard Vartabed's voice was gentle, but broke Whit's reverie.

As Whit regained his awareness, he responded, "No, not at all, please sit down." Aside from the priest and the host in the tabernacle behind the altar, the Church was devoid of any human presence. "You look tired, Vartabed, are you ok?"

"Yes, yes. It was just a long day. How are you, Whit?"

"Fine. I . . . wanted to stop by to show you something." Whit removed the paper from his pocket on which he had scrawled the letters that had been carved into the bleeding man's chest. The priest took them from him, and raised his eyebrows as he read it.

"Well, they are from the Book of Daniel." Then the priest looked at Whit's Bible, noticing it was open to Daniel. "But you seem to know this?"

"Well, I can't find it."

"Yes, they're from a strange story. King Belshazaar had a banquet, and the King's court brought out the sacred possessions of the Jewish people who were in exile, using them for the banquet and violating their sacred nature. But the King, suddenly, sees a hand – just a hand, no person, writing on a wall." The priest motioned, as if holding a pen and writing some imaginary message.

"It writes several things, but not in the King's language, so he calls forth Daniel, a Jewish servant, to interpret. There were just three words on the wall, but Daniel interprets them as words with fuller messages. He explains that the message is from God to the King and his Court, a Court of sinners, as the case may be. These symbols you have written are one of the words Daniel interprets." The priest looked at Whit, whom he could tell was not yet satisfied.

"How did Daniel interpret it?" They were silent for a moment.

"Daniel interpreted the symbols as the word tekel, which he said means, 'You have been weighed on the scales, and found wanting.'"

Whit felt as though his stomach had been pierced with a hot iron and his doubt erupted like a volcanic plume, searing that place inside where emotions had a physical presence. Gaspar Vartabed could see Whit's pain, having seen it in so many faces in so many ways – a loss of orientation magnified by man's ceaseless questioning. How fine the line was, he thought, between despair and triumph. Man could never really find his way to God without questioning; but too much questioning, and he could lose himself in the thicket.

"Where did this come from?"

"You'll think I'm crazy." But he saw the way the priest looked at him, inviting him to speak. "You know the man that you are . . . helping?"

The priest thought, and replied, "I'm afraid you'll have to narrow . . ."

"I mean the possessed man – with the bleeding chest . . ."

"Oh yes. This is from him?"

"I guess so." Whit said hesitantly, hardly believing his own story, "I've seen him other places. I mean, just strange situations, almost as if they were dreams, but real."

Gaspar Vartabed nodded without speaking.

"And, you saw," Whit continued, "he's frequently . . . bleeding."

"Yes."

"Well, I thought back and . . . just wrote down what I had seen. The different cuts, that is. This was their shape."

The priest looked down at the Bible again, "Do you think this was meant for you?"

"Maybe not, but . . ." Whit grew quiet.

"But what?"

"The most recent time I saw him – it was, there was just no other way. It had to be for me. There was no one else around. It was . . . haunting."

"Whit, this man is possessed by demons."

"Yes."

"Scripture tells us that their master is the father of lies."

Whit nodded slowly.

"Jesus tells us that there is no truth in the devil."

Whit peered towards the altar, leaning forward with his elbows on his knees and his chin resting on his thumbs, his mouth touching his knuckles.

"So, you cannot listen to what he says, even if it is something that sounds true. That is precisely how he works. He speaks in half truths, to tempt you into confusion."

Whit continued slowly nodding.

"He takes the truth, and twists it, so that a lie feels familiar, but works evil within you."

"But it's almost as though he saw something true in me, and took it a little further – maybe something I couldn't see."

"He plays on the fears and emotions that all of us have. He plays on our confusions, and our questions, and our anxieties. That is how he works – he knows man well, because he tempts him in the deepest recesses of his being. The evil one will never communicate God's truth to you, Whit, there is no truth in him." The priest paused, then continued, "The devil lies to keep us from God. Evil speaks a message without hope, and without hope we despair, and despair is the greatest stumbling block of all. If one speaks a message without hope, then what he speaks is from the evil one."

Suddenly, Whit remembered the first night when he had seen this man. He remembered what he had said, "Do not hope."

"How do we know the truth, Father, when so much is wrapped in lies?"

"Because there is life in it, Whit. And because there is hope."

The priest, seeing Whit nodding, smiled and looked towards the altar. Whit checked his watch.

"I've got to go, Father, can I use your phone?"

"Of course."

# CHAPTER THIRTY-SEVEN

Farouk adjusted his spectacles and paced back and forth in the darkened room. "You couldn't get anyone in Yanta to tell you whether he was there?"

"All they would say was that they didn't see him," Marduk, Keswani's old companion from Roumieh, now free, said to Farouk.

"So at this moment, he is completely gone, and we have absolutely no idea where he is?"

Marduk shook his head. "Whoever went into the camp really had some firepower. The whole thing is destroyed – there is not a stone left standing."

"And no one left to tell us who was there?"

"No. Our guy in Yanta just tells us he saw one man with the boy and the girl. That's it, he can't even describe him that well."

"I don't care how long it takes us. We have to find out who this man is. Did our guy tell us anyone in Yanta they had contact with?"

"Yeah – but how the heck can we get to him?"

"We have to find a way."

"That much firepower, Mister Farouk. It had to have been the Israelis. If they have hi--"

"Find this guy in Yanta!"

"And what about our plans for the Prime Minister? We've been on him for months."

"Dammit! It doesn't matter what happens to the Prime Minister until we find Jawad."

"Yes, sir."

# CHAPTER THIRTY-EIGHT

Boutros held the passports in his hand, leafing through them one by one, seeing one by one a lifetime of possibility unfurling before his children. The possibilities ran wild through his imagination. Hope, like dawn's light, flooded, at first hesitantly, and then unbound, across the long forlorn plains of his heart. His eyes began to moisten as excited anticipation, an emotion he had not known for so long, filled his heart.

"I don't . . . I don't know what to say."

"Say nothing," Whit said. "Just go."

"Of course. This . . . is . . . what we've wanted for so long." He spoke, disbelieving the reality that was settling upon him. "Of course we'll go." He spoke in a baffled tone. "The airport is shut down.  I . . . I am not sure how right now . . ."

"Could you be ready to go tonight?"

Boutros laughed, and then sobered quickly as he saw Whit wasn't joking.

Whit continued. "I know with certainty I can get you out tonight. After that, I can't make any promises. With the fighting, there's no telling when the airport will reopen and . . . I can't provide any tickets to the U.S. from there." Boutros raised his arms, clasping his hands together behind his head.

"It is time, Whit. We will be ready." They sat silently as the smell of coffee wafted around them.

"Najwa told me, Whit. About what you did." Whit waived his hand, as if dismissing it.

"No, I know you can't talk about it. But I want you to know . . ." Whit held up his hand again, pleading without words.

"Whit you have to know how . . . It means everything to us. You mean everything. I don't know why you've done all this for us. I don't understand it at all. But . . ." a tear rolled down his cheek as he laughed with embarrassment, "Thank you. It's so inadequate. But thank you."

"Not inadequate at all," Whit said in a somber tone.

"Najwa told me . . . everything else . . . about you." Whit stared grimly at Boutros, who shifted uneasily.

"I mean, you . . . we don't need to talk about it. I just don't understand."

Moments past. "Understand what?"

"C'mon, Whit. I've been around long enough in Beirut to know no one in . . . your profession . . .does anything without a reason."

"I have my reasons."

"What? You have asked nothing of me."

"I didn't want anything from you."

"I owe you now, at least, that is for sure."

"Nothing," Whit raised his voice. "You owe me nothing but what you have already given me."

"But what on earth is that?"

Whit pushed his coffee away, shaking his head in disbelief. "I guess I didn't expect you to be such a good man, Boutros."

"What is that worth?"

"More than you know."

Boutros let the look of confusion ease from his face, though he didn't understand, he accepted it and refocused. "What are you going to do next, Whit?"

"Well," Whit leaned back in his chair uneasily as he rubbed his hands briefly on his thighs. "I have to stay here . . ."

"What?!" Boutros said, incredulously. "Why?"

The corners of Whit's mouth pursed in consideration, "I started something that I need to finish."

"Whit, as your friend, I just want what's best for you. Is that really here?"

"You know," Whit said, looking again out the window, having difficulty making eye contact, " . . . sometimes I look back and it's as if I'm standing on a mountain and can see a long spider web of pathways stretching back into the distance. There are all these decisions – forks in the road – along the way. Sometimes I wonder if I took the right ones."

"Or the right one, in particular?"

"Yeah, the right one. Do you ever think about that?"

After a brief moment, Boutros blurted, "No!" They laughed at his certainty and sat silently for a few moments longer, then Boutros continued, "A week or so ago, you told me about that scripture passage. Pilate asked Christ, what is truth?"

"Yeah."

"If I remember correctly, before that Christ said, 'I came to testify to the truth.'"

"Yeah."

"I may be a simple man, but I just think you don't have one path through life and either you hit it, or you miss it. Every decision you make – your life either testifies to the truth, or it doesn't."

Whit nodded, considering it. "Well – I guess you better get home and testify." They exchanged a smile. Whit dropped money on the table.

"You can come inside and show everyo - "

"No," Boutros was startled by Whit's sudden retort. "No, this is your victory."

"No, Whit, I insist, you –"

"Please – you earned this for them."

Boutros closed his mouth, shaking his head again.

"But, if you'll permit me just to hang outside. I just, I just want to hear them." Boutros felt pity for this young man whom he thought he knew, but whom he realized was still so alone.

"Of course, Whit, of course."

They walked the few short blocks back to the Khoury's apartment. "We are evacuating with the Americans tonight – I need to get you on that boat. From there you'll get to Cyprus and there will be flights to the States. I'll call you tonight. I don't know what time yet."

"Ok. Ok. We will start getting ready immediately."

They embraced at the house, and Boutros hesitated.

"I'll see you tonight, Boutros."

"Ok," he said, "oh and Whit,"

"Yes."

"I saw Kadir when I was leaving to meet you." Whit's curiosity was heightened.

"Oh yeah?"

"I told him I was going to see you. He said you had asked him some question. He told me to tell you that that the answer is yes." Whit smiled, and gently patted Boutros' shoulder, "Get inside," Whit said, laughing. Boutros turned and bound up the stairs.

Whit leaned on the wall outside. From there he could hear Boutros scream "I'm home and have a present, everyone come around the table." Whit stepped away from the wall and crossed the corner where he could see the family huddled over their kitchen table. Boutros pulled the paper bag out. "Everyone close your eyes." As they did, Boutros situated each Khoury's passport in front of them, opening it to the visa page.

"Ok – open your eyes." Nadia screamed first, "VISAS!!!!" The family broke out in a jubilant cry, hugging one another.

Boutros looked towards the street and his family's reflection in the glass caught his eye. Through the reflection he could see the outline of Whit's figure outside, walking into the distance. He held up his hand, unbeknownst to the rest. Whit stopped for a moment, held up his hand, then turned, continuing on into the darkness.

# CHAPTER THIRTY-NINE

Whit decided to leave his car near Boutros' home and continue walking. He walked through the city, but once outside Ayn al-Roummaneh, felt he was traversing a bizarre carnival where only the evil came out to play. The city had transformed into a hate-filled hollow of dark spirits who prayed on the weakness of mankind.

Whit could hear screams in the distance; then suddenly, nearby. Faces, lit intermittently by explosions flashing across the windows, were distorted with envy, doubt, and fear. Gunfire rang out, echoing off the walls of the buildings. Whit passed one street where tires burned, but the street sat empty, except for one, solitary man who lay dead on the ground. A pack of stray dogs ran across the road in front of him. The wind, cruel and relentless, offered no quarter as it beat mercilessly against Whit's face. Even the ocean roared in the distant darkness, unseen yet taunting those ashore in its unfathomable power.

As Whit arrived at Jerome's Bakery, its glass facade reflected flashes across the Beirut skyline that lit the low-hanging clouds. He walked to the door and gave two quick taps, waited two seconds, and gave two more quick taps. The door opened, but no one was behind it. Whit walked to a second door, removed a key from his pocket and opened it. Behind it a room bustled with people running back and forth.

Royce emerged from the thick, "Thank God you're ok. I shouldn't have let you come – it's chaos. The Marines are already hitting the shore. We're trying to get everyone out before dawn." Whit started forward, checking his watch quickly, but froze as Royce continued.

"But they've set us on a collision course. They landed on the western shore because of all the stalled boats blocking the harbor." Royce was speaking quickly and nervously as he walked Whit hastily to a room in the back. No one in the room said a word to him besides Royce. As the door shut behind him, Whit began to speak.

"Why is that a problem?

"We got Abou Ammar and the General to the table, but we already agreed to meet at the Melkart." Whit grimaced. The Melkart was right on the water by the western shore.

"I heard from the Prime Minister's people. They're ready to meet. What's the plan?"

Royce swung a chalk board around with a map of the city, and pointed at a spot where numerous roads met in a hub and spoke pattern.

"Are you sure you want to go there?"

"It's the most neutral ground we could find."

"Yeah, which is its biggest problem. It's fairly accessible from virtually every direction in the city." Whit put his finger on Tal Za'atar and traced a line to the Square, "There are several different roads leading straight to it from various quarters. The fedayeen will come from here." He picked a spot in Ayn al-Roummaneh and drew another invisible line with a few moves, "The Christians will come from here," drawing two invisible lines quickly he said, "the military is likely to come from here and here," and another line, "Add the Marines into the mix . . ."

"Yeah, yeah, we see it. We just don't have a choice."

"Let's just hope the Marines are out by that time. Otherwise we're going to get further drawn into this."

"Are we front-running the agreement terms so there are no surprises?"

"Yes," said Royce, handing an envelope to Whit. "This is the draft terms the General and Abou Ammar have received. We just sent one off to the Prime Minister."

"Alright, I'll be out there. The only way to keep it all from falling apart is to either hold off fire, or isolate and overwhelm the fringe fedayeen groups that are going to try to turn it over."

"And your third force?"

"I can only fight the enemy I can see." But Whit was visibly frustrated.

"Anyway, most of the PFLP got away. We've been getting reports of random acts, and then all hell will break loose in a given district. Name any one. The army finishes putting out that fire and then something blows up somewhere else. All day, every day." The two stood for a moment, looking at the map.

"Whit – you know – you don't have to be down there. This is on them if they can't hold the Melkart long enough."

"No. This is the chance. Besides, I've got other reasons to be down there now, anyway.

"You gotta get your friends down to the Marines?"

Whit nodded.

"They must be some special friends."

"That family, Royce, is the only thing that makes sense in all this."

"There's lots a families out there."

"All the more reason we can't give up on them."

"So you going to drag them right into the middle of hell?"

Whit laughed, shaking his head.

"What?" Royce pressed.

Whit spoke, but quietly, staring at the map. "I didn't say it was good."

"That's for sure."

"But it's their only way out of it."

"Yeah, well, at this point, it's the only way out of it for all of us. And another thing, you better go get whoever it is you get – and keep the PFLP from lighting a fire to the hotel."

"You don't think the military can handle it?"

"If they can't – and the fedayeen overrun the Melkart, do you think Lebanon can deal with the fallout?"

"If the military can't handle it and the militias get involved now – I guess I'm not sure what the difference will be."

"Maybe," Royce said, shaking his head, "but you're going to need everybody on your side you can find."

"Alright – do you have another car I can use to get back to my place. I left mine a ways away because of the situation."

Royce tossed some keys to Whit, "The old BMW a block down on the left." Whit nodded, and reached out his hand to Royce, who took it, shaking briefly. Royce watched as Whit walked to the door without speaking with anyone. After the door closed behind Whit. Royce threw his pen against the wall in frustration and looked at the map for a moment more. He checked his watch and went back into the bustling, open room.

# CHAPTER FORTY

Sayyid took the receiver from the young foot soldier, "Yes, what do you have?" He waited, nodding his head. "You're absolutely sure?" He waited a few moments longer and hung up. Turning to the group in the room, "Alright, get everything we have. They're meeting at the Melkart. Bashar, you take a group on the East side. I'll go at it from the West."

The men all turned and ran outside. They piled into cars and started off in one direction. Sayyid hopped on his motorcycle, and additional cars followed him the opposite way.

# CHAPTER FORTY-ONE

The Khoury's were packed when Whit arrived. Najwa opened the door, and seeing Whit, embraced him, refusing to let go.

"Are you going to come with us?" she asked. Before he could respond, Martha was beside them, "Whit, isn't it wonderful? Isn't it wonderful? Did you know about this?!"

Whit looked back into the room where Boutros stood with the rest of the family, "Only when Boutros called me to drive you guys. It is so wonderful, I hardly know what to say." Nadia sprinted towards him and jumped into his arms, "You are going to love America, little girl."

"Whit, is it true that the kids eat cotton candy for breakfast there?"

"Only the ones who walk around turning purple with really bad stomach aches, my little beautiful," she giggled and dropped down to sprint to her room.

Then, seemingly out of nowhere, they heard a wild, female scream. Martha grabbed Whit's arm as she turned to Boutros, "That's Emin." Martha turned and ran out the door and down the hallway.

"You all stay here. We'll be back." Boutros went after her and Whit closed the door behind. Najwa turned to Whit, "Mama said Emin's baby hasn't turned yet, and she could be in real trouble." Whit nodded and asked, "How is Khalil doing?"

"He's ok, but still really tired. He went to bed an hour ago just to have energy for . . . the trip."

Boutros burst into the room, "We have to get her to the hospital."

Whit turned towards Boutros, "I've been out tonight – the city is a wasteland."

"Martha thinks if we don't get her there, she could die."

"Ok – let me think – we may not have enough gas to get to the hospital and the port." They looked at one another. Another scream followed.

"Alright, Najwa, you stay here with Khalil and Nadia."

"No, I…" and Whit and Boutros both stared at her simultaneously.

"Honey, after all that has happened," Boutros said, "you have to stay safe."

"We'll be back," Whit followed.

She looked down. "Ok."

Kadir and Boutros carried Emin out the door of the apartment building as Whit opened the rear door of the car. They sped through the streets and at the hospital Whit got out and ran around the car. Boutros and Kadir lifted Emin inside to the waiting room and disappeared around the corner once they got inside. After a few moments, Kadir emerged from a side room with Emin in a bed and several doctors walking with them. Then, at the end of the group, Rafqa emerged. She stopped upon seeing Whit, smiling a little, then turned with a determined focus down the hall.

Boutros, Martha, and Whit stood and watched the group move forward.

A few minutes later, Kadir entered and asked them to come back to the room. But Whit stayed seated as Boutros and Martha rose and Martha walked down the hall without further word.

"You, too, Whit." Whit rose and the three men walked down the hall. Kadir ran ahead as another scream emerged from Emin's room.

Walking in, Whit could see Rafqa working fervently. She had her hands on Emin's stomach and was pushing aggressively. Emin screamed as Rafqa pushed. Emin sweat profusely, her hair sticking to her forehead and sprung about, evidencing the pain. Martha whispered to Whit, "It's pretty bad for both the child and Emin. She's lost a lot of blood, and the baby still hasn't turned."

Kadir watched helplessly as nurses ran in and out of the room.

Then, as if a sinister plot had been hatched against the birth of this child, and in the midst of Emin sitting nearly straight up in the bed and screaming, the electricity in the entire hospital failed. Emin screamed again, and Whit vaguely made out through the darkness Rafqa closing her eyes, placing her hands in a different position. Then she spoke calmly and directly.

"Don't give up now Emin – we are almost there. Start pushing when I tell you, Emin, in three, two, one . . ." Emin screamed as Rafqa, eyes still closed, moved the child, inch by inch, from the side, to a position facing directly downward within the womb.

"Kadir, stand there so her right leg is on your side, and Martha, here on the left." Rafqa moved to the end of the bed directly in line with Emin and pushed her legs up onto Kadir and Martha. Whit saw Kadir stumble as blood surged forth from Emin, and Boutros moved quickly towards Kadir as he began to faint. Whit slid over and grabbed Kadir first and Boutros, responding quickly, moved up to support Emin's leg. Whit set Kadir down on a chair and a nurse came immediately with smelling salts. When Whit saw her approaching, he moved back to his original spot near the door. Kadir came to, and immediately got back up to Emin's side.

"Push again, Emin," Rafqa said hurriedly as Martha held Emin's hand and Kadir replaced Boutros. Emin screamed. "Push again," she said and another scream followed. Whit's view was obstructed, but he was watching Rafqa. Whit watched as Rafqa focused on bringing forth one life and saving another. Through the darkness he watched the movement of her body, determined to succeed.

Lightning flashed again, momentarily electrifying the room, and at the end of one, prolonged scream, Whit thought he discerned another. Out of the darkness, a baby's cry ushered forth again, and Rafqa pulled to her chest a crying child, soaked in the blood of her heritage.

Rafqa handed the baby to Kadir. He was shaking with the joy that only parents can know, but which they can never properly express to another. Some things in life cannot be explained, only experienced. He shook as he took the baby the few feet to Emin's outstretched hands, and her high-pitched utterance, indecipherable as a word but communicating so clearly the resonant joy coursing through her veins, filled the room. Lightning flashed outside and the couple embraced their child as nurses wiped the baby clean and tended to Emin.

After a few more minutes, Rafqa stepped back, as well. She wiped her hands on a towel and turned and stared at Whit. Simultaneously, the room was lit with an electric glow that seemed to resonate from her eyes as much as from the rain-soaked wilderness beyond the window. A tremulous aura surged forth from her like the fire of God descending upon Whit, searing every unwholesome corner of his being until the only remnant was a naked, unspoiled innocence.

Whit turned into the hallway, and walked slowly away. He walked until he came to a series of glass windows facing into an internal room, and as he approached it, he could see clearly it was the nursery. The soft lights there that must have been hooked up to a backup generator, left tiny faces, hands and feet intermittently discernible in bassinets spread throughout the room. Whit lifted his hands to the glass as if to touch one child sleeping just beneath the window. The child was hooked to tubes and appeared more vulnerable than the others.

Whit's mind buzzed in contemplation. What is man, born of woman, that he, from birth, must struggle with his very nature? What truth resonates within him that, deprived of it in its purest form, he spends his life trying to find it? Why, so deeply imbued with that truth, do we still find it so elusive, so difficult to grasp?

As Whit watched, the baby opened his eyes, and looked straight at Whit.

Whit felt a hand clasp his arm just a few inches above his elbow, and he turned to see Rafqa, looking at the baby beside him.

"Are they ok?"

"They are going to be just fine – Kadir may be the worst off." Whit smiled, but lost the grin when he turned back to the child.

"What's wrong with him?" Whit asked tapping the glass as the child moved his head in recognition.

"The same thing that's wrong with all of us, I guess," she said as she leaned her head against Whit's shoulder.

"What's that?" Whit asked.

"Hard to say, Whit. Something he got from his parents." Whit shifted his hand so that it sat against the glass in its entirety, rather than merely his fingertips. "If I could heal him, I would."

"You can, Rafqa. Just like you saved Emin and their child"

"No, I. . . ," she paused, uncertain how to respond.

"Watching you in there with Emin . . . what you have is a gift, Rafqa. My God, it's amazing. You're just, you are so . . . beautiful." Rafqa squeezed his arm tighter. "Rafqa – "

"Yes?"

"This is where you're meant to be. This whole nation may come crashing down upon you, but you have to choose this. You know, choose . . . life."

She stared at the child. "It's happening tomorrow, isn't it?" Whit stared at the child, too.

He was silent for a moment, as his hand slid so only the fingertips again were on the glass.

"What will you choose, Whit?" He said nothing, and she continued. "You don't have to do this either. We can . . ." He looked at her and she grew quiet, these two uncharacteristically fierce personalities humbled by one another's presence. "We can both choose life." He nodded slowly, still not speaking. He turned to the child.

As he began to open his mouth, light flooded the hallway. Almost instantaneously, a nurse emerged from the room further down the hall shouting, "Doctor, doctor." Rafqa was startled, but looked back at Whit, waiting for him to speak.

"You better go." Her eyes reddened as she walked and then jogged away. Before she entered the room, she turned back to look at Whit and saw him with his hand still placed on the window, staring down at the child. A tear rolled down her cheek as she entered the room. He looked up towards her in just enough time to see her disappear.

--

Across Beirut the people prepared for the gathering storm. George, Camille and Col. Chartouni stood in the square near the Melkart and directed men to various nearby emplacements. On the shores, boats carrying United States Marines landed. The Marines fanned out across the coast and cordoned off a section, erecting barriers. Royce emerged from the night and shook the hand of the squadron leader. In the streets outside the Melkart, Musa Rasoul and Salman ducked behind a car, exchanging fire with a group in the darkness. Sayyid sped through the same streets, firing his gun wildly and directing various fedayeen to take positions and fire on the Melkart from different vantage points.

The storm-ridden Mediterranean shorelines, crawling with Marines, fedayeen, militias, and the innocents, were a mirror of human time. The faces and the names changed. The story remained the same. The story is one of man's unceasing effort to conquer himself. And God moves swiftly over the waters.

# CHAPTER FORTY-TWO

It was still dark when the family struggled down the stairs with their belongings. The women got in the car, and Whit pulled Boutros and Khalil aside before shutting the door.

"Guys," Whit said to Boutros and Khalil, "the plan has changed a little bit." In the distance, down towards the water, gunfire and flashes of light exploded throughout the city. Boutros and Khalil exchanged glances and looked intently at Whit. "The Marines have been pulled into firefights. They are picking people up near the Melkart Hotel, but it's gotten pretty bad there. It's going to be . . . incredibly dangerous to get down there."

"How are we going to get through the fighting?" Boutros asked. The three were silent for a moment, and Khalil kicked an imaginary rock on the ground, then looked up.

"Today's our chance, Whit. You said it yourself. This is all we've got."

They all looked towards the explosions in the distance, and the one by one, hopped into the car. Whit occupied the driver's seat and revved the engine, tearing out into the street. For the first several blocks there were only the occasional onlookers, waiting aimlessly for some uncertain fate to come closing in upon them. Then, as an open street came briefly within view on the left, out of the corner of his eye, Whit captured a snapshot of a group of fedayeen youth sitting on top of a pick up truck half a block down. Though he was past the block too quickly to see it, he new instinctively what would happen. The youth, though not knowing for what or after whom, decided to give chase. They piled into the rear and cabin of the truck and jolted forward in chaotic pursuit.

Whit oriented himself towards the flashes of light erupting in the distance, but Boutros took over, shouting directions as Whit rushed through the streets.

"Left here!" he yelled as the whole family pressed against one another. After ripping around the corner, Whit could see the pick-up truck veer wildly in hot pursuit. One of the fedayeen almost fell off, and the group pulled him back on. The youth fired wildly.

As they wound through the streets, the Khourys ducking in fear, Boutros guiding Whit down towards the coast, the fedayeen flailing along behind them, Whit noticed something strange. The youth weren't really firing at his car, they just fired their weapons into the dark night. They hit buildings, cars, and light posts. They seemed to hit everything except the family's car. Hurtling through the streets of Beirut, they fired without aiming; and pursued without any sense of conviction. Indeed, as the cacophony of explosions around the Melkart neared, and the sonorous, evil hymns of violence grew close enough to rattle the windows of the car, the fedayeen car began to slow.

Moving along the streets now more smoothly, Whit beheld in the rear view mirror an apparition of fear and uncertainty. The youth stared ahead of him, their terror filled faces lit by the occasional flare launched into the night sky. They stopped firing. They grew more distant as their car slowed down, and eventually Whit realized they had given up the chase. He drove towards the vast, impenetrable darkness ahead. The car grew silent as its inhabitants, filled with fear, wandered whether there would emerge from the darkness alive.

Whit could see the Melkart's dark outline in the flashing night. In the distance lay the coast. A Marine ship sent forth a series of flares that exploded in the air, lighting the coast and the surrounding city block for a half a minute or more as clusters descended gracefully from their peak. As its warmth faded, the faces of all the Khoury's, whom Whit turned to check, looked bemused, crestfallen, and desperate. Panning the vacant streets into which he now silently rolled, Whit saw movement coming from the right side of the car. Then, he saw three flashes of light. He turned to Khalil.

"Quick a flashlight."

"Yes." Khalil scrambled.

"Quick. Flash it three times out the window. Hurry." Khalil fumbled through his bag, and Whit saw three more flashes of light.

"Hurry, Khalil." Khalil found the flashlight and shined it out the window three times.

"What's going on?"

"Just wait."

From the darkness, a figure moved swiftly towards the right side of the car and slammed into the side, sliding down to his knees, looking around wildly underneath a large helmet. Martha embraced the girls in the back, and all gave a shocked utterance as the figure, whom Whit could clearly make out as a Marine, tapped on the window. Whit motioned for Boutros to roll the window down.

"What are you doing here?" Whit said calmly.

"Americans?"

"Yes, I'm with the Embassy. What's your name?"

"Captain Carole, sir. You guys gotta get out of here. We've been pinned down in a firefight. The rest of our platoon got out with the civies and are probably out on the boat."

"Are they coming for you?"

"Hell if I know, sir – we lost contact when they blew up our radio." The man nervously glanced in front and behind the car, as if he was expecting fire any moment.

"I've got a weapon. Your guys and I will flank the car on foot and make our way up to that building," Whit said, pointing towards the Melkart.

"I don't know sir, we've been fighting in these streets for hours and that hotel seems to be the focal point of a lot of sh-," he stopped himself, noticing the rest of the family in the back for the first time, "a lot of firepower."

"It's the only place where we can regroup and try and get contact with your guys, Captain."

"Ok, sir."

Whit turned to the family. "Ok guys. Your dad is going to drive," they all nodded. "Khalil, take this gun," Whit said, handing him his gun, "You do whatever you guys have to do to get through to the Melkart and then down to the water." Whit said as he pointed out into the darkness.

"Whit, we're not going without you," Najwa said.

Whit looked briefly, then hopped out of the car, pulling a small machine gun from under the driver's seat. He shut the door as Boutros slid over. The group started moving slowly. Khalil slid into the front and slapped Boutros on the shoulder with confidence.

The streets were strewn with the dead, the flashing light intermittently revealing faces, hands, and legs. On one body, Whit saw something familiar, though he couldn't immediately place it. It was only moments later that the image crystallized in his mind. The watch on the dead body – a red Kiple – glimmered faintly under the moonlight.

They jogged on into the darkness. Whit couldn't be certain if he was witnessing reality or some distorted vision of future chaos. Nothing visible, save this small band, was alive. Most of the dead appeared to be fedayeen. Bodies were laying across the curbs, leaning against walls, hunched against one another, strewn in one last pantomime of agonized shock. Death animated this dark roadway, haunting Whit with an awful, sentient sense as much premonition as memory.

Gunfire grew more audible as they neared the Melkart, now three blocks away. Suddenly, the right side of the Khoury's car lit up in sparks when a few shots broached its side. The Khoury women screamed and the Marines on that side dropped and began firing at a fedayeen position some fifteen yards down the block in the darkness. Whit motioned for Boutros to stop, but the oncoming fire had already ceased.

Whit signaled for the Marines to move forward and held out his hand for Boutros to hold. Then, his heart stopped cold as he suddenly heard a pleading, familiar voice from behind a burnt out shell of a car towards which the Marines had fired. They moved in towards it, and Whit yelled,

"Stand up with your hands in the air."

Whit heard only a low sobbing.

"I said stand up, dammit," he yelled again in Arabic.

Then, in the fluttering silence, he made out the voice clearly, "You can come kill me! I'm not standing up!" My God, Whit thought, it was Salman.

"Salman?" Whit yelled. "Salman is that you?"

"Who's there? Who's there?" Salman's terrorized voice came back.

"Salman it's W –, it's Michel."

"Michel, what are you doing? Come help! I can't move. Uncle is shot."

Whit sprinted the last few yards to the car and, as he rounded the corner, beheld a gruesome site. Musa Rasoul had been shot in the stomach and lay, eyes closed, on the ground. Salman's right leg was bleeding, and blood splattered the ground all around them.

Salman looked perplexed, but too exhausted to fight. "We've been here all night. Abou Ammar ordered us to defend the Melkart. The PFLP and God knows who else is running wild all around. We fought them for hours and ran out of ammunition."

"Ok, Salman," Whit said, picking him up, "just stay quiet now, we're getting you some help." Whit motioned to the Marines, and two of them picked up Musa Rasoul, who stirred slightly with pain.

"Be careful, he's . . . they shot him before they overran us."

Gunfire erupted in the distance, and explosions sounded close, then further away.

"Salman do you remember how many of them there were or where they went?"

"I don't know. They went off towards the Melkart."

The group turned towards the Melkart. Flames licked the window frames of the buildings on the other side of the hotel. Whit motioned Boutros onward and the Marines carried Musa Rasoul, as Salman hobbled, one arm over Whit's shoulders.

"Do you think uncle's going to make it?"

"Stop!" A voice yelled in the distance in Arabic. "On your knees and drop your weapons." Whit waited a few moments, then knelt.

"Not dropping our guns, sir." Captain Carole said to Whit, as the men kneeled, aiming.

"Hold on up there," Whit yelled, "we're friendlies."

"Sir, how do you know who these guys are?" Captain Carole whispered as they all hovered close to the ground.

"It's gotta be the army. We're too close to the Melkart, they're in a defensive position. The fedayeen must have worked their way around to try and find a weak spot on the other side."

"We're Americans, trying to get down to the coast," Whit yelled. A bright light shown on the group. A lone man came out towards them.

"Just put your guns down, I'll bring you in." The Marines lowered their guns, and as the figure approached, Whit could clearly see it was Qustantin.

"I know you." Qustantin said as a look of recognition came over his face.

"Yes, you do," Whit responded, "I need to see Col. Chartouni."

"Ok, let's get everyone back behind the line. And ditch the car." As they walked, Qustantin continued, "you picked a hell of a time to come. We've been holding out all night, but we're running out of ammunition."

"We're not sure how much longer we can last. The men are starting to get nervous." They walked through a narrow fortified pathway where sandbags had been stacked to form an above-ground bunker. Several soldiers manned the barriers and glanced briefly at Qustantin and Whit's group as they passed by.

"We thought the Marines might make it up this far." Qustantin said more loudly over Whit's shoulder. "But your guys all started pulling out an hour ago, I don't know what you're still doing here. There's a wall of fire between us and the coast. You're going to have to break through the fedayeen lines to get there."

Qustantin turned to the center, "Off there straight ahead you can see the square. The Colonel's headquarters is set up right in the base of the Melkart, the building to the left. The politicos are in there negotiating this thing with Abou Ammar right now."

Whit shook hands with Qustantin, who said, "I never got your name?"

"Cordell Whitaker."

"Mr. Whitaker, heading towards the coast is about the last place in the world I'd want to be tonight."

"Well, sometimes we don't seem to have a choice, do we?"

Qustantin looked at Whit, and gazed across the faces of the Khoury family and Marines.

"Good luck."

Whit motioned the Marines and the Khourys to follow, and turned and started walking towards the headquarters. The open square stood off to the side of the confluence of several major roads. Not a soul could be seen, and the street was littered with trash. A slightly chilly ocean wind picked up, swaying the palm trees that lined the side of the street in the strange formation of ominous serenity that was a haunting harbinger of dark storms headed for landfall. Flames surrounding the square left an intermittent glow.

The square sat in silence but for the breeze flowing through it like the waves crashing against the rocks within earshot, but out of view. Broken windows littered the lower two levels of the buildings, and shards of glass skipped lightly along the road. As Whit neared the center of the square, a loose newspaper blew against his ankle, and he bent over to pick it up, reading the headline "Unknown Assailants Start New Round of Fighting." Thunder boomed in the distance. Whit looked around, and at the mouth of each street, saw an army barricade. The square had been converted into a makeshift fortress.

They made their way towards the entrance to the Melkart, and upon reaching the door, were frisked. Just inside, Whit spotted Camille near the back wall talking with someone. Whit started walking closer and, as the figure turned, he was shocked to see that it was Gaspar Vartabed.

"Whit," Camille bellowed as he approached, "do you know my friend Gaspar Vartabed, from the Armenian quarter?"

Whit reached out to shake Gaspar's hand, "We've met before, Camille. Gaspar Vartabed, what on earth are you doing here?" The priest began to speak, but just as he did so, Camille interrupted,

"We've had a little problem with someone who got onto the premises, Whit, but you are a Westerner and couldn't understand."

"No, Camille," the priest began speaking, "he understands quite well."

"Well then," Camille said abruptly, "there's a lunatic running around the hotel whom," Camille paused incredulously, raising his eyebrows, "my soldiers think is possessed. But hell if we can't find him anymore."

"He is." Whit said, stone-faced, as Camille looked at Whit in disbelief. "What do you need Father?"

"A quiet room away from all this."

"Father, we can't get you out of the hotel now. We think the fedayeen are already surrounding the area. Whit we need you out there."

"Are they still negotiating?"

"We have refused to concede on several points, and low and behold, Abou Ammar stormed out and moments later the bombardment started. They're going to his room now. It will quiet down, no doubt, but I'm not sure we can hold much longer if it picks up too much."

"Ok, where's the weakest spot?"

"Right where they're attacking."

"The only chance left is to do a counter." Whit said coldly.

"What?"

"Punch out right at them. They won't be expecting it. If you just sit and wait, eventually you'll collapse in. Who is it, anyway? Sadiq and PFLP?"

"Sadiq. Sayyid. Nuri. Adib. What does it matter? They're all the same. There are several other groups converging from different camps as we speak. We're putting up sporadic firefights to slow them down, but Hadad is nowhere to be found, and so we're left with Colonel Chartouni's men. Oh, and George is here with his people." Whit paused momentarily to consider the information.

"Ok, get Chartouni and a contingent down to the walls facing the coast. I'll have the Marines. We've got to go out there."

"What about this family you brought?"

"Once we punch out, it should create an opening. Then we'll have split them in two and if they're still fighting we can start to work on them separately. While we do that, send Qustantin through with the Khourys and any other civilians down to the coast."

"Ok."

Whit walked back to find the Khourys and the Marines.

"Alright guys, we need to wait just a little bit longer until we can speak with some of the officers."

"Yes, sir."

"Where did they take Salman?"

"Who?"

"The Palestinian."

This time Boutros answered, "Back into those tents, Whit, where they are treating all the injured."

"Ok you guys wait here, I'll be back."

Whit walked into the tents, and saw the grotesque horrors of battle lit by the candlelight. Suddenly, behind him he heard a soft voice.

"And so the American came back to save the world?" Rafqa grimaced indignantly as he turned.

"No," he said, "just to be with my friends when it burned." Her grimace disappeared as they awaited each other.

"Oh, Whit, I can't be angry. I was afraid maybe you had left. But I didn't want to see you here, either."

"Rafqa! Rafqa!" Someone shouted from across the tent. "We need you fast." She turned and ran with Whit following after her.

"Salman," Whit said, as they arrived to the other side.

Salman turned, not seeming to recognize Whit, and then a wave of amazement seemed to pass over his face. Whit saw Rafqa was already working on the ground with another soldier. Salman's golden gun was at his side, and he was clinging to it. A soldier from the hotel grabbed it to remove it, but Whit stopped him. Musa Rasoul remained unconscious, his face pale from excessive blood loss.

Rafqa was moving between patients, telling attendants which to treat first, which to treat next, and which to leave because there was nothing left that could be done. When she arrived at Musa Rasoul's side, she saw Whit holding a cloth over his abdomen, and checked the wound. Whit noticed confusion on her face.

"Lift him," she said to the two attendants, and when they did so, to Whit's horror, his back had been riddled with bullets. She shook her head, and they laid him back down gently, moving to Salman.

"Help him," he said, struggling as the attendants inspected his legs and Rafqa instructed in hushed tones how to treat his leg wounds, "Doctor please help my uncle." She stopped speaking to the attendants, "I am sorry, but your uncle is hurt very badly."

"No," Salman again uttered, wincing in pain and heartbreak,"No, doctor, he can survive." She moved away while a tear ran down Salman's cheek. Whit saw Gaspar Vartabed leaning over a soldier who was laid out on another cot. He crossed the soldier and held his hand on the man's forehead as he prayed over him, touching the man from time to time with his stole.

The air began to thicken with a murky, grey moisture that had accumulated from the sea. It enveloped the city with a thick layer of memories. Gunfire could be heard from various quarters, but the sounds were muffled in a shroud of ceaseless repetition, where the fight seemed to ricochet endlessly off the floating walls of the fog. A dull boom signaled explosions and the powerful fire of the army's new weaponry. The staccato crackle of the fedayeen's AK-47s swirled together with the larger booms as they simultaneously died in the fog, only to be reborn with each new malevolent act.

Suddenly, Whit noticed Musa Rasoul's hand was in the air, hanging limply as his elbow sat on the cot. Whit reached out to grab it, and Musa spoke in a low mumble, his eyes closed, but intent on saying something. Whit could not tell his intended audience, but Salman propped himself up on his elbow, looking at Whit and listening intently.

"It could have been . . . so different." He squeezed Whit's hand. Salman, looking straight at his uncle, instead of the countenance of fear and hesitation that usually occupied his face, he appeared to fill with a certain resolve. Then, Musa's hand slipped slowly from Whit's, and fell gently across his stomach, sliding an inch before coming to a permanent resting point. The rise and fall of his torso ceased. Whit lifted the cloth; no more blood issued forth.

They sat for several minutes without speaking. "Who was it?" Salman and Whit turned towards Camille, who had appeared with Colonel Chartouni, then looked quizzically at one another.

Whit started to speak, then Salman, somewhat combatively, said, "What?"

"We talked with some of the soldiers here. We know you guys were fighting along with us. Who did this to him?" Salman looked off into the distance.

Then, he said, vacantly, "Does it matter?"

"The negotiations upstairs are failing, and we're losing men out in the streets. They can't hold much longer, and by the morning we'll be finished, without even knowing who or how many are out there. So, yeah, it matters." They turned to Salman.

"I don't even know."

"Bullshit." Camille said.

"Alright," Whit said, "alright, hold on. Salman," he said, lowering his voice, "do you remember who you saw out there? What they looked like?"

Salman was silent for four or five seconds, but it seemed like an eternity to the others. "I . . ." he murmured, "can't say." Camille and the Colonel shifted with displeasure. "I mean, they would just come out of nowhere, and then disappear again."

The Colonel said angrily. "Whit, this is bullshit." Then turning to Salman, "My friend, when they find you here, they'll treat you just like they treat us."

"Guys . . . hold on!" Whit raised his voice sharply, staring at the Colonel and Camille before turning calmly to Salman.

"Salman, did you see your uncle get shot?" They were silent again. Salman simply shook his head no. The Colonel grabbed Salman's gun contemptuously stripping it away from him.

Salman pleaded, "No, I need it, you can't . . ."

"A coward doesn't need any bullets," the Colonel said, and removed the magazine and the bullet in the chamber. Salman looked back to the sky and then to Whit.

"You will never understand," he said, turning to Camille and the Colonel. "It matters to you who, but why? It could be anyone. They're still there. The PFLP, maybe. They want to kill us. Maybe it was the Israelis. Maybe it was the Deuxieme Bureau in street clothes, you hate us, too. Of course, it could have been the Syrians. Or, maybe it was the Americans," now waving his hand towards Whit. "My uncle is dead. And I'm a coward who hid behind a car without firing a shot. Just like I've always been. Hiding and hoping it will go away. But it will never go away."

They all stared, appreciating his frustration in different turns, but none knowing it as fully as Salman. "Well, Whit," Camille said, "do you have your answer?" Whit looked at him quizzically. "Whit's a journalist, you know, Salman. He was going to write a big article," Camille said, swiping his open hands to signify the headline floating invisibly. "The Pulitzer goes to Cordell Whitaker!" He shouted angrily, "Who was the third force? It doesn't matter, he wrote." Camille looked back at him contemptuously. "I'm sorry, Mr. Salman, but I think it does matter. I think you have to know what you're fighting for and who you're fighting against."

"Well, I don't know anymore." Camille and the Colonel turned silently and walked out. Whit sat a minute longer and then, patting Salman on the shoulder, got up to leave.

"Michel," Salman said, and Whit turned to look at him. "Whit?"

"It's a long story, Salman. But it doesn't matter."

"You're probably right. Whoever you are . . . can you give me a bullet?" Whit's heart plunged into his stomach. He hadn't asked for his bullets back. He hadn't asked for a new loaded gun. He had asked only for one bullet. No man needs just one bullet.

"Salman," Whit said, "that'd be just another way to hide." Whit looked at him, and then turned and walked away.

Salman, tearing up, watched as Whit crossed the courtyard in the direction of one of the barricades. After a few moments more, Salman's attention was drawn to a nearby soldier, hobbling past on crutches. "My friend," he said.

"Yeah."

Salman said, "They say we're going to be surrounded soon." Lifting his gun and showing the man, he continued, "I don't have any ammunition left and my leg is injured." The soldier shifted uneasily, but waited, "Can you give me just one bullet, in case they make it all the way here? I don't want to go down without a fight." The man looked around, and slipped a bullet from his belt, handing it to Salman, who smiled blankly. "Thank you." When he looked back towards the city, he caught a final glimpse of Whit's distinct figure disappearing, purposefully, into the fog.

# CHAPTER FORTY-THREE

"I can't see anything."

"What are you looking for?"

"I don't know."

"Well no wonder you can't see it." Camille directed a befuddled gaze towards Whit and handed the night vision goggles to Col. Chartouni as the two men, along with Whit and George, scanned the streets between the Melkart and the coast. What few street lights had not been destroyed by days of fighting were all but extinguished by the thick fog that had set into the blackness of the early morning hours.

"Dammit. The air is so thick you can't see even a few feet in front of you."

"Then they won't be able to see us coming, either." Whit responded.

"Precisely," said Camille, "They're bound to hold off until this clears. We could still have time."

George said, "Yeah, but Abou Ammar will just refuse to negotiate until he has leverage again."

The three were silent, looking and contemplating.

"Alright." Suddenly, Captain Carole jogged across the square.

"Sir," he now spoke to Colonel Chartouni, "my commander is down on the port. He says they're willing to put suppressing fire where we need it, but that they're pulling out in about thirty minutes. He's almost got the last of the civilians loaded up and out in the boats and they're just getting the rest of our guys and gear taken care of. I told him we have some more to get down there, and he's waiting."

"Alright then," now Chartouni spoke, "Whit and George, we'll know pretty soon where they are once you guys get out there. You charge the center and we'll call in the coordinates to the Marines."

"We're going too, sir," Captain Carole said. Chartouni nodded his assent. The Colonel and Camille shook hands with the men and headed back towards the hotel. George strode over to a group of about ten men, speaking to them, and Whit approached Boutros. As he did so, Khalil came up to his side.

"Alright guys. This is it. George, his guys, the Marines, and I are going out first. We have to break through this barrier. As soon as we get an opening and it's safe, Qustantin is going to lead you guys down to the water. The Marines know you're coming, and it's just about four blocks away. It's going to get pretty dicey, but we're going to get you out of here. Whatever happens, you just get down to the coast."

The men nodded. Whit walked back to the barrier.

"Whit," Whit turned to Boutros, "I, I don't," his words came slowly, "know wh-"

"You don't have to say anything Boutros. You just get your family to the Marines no matter what happens.

You don't stop and you don't turn around. Promise me that?"

"Ok, I promise."

Whit nodded to Captain Carole, who spoke into the walkie talkie he had acquired. After a few moments, a bright flare burst in the sky. The light showed the thick set fog and the black night. A row of cars was barely discernible. In the distance, Whit heard the sound of a motorcycle engine revving.

Whit paused, then motioned to George. George turned and motioned to his team, who brought a bazooka up to the barricade wall.

"Alright, once you light up the center of that blockade, covering fire and then we hit it on foot. We form a half circle once we breach it, and take them down." George nodded, turned to one of his men, and motioned towards the barricade.

The bazooka man lifted the weapon to his shoulder, took aim, and just as the next starburst exploded over the night sky, pulled the trigger. A solid bar of flame erupted towards the cars, and a moment later a massive explosion rocked the ground. Whit lunged over the barricade with George, his men and the Marines following. Qustantin and a number of soldiers fired towards the wall, from which a dense thicket of gunfire now exploded back towards the oncoming rush.

As they ran and fired, bullets exploded on the ground all around them and the dense fog and night was aglow. They had only the blaze in front of them to guide them, and when they burst through it, they found the fedayeen in disarray. Some still lined the car barricades and fired towards the square, others lay disoriented on the ground, and numerous others were strewn about, injured or killed.

The fedayeen, at first shocked to see this group so suddenly in their midst, reacted slowly. Whit's contingent took a half circle position and fired at fedayeen all around them. The fedayeen fled in both directions. Ahead in the distance, as the fog began to break intermittently and another flare lit the night sky, Whit could see the water and the Marines.

Gunfire ripped across the ground just in front of Whit, and as he turned to his right he saw Sayyid atop a yellow motorcycle speeding away towards the water and firing back.

Whit motioned his team forward. They rose and began running, firing ahead, to their left and right. The fedayeen melted into the side alleys and streets. Whit fired at the motorcycle as he ran and saw its rear tire burst into flames. The flames disappeared in a thicket of fog.

Whit's group charged forward. Moments later, the firing from both sides subsided and the group hit a grassy, open area that, though the fog was thick, they knew signaled their proximity to the water. Whit motioned for the group to halt and again circle. As they did so, he nodded to Captain Carole, who spoke into the walkie talkie, warning the Marines they were about to approach. Carole nodded back and the group jogged forward for another fifteen seconds until the outline of a thick group of Marines emerged, hunkered behind the low brick walls that protected the walkways along the water.

As they met the group, one man stood, "Welcome to the water gentlemen. I'm Lieutenant Colonel Evans."

"Sir," said Carole, "we need mortar fire as directed by," static burst forth over the radio, "wait here it is . . . ok they're calling it in at two points. Sir, one hundreds yards east, twenty yards north, and a second barrage, one hundred fifty yards east, thirty yards south." Evans called it in, and the group could hear firing back towards the target areas. They had succeeded in splitting the fedayeen and from the way fire continued to erupt from the center, it looked like a contingent of Chartouni's men had followed them out and was attempting to hold a middle position to then follow on the barrage.

Mortar rounds burst to either side, sending the group ducking behind the walls. As the shells crashed into the target areas, explosions again lit the night sky. The gunfire erupted toward the Marines' position on the coast. The Marines and Whit's crew, behind the barricades, began firing back.

"They must be fleeing back this direction from the mortar fire."

"Sir, sir" Captain Carole yelled, "they're saying they reached agreement in the Melkart. Abou Ammar is calling off his men."

"Tell them that!" Whit yelled, as he fired over the wall.

As the firing quieted, and sporadic gunshots rang out, the fog grew thinner, but still rested on the city.

Evans grabbed Whit's shoulder. "Alright, they're telling me we gotta pull out. Last boat is heading out in ten minutes." Evans turned to all the Marines and made some hand gestures.

Whit turned to Carole, grabbing the walkie talkie.

"Camille,"

"Just a minute," a voice on the other end responded.

"Yes, it's me."

"Ok, time to send them through. I'll come back up there and meet halfway in case there's firing."

"Ok, on the way."

Whit turned and shook hands with Carole, nodding at Evans.

"Aren't you coming with, sir?"

"No, I have to stay back."

"We're supposed to get all Americans out, sir."

"I'm with the Embassy."

"Ok, got it. Good luck to you."

Carole looked at Whit, shaking his hand, "Thanks again, sir."

"I'll see you around."

"Yeah."

Both turned to head in separate directions.

Whit and George's men proceeded deliberately. Whit used the fires burning on the left and right, visible intermittently through brief openings in the fog, to orient himself. After what seemed to him an interminable time, he heard a muffled voice calling out, "Nadia! Nadia!" It was Martha, yelling in sheer terror. Whit began sprinting and found himself almost immediately upon Qustantin and the Khourys; but not all of them.

"Whit, my God, Nadia got away from us somehow, we don't know where she is!"

At that moment, Whit heard the rev of a motorcycle engine. He glanced all around, but could see nothing through the fog.

"Ok, ok, we're going to find her. Martha and Najwa, you have to keep going down to the water."

"No we could n-"

"It's not up for debate." Whit raised his voice. "Time is running out. You can't stay here and we have to know where you'll be. You go to the coast so we know where you are – the Marines will wait. Boutros, Khalil, you walk on the left, back towards the Melkart. I'll w–"

Gunshots erupted, but the firing ceased just as quickly. The Khourys all looked frantic.

"I'll walk on the right and once we find her, you get back down to the coast immediately. Got it?"

"Ok."

Najwa embraced Whit a, a tear breaking down her cheek. Whit grabbed her shoulders, then he pushed her gently towards Qustantin without a word. She cried his name as he ran into the dark fog and Qustantin pulled her and Martha towards the coast.

"Nadia," Whit yelled, and heard Boutros and Khalil doing the same. The firing had stopped, and Whit heard only the deafening silence and the intermittent revving of the motorcycle engine. The revving seemed near as Whit passed an open block. It receded again.

"Help!" a pleading, desperate voice came lightly through the fog. Whit heard the motorcycle speeding nearby, but could see nothing. Then again. Then quiet.

A frantic scream, "Daddy, I'm lost. Help me!"

Whit heard Boutros yell, "I'm coming swee -" and the fog swallowed the rest.

Then, as if some divine relief passed over the land, in the distance through the fog, Whit could see the first hint of light. A slight breeze emerged. It pushed the fog in waves more swiftly across the earth. Whit saw a child about fifteen yards away, standing and facing the other direction. Then the fog enveloped the child, wrapping its occlusive arms around as though keeping a secret that Whit could not uncover.

Fearfully and faintly through the fog, he heard a voice, "Help me!"

"Nadia, it's Whit! Stay right there, honey, I'm coming to you!" As he ran towards where he had last seen the child, he found the spot empty.

Suddenly, a flash of fire erupted in Whit's peripheral vision as the high-pitched roar of a motorcycle blew through his eardrums. He caught, in his sight, momentarily, Sayyid, distorted with rage and firing wildly. Just as soon, he was gone.

"Nadia?! Nadia?!"

"Help me!"

Again an opening, and a motionless child facing the other direction. Whit sprinted, and suddenly heard the motorcycle hurtling towards him. The fog opened up in time for Whit to see the ground exploding all around him. Sprinting again, he closed in on the child. Whit reached out as the child turned towards him. He saw Nadia's face in the instant before he embraced her and a yellow blur simultaneously exploded nearby. The sound of the motorcycle and the sound of gunfire broke instantly upon Whit's senses.

Silence.

The smallish light that had been resting on the horizon began reaching its wakeful arms into the sky. A breeze swept across the coast and the fog lifted across the city, uncovering the entire scene like a curtain lifting for the final act. It uncovered the Lebanese soldiers and Camille and Chartouni poised at the edge of the barricade. Fedayeen, lining the side streets, pointed their guns towards the soldiers. The groups stood locked in mutual apprehension. But as they pointed their weapons, all looked to the center of the street. There, Whit lay over the top of the child.

The bullets that had ripped through Whit's side and arm had hurled him to the ground. Nadia lay beneath him, unscathed. Sayyid, stationary roughly fifteen feet away, revved his engine. He dropped the kickstand and stepped off the bike with a malignant grimace. Whit struggled up to his knees, watching Sayyid. He felt for his weapon, but could not find it. He pulled Nadia behind him with his arm that had not been pierced.

"Whit, Whit," he heard Nadia say through sobs. The fedayeen and the army were transfixed, holding one another at bay. Sayyid slowly walked towards Whit, pointing his machine gun.

"It's going to be ok, Nadia," Whit said, as he coughed blood.

"You never should have come here, American."

With his other arm, bloodied and visible to all, Whit raised his hand towards Sayyid, his index and middle fingers outstretched, the outer fingers curled down to his palm. Sayyid stopped and raised the gun, momentarily pausing as he aimed at Whit's forehead.

Whit knelt motionless even as the shot was fired. And after the shot rang out, no one, on either side, moved. All stood, captivated, except Sayyid. Sayyid fell to his knees, and hunched over backwards, smoke rising from his forehead. His hand dropped to his side, and his gun clattered against the cement. Salman, ten feet away, slowly lowered his golden gun, smoke still rising from its barrel, and looked with utter shock at his doing. As Salman lowered his gun, the fedayeen on both sides of the street, and then the military, followed suit.

Rafqa, appearing at the barrier, stopped and screamed. Gaspar Vartabed crawled over the barrier and began running towards Whit, saying with determination, "No, no, no." He bumped Salman's shoulder, who looked from Sayyid's lifeless body to the gun he held, and in disgust, threw it to the ground. He turned slowly, as if in a trance, and began to walk away.

Boutros and Khalil emerged and ran to Whit's side. Khalil grabbed Nadia and Boutros embraced Whit, whom he laid down on his back.

"Whit, we have to get you help." Gaspar Vartabed arrived to Whit's side. Whit locked eyes with Khalil, and glassy eyed, gave a slight twitch of his fingers towards the water. As he did, the sun peaked above the horizon.

The soft glow of the sunrise flickered in Khalil's mind, and he remembered the promise he made to Whit. He nodded slowly as Whit stared into his eyes, unspeaking.

"Dad, we have to go," Khalil grabbed Boutros, pulling him, "we have to go," and George and Qustantin emerged, grabbing and pulling Boutros as he fought them.

"No, we have to help," Boutros yelled. "No, we have to help him." He yelled again as they pulled him away, and the group finally turned towards the water, Boutros fighting them as they disappeared.

"Whit!" Rafqa screamed, in one, prolonged cry of anguish, as she ran towards him. "No, Whit, you can't!" She lunged down at his side, she took the other half of Whit's torso and plugged her hands on the wounds she could find.

The priest spoke next, "Whit, do you reject Satan, and all his works, and all his empty promises?" Behind them, the bleeding demoniac walked languidly. He stooped over the golden gun, slowly bent down, and picked it up. Straightening quickly, he turned to look around, then shuffled toward the side of the road.

"I," Whit coughed again, blood coming forth, and Rafqa, crying, placed her hand gently on his mouth.

"Just nod," she said, crying as pain rent her beautiful features. Whit nodded and her hand smeared his own blood on his cheek as she gently brushed his face.

"Do you believe in God the Father Almighty, creator of heaven and earth?" Gaspar continued.

Whit's eyes glowed with the rising sun. The lines along his temples compressed, his torso squeezed, and the blood from his side spoke the words that he could not.

"No, Whit, you can't go, Whit . . . Whit, you are going to live." Rafqa whispered softly, choking down an unbearable torment as she held her hands on his side and on his face, blood now more slowly issuing from both. She cried out, loudly, between tears, "You are going to live!"

The Third Force is Brock Dahl's first novel. He has written extensively on national security, cybersecurity, international law, and literary topics. His writings have appeared in *The Military Review*, *Small Wars Journal*, *Lawfare*, *National Review Online*, and more.

Originally from Wichita, Kansas, Brock has performed field research and worked professionally in such places as Lebanon, Afghanistan, Iraq, and the tribal regions of Silicon Valley. He is an attorney in Washington, D.C.

86240285R00205

Made in the USA
Columbia, SC
30 December 2017